"KISS ME," THE WHITE WOMAN WHISPERED.

She reached up, sliding her fingers through Tykota's long black hair.

A raw urgency built in the pit of his stomach and spread through his veins, his mind, his whole being.

It didn't seem to matter that his mortal enemy, the Apache, were nearby, or that he and this white woman might die at any time. Just one kiss was all he wanted.

But when Tykota's lips touched Makinna's, he knew that would never be enough. His mouth ground against hers. His tongue explored her, stirring the heat in his belly. He wanted to know her in every way a man can know a woman. He wanted to unveil her hidden beauty and kiss every part of her body.

Wild, primitive emotions tore through him, and he was on fire.

And, in that moment, Makinna became his woman.

His to protect. To love. To take . . .

TYKOTA'S WOMAN

CONSTANCE O'BANYON

LEISURE BOOKS   NEW YORK CITY

A LEISURE BOOK®

May 2000

Published by

Dorchester Publishing Co., Inc.
276 Fifth Avenue
New York, NY 10001

ISBN 0-8439-4715-2

This is for you, Courtney Melton, my delightful grand-daughter with the bright blue eyes, infectious smile, and loving heart. I love you, sweet one.

And for my dear friend Helen Owens. Thank you for your cheerfulness and support during difficult days. It's always nice to know that someone understands how reclusive a writer can be when she's on deadline—and still like her when it's over. You are a blessing!

And for Lynsay Sands, who made me realize more than ever that friends are treasures and can cheer you on when you most need it.

And Marisa Yanes, my little friend South of the Border. Thank you for your help with research—your input was invaluable to me and is much appreciated.

El Paso
Tykota's Woman

The Legend

There is a legend that grew out of the West, carried on the dry, restless winds past the vast deserts of El Paso. It is whispered among the Apache that a mighty tribe, the Perdenelas, dwell in a secret place called Valle de la Luna, a lush, green paradise by the Mountain of the Moon. The Apache speak of untold wealth hidden in a sacred mountain, its secret location passed down from the chief to the son of his choice. The legend warns that anyone attempting to steal the gold will die a horrible death. The Apache sing songs of honor about a great young chief of the Perdenelas who turned his back on the treasure for the love of a white woman.

Or so the legend goes . . .

Prologue

Valatar, chief of the Perdenelas tribe, stood
on the red rock cliff, his gaze sweeping across
his vast tribal land. He was no longer a young
man; his long hair was laced with gray, and
his brow was furrowed with worries. But he
carried himself straight and tall and dis-
patched with honor the obligations of a powerful chief. He wore an unadorned
breechcloth, as did the other men of his tribe.
But his leather headband, unlike those of the
the others, bore a carved golden eagle.

His gaze moved to Mangas, who stood
silently beside him. Mangas had been his child-
hood companion and was now teacher to his

youngest son. "Find Tykota and bring him to me. Then tell my other two sons and their mother to come to the council room."

The old man left to do the chief's bidding, and Valatar returned to his thoughts.

Tykota was only in his sixth summer, but he was the son of Valatar's heart and destined to be chief. Tykota had been born to him from his first wife, Llena, long after they had given up hope of ever having a child. Although she had gone to the spirit world four summers ago, Valatar still thought of her daily and missed her deeply.

Again he gazed out over the Valle de la Luna, now bathed in silvery moonlight. The Perdenelas were cliff dwellers, and their homes had been artfully carved into the granite face of the Mountain of the Moon so they would blend in as a part of it. With its harmonious passages and family chambers, Moon Valley and its surrounding mountains had been home to the tribe for as far back as the Old Ones could account, long before the first white man had set foot on the continent. Legend had it that the Perdenelas had once lived many miles away but had long ago been forced to abandon their homeland because the river had run dry. The accounts handed down through the ages recounted that a giant eagle with golden eyes had led their forefathers across the desert to this hidden paradise.

The chief sighed, his heart heavy over what he must do tonight. When any of his tribe went against the laws, the chief had to dispense retribution. Over the years, many had suffered his stern judgment for their transgressions, but never members of his own family. Until now.

His gaze moved westward to the mountain passage that led, between twin peaks, out to the arid track of land his people called the desert of a thousand deaths. But within the valley, in the bright moonlight Valatar could see the swift, clear river that nurtured the fruit and nut trees and the blue moonflowers that dotted the meadow with their brilliance. He loved this land, and he loved his people. He would do what he must to preserve their way of life.

Valatar's footsteps were heavy when he entered the council chamber, where the Old Ones had already gathered. Age and wisdom were revered among his people, and a warrior had to live many winters before he was considered wise enough to counsel the chief. Each man greeted Valatar with respect, and, he thought, sympathy, because they knew he felt tormented for having to judge his own family.

There was also a white man present, an unprecedented event, especially in the council room, which was normally reserved for only the most powerful tribal advisors. Valatar acknowledged George Silverhorn's presence with a nod and seated himself on the white buffalo robe reserved for the chief. He silently motioned George to sit to his left, a position of honor. He would ask much of their friendship tonight.

There was a commotion at the entrance as a woman and two boys noisily entered the hallowed chamber. Petera was the second wife Valatar had reluctantly taken when his beloved Llena had seemed incapable of producing the necessary son. And since Petera was a Chiricahua Apache, Valatar had hoped that the union would end the bad blood between the two tribes. Although she was not as tall as Perdenelas women, nor graced with the high, delicate cheekbones or slender stature typical of the tribe, she was yet a handsome woman. Her forehead was wide, her face round. Her large dark eyes, her finest feature, now held a guarded expression as she cast a haughty look at the gathered men and stopped in front of Valatar.

"Why have you called me and my sons here?" she demanded.

Valatar stared at her, almost hating this woman who had given him two sons. "Woman, you will not speak unless I ask it of you!"

She fell silent, but her mouth pursed, and her brow creased in anger.

Valatar looked at the two boys. The elder, Coloradous, was tall and had the features of

14

the Perdenelas, while the other, Sinica, was shorter and resembled his mother's people. Valatar had never felt close to either of them, although, as his eldest son, Coloradous should have held a place of honor in the tribe and in the chief's heart. Coloradous looked with uncertainly into his father's eyes, while Sinica's brooding expression mirrored the one his mother wore.

All heads turned as Tykota and Mangas appeared at the entrance to the chamber. The chief's youngest boy was intelligent beyond his years and had the look of his mother about him, reminding Valatar of his beloved Llena. The young boy stumbled, almost fell, and leaned heavily on Mangas. And fury raced through the mighty chief when he noticed how weak and shaky Tykota was.

Tykota had been suffering agonizing stomach cramps, and although he was well enough now to leave his chamber, he had not yet regained his strength. He hoped he would not shame himself before his father by showing weakness. He took a deep breath to ease the pain still gnawing inside him. It wasn't often that he was allowed into his father's council room, and he did not know what to expect.

Valatar gave a small smile in encouragement. "Sit beside me, my son. The matters we discuss this night concern you."

Tykota stared at his stepmother and his two half brothers. Why were they standing before the chief when he was allowed to sit? Perhaps it was because he had been so ill.

Valatar turned his attention to the gathered elders. "You all know why I have called you here today. Petera, step forward."

Sullenly, she obeyed.

Valatar continued speaking. "Know you this, Petera—I have judged you to be a criminal, without honor. Therefore, you will be sent from this place to dwell once more among your own people."

She glared at Valatar. "You would shame me so?"

"You have brought shame upon yourself and your sons, who must share in your disgrace. Although they may share your guilt, I shall allow them to remain in Valle de la Luna. But henceforth let no man honor them."

Tykota gasped. He did not know why his two brothers should be shunned by the tribe or why their mother should be sent away.

He met the pale gaze of the white man, who seemed to be studying him intently. George Silverhorn smiled at him and nodded. Tykota was troubled and turned back to his father.

Valatar was now speaking to Tykota's half brothers. "If either of you choose, you may go with your mother. But know this: If you remain, neither of you are to call me Father."

Tears stung Tykota's eyes. Why was his father doing this? He felt pain in his heart because of the humiliation his half brothers were suffering. He met Petera's gaze, and she glared at him with hatred. He did not know his stepmother very well because he had lived mainly with Mangas since his own mother's death. But only a week ago Petera had brought him honey cakes, and, at her urging, he had eaten them all to please her.

His father was speaking again, this time directly to Petera. "You know why I send you away."

Her gaze bore venomously into Tykota. "I know."

"You wanted my son by my first wife to die so that one of your sons would one day be chief. Do you deny this?"

"You have already found the poisonous berries in my bedroll. Why should I deny it?"

Valatar's eyes narrowed, and she actually took a quick step backward.

"If you were a Perdenelas," he said fiercely, "you would have to die for what you did to my son."

"You have three sons," she replied through clenched teeth. "But you have never seen my sons as a father should. You think only of your poor, dead Llena and the son and daughter she gave you. I spit on you all!"

"These two are *your* sons, woman. I no

longer know them." His eyes shifted to Coloradous, then to Sinica. "I do not know if either of you caused the other two accidents that almost took Tykota's life, but I have my suspicions that one of you aided your mother in this effort. If I know for sure who was guilty, he would die." He waved them away. "Leave me now. Go from my sight!"

Tykota's brow furrowed. Before his illness, he had been pushed into the deepest, swiftest part of the river by someone he had not seen, but he had managed to swim ashore. Did his father think his stepmother and half brothers were responsible?

Without thinking, Tykota jumped to his feet. "Please do not send them away, Father. You are wrong about my brothers."

Valatar's expression was fearsome, and his voice held a sharp reprimand. "Do not speak further of this, Tykota! I have made my judgment, and that is how it will be."

His eyes shining earnestly, the young boy said, "I do not believe Sinica or Coloradous would harm me—I am their brother!"

Sinica stared into Tykota's eyes with such a deep, dark hatred that Tykota drew back.

Coloradous hung his head and stepped forward. "Even though I bear shame for what my mother has done, I wish to remain with my people, Fathe—I do not wish to live with the Apache. Valle de la Luna is my home."

18

For a moment Valatar's eyes seemed to hold pity that he had judged his sons so harshly. Perhaps the guilt belonged to their mother alone.

Then Sinica spoke. "I go with my mother, and I am glad to leave this place. I curse the blood in my body that came from the Perdenelas. If it were possible, I would drain that part away."

Valatar stood, speaking in a decisive voice. "Go from my sight. Petera and Sinica, you will leave tonight and never show your faces here again. Coloradous, you may stay in the Valle de la Luna, if you choose, but my judgment stands."

Coloradous looked sad as he walked to the exit, but the malice etched on Petera's face was echoed in Sinica's expression.

Valatar raised his voice so that the guards standing outside the entrance would hear it. "Escort Petera and her son, Sinica, out of the valley and send them on their way. Coloradous will be allowed food and water and to remain in the valley, but he will not live among us."

Tykota wanted to protest, but Coloradous met his young brother's eyes and shook his head, accepting their father's judgement. He walked, straight and tall, out of the chamber, while his mother and brother were led away by guards.

Sinica stopped near Tykota and said in a

voice that only the boy could hear, "One day, you will feel my blade at your throat."

Tykota trembled in shock, but soon after the three had gone, Valatar spoke again. "Is there any here who disagrees with my judgment?"

There was silence; no man opposed him. Tykota opened his mouth to voice his objections on behalf of Coloradous, but the hard look Mangas gave him sealed his lips.

Valatar looked at the revered members of the council. "I have chosen to show Tykota the secret of our sacred mountain."

Tykota's eyes widened in wonder. Of what secret did his father speak?

The elders nodded in approval.

Valatar continued. "I have called you all here tonight because I want every one of you to give Tykota your pledge of faith. I want to watch each man's face as he promises to honor my son, so I shall know if he speaks true."

The chamber remained silent until Mangas stood, bowing his head. "I will honor Tykota and keep faith with your will, my chief."

The others followed, each in turn, while Tykota watched in confusion. Why was his father doing this? Coloradous was his eldest son—he should be chief after their father.

After each member of the council had complied, the chief told them to depart. They filed out in an orderly manner until only Tykota, Mangas, and George Silverhorn were left.

When Valatar was satisfied he would not be overheard, he spoke quietly. "Tykota, my son, when George Silverhorn leaves here, you will accompany him. You will dwell in his land and listen to his voice as if it were mine. There may be other enemies among us. I will send for you when I feel it is safe for you to return."

Again Tykota wanted to protest. He did not want to leave his home. He did not want to live with the unfamiliar white man, George Silverhorn. He did not want his brothers to be sent away in shame. And he did not even want to stand in his father's place.

He thought of his young sister, Inea, who depended on him to look after her. "Will Inea go with me?"

"No," Valatar said. "Where you go, she cannot follow." Then his voice softened. "I know you are confused by what happened tonight, Tykota. One day you will understand why I must send you from your home, even though I do not wish it." Valatar laid a hand on Tykota's shoulder. "When my eyes are closed in death, and you stand in my place, I charge you to always put the good of the people ahead of your own wants."

There was an aura of power around Valatar, and Tykota was a little frightened of his commanding presence. He had been taught, as all the Perdenelas were, that the chief's word was law. "I do not understand."

"Understand this. You are the son of my heart, Tykota. You came to me late in life, but I have always known that you would one day have the strength and courage to stand in my place. Listen to my voice, and take heed of my words."

Tykota blinked and stared up at his father, astonished. He was not aware that his father had given any thought to him at all. Sadly, the realization came to him that his father was showing his feelings because he did not believe that they would meet again in this life.

Valatar glanced down at the boy and spoke softly. "My son, your mother was my first wife, and the one who still dwells within my heart. She was childless in her younger years, but you, Tykota, came to us as a gift from the Great Spirit. Then your mother also gave me a daughter but she died the night Inea was born. I have long felt your mother's graceful spirit dwelling within you. She was a great princess, and you must always be proud that you are her son." Valatar paused, then spoke with feeling. "You, Tykota, are my choice to stand where I now stand. You will look after our people when I am gone."

Tykota's eyes widened. "But, my father—"

Valatar placed a finger over the boy's lips, silencing his protest. "You must remember that no sacrifice is too great if it is for your people." Valatar sighed. "No sacrifice. For the future good of our people, I am sending you away. You, my one joy." He sighed again.

Tykota glanced at George Silverhorn, who smiled at him. But Tykota hardly knew the white man, and he was afraid of him and his world outside the twin peaks.

"What have you to say, my son?" his father asked.

Tykota began to object, but at Mangas's nudge, he said simply, "I will do as you say, my father. But must I stay away long?" he couldn't help adding.

"If I think it necessary. George Silverhorn lives in a place called England far across the big water to the east. I believe that you will learn much there, and I expect you to respect my friend as if he were your father."

The boy fought back his tears. "Can Mangas go with me?" he blurted, then feared he had offended his father by showing weakness.

The chief nodded. "Mangas will go with you, and he will continue teaching you our ways, but you will also go to the white man's school and learn about their world. There will be hard times ahead for you, my son. But I charge you to always remember what is expected of you— to always remember who you are and who you must become."

Tykota's lips trembled as he looked into his father's eyes. "*Must* I leave?"

"Yes. You must."

"But who will take care of Inea when I am gone?"

"Your sister will be well taken care of—I will see to that."

"I do not understand the events of this night."

"Tykota, you may be in grave danger if you remain here in our valley. You have enemies. One was your stepmother, but there may well be others, and if you remain, they may succeed in ending your life. That is one sacrifice I am unwilling to make."

Tykota had much to think about for one so young. He wished his father had not sent his brothers away. Coloradous had always been kind to him, and even though Sinica sometimes bullied him and this night had made a threat, Tykota was sad to see them so shamed by their father.

Valatar held out a hand. "Come with me, my son. There is a secret I will reveal to you—a secret none but you must know."

Chapter One

Texas, 1868

Weary, Makinna Hillyard leaned her head back against the worn leather seat, her eyes closed. The stagecoach rocked and swayed down the bumpy road, and her body felt every rut. The sound of a whip cracking to urge the mules forward was quickly swept away on the blistering desert wind and the waves of breath-stealing heat.

Opening her eyes, Makinna gazed at her traveling companions, glad that she could study them through her black mourning veil but that they could not see her through it. There were three men on the stage with her. Mr. Horace Rumford was a distinguished-looking gentleman with white hair, a neatly clipped white mustache, and, above his gray eyes, thick white eyebrows. She had learned from his conversation that he was an agent for the Butterfield Stage Line. The passenger sitting beside Makinna was Alvin Carruthers, a short, balding man with a nervous habit of blinking constantly. He was evidently a clothier from St. Louis.

Reluctantly, her gaze fell on the man directly across from her. Since he'd been asleep when she boarded the stage at Whispering Wells, she knew nothing about him. She assumed from the fine cut of his black suit and the quality of his European-made leather boots and gloves that he must be a man of some consequence. His wide-brimmed hat was pulled low over his face, and he still appeared to be sleeping. Although she could not tell for sure, she thought he must be younger than the other men. She could see the broadness of his shoulders, and he looked decidedly taller and more muscular than his fellow passengers.

Horace Rumford glanced out the window, his gaze traveling the parched land. He frowned as he turned back to Alvin Carruthers. "If trouble comes at us, it'll be on this godforsaken stretch of country from here to El Paso."

"Indian trouble?" his companion asked anxiously blinking rapidly with concern.

"The worst kind of Indian trouble—Apaches.

That's why we have two men riding shotgun instead of the usual one. But I don't expect any trouble on this trip."

Alvin Carruthers's eyes darted nervously to the window, as if he feared an attack at any moment. "Why this stretch of land? And why Apaches? I'd always heard that the Comanches were the fiercest tribe in Texas." His voice trembled, but he managed a tight smile. "Before I left St. Louis, I was assured that the army's presence here would keep the journey safe from Indian attack."

The agent's smile was not reassuring. "Even the Comanches stay clear of these parts, lest they tangle with the Apache. As a rule, the army's presence in El Paso has made things a good deal safer, but the Apache never follow the rules. They certainly don't abide by our laws.

"This was *their* land before we took it from them," Makinna said with a conviction that surprised the two men. Expressing her opinion so fervently surprised her, as well. "We are the intruders here, sir."

"Please pardon me, ma'am," Mr. Rumford said kindly, "but that is a mistaken notion. We make the land habitable with farms and ranches. We start settlements, develop towns, build schools, and bring civilization to an otherwise inhospitable locale."

Makinna sank back into silence for a

moment. She certainly knew next to nothing about Texas or its inhabitants, and like everyone else she'd heard terrifying tales about the Apaches. Still, the arrogance of certain attitudes annoyed her. "It just seems to me that the Indian has done very well for hundreds of years without interference from us."

Mr. Rumford gave her an indulgent smile. "May I introduce myself, ma'am? I'm Horace Rumford, and this is Mr. Alvin Carruthers." He nodded toward the sleeping passenger. "I don't know that gentlemen. The log says his name is Silverhorn. He was asleep when I came aboard." His smile widened. "And he still is."

Makinna smiled, too. "I'm pleased to meet you both. I'm Makinna Hillyard."

Mr. Carruthers looked at the black clothing hotly swathing her from head to toe. He spoke kindly. "May I respectfully inquire, madam, if you have recently suffered a bereavement?"

Makinna hesitated a moment. "Yes. I lost my brother and my mother within a month of each other."

"Please accept my heartfelt sympathy, ma'am," Alvin Carruthers said earnestly, blinking. "Such a great pity."

"And accept my condolences," Mr. Rumford echoed, glancing down at her wedding band. "It's unusual for a woman to travel alone in these parts, Mrs. Hillyard." He leaned back and studied her intently. "Of course, there's nothing wrong with it," he quickly added, "but it takes more courage than most women have."

"I am not courageous, sir. I had no choice in the matter. Left so suddenly alone, I am going to San Francisco to live with my sister. I didn't know how arduous the journey would be. As an agent for the stage line, do you think we'll experience any more delays?"

"You can trust the Butterfield Line, ma'am," Mr. Rumford said with confidence. "We pride ourselves on meeting our schedules."

"Not always, sir," she said softly. "The stage I was on before broke an axle, and I had to spend a week at Whispering Wells waiting for another stage."

"Regrettably, the unforeseen sometimes happens," the Butterfield agent stated. "Today will be a tedious one for you, Mrs. Hillyard," he said, "for we won't reach the way station at Adobe Springs before nightfall. However, tomorrow night we reach El Paso, where you'll enjoy some measure of comfort before we continue on to California the following day."

Makinna sighed wearily. She had been traveling for over three weeks, and it seemed she would never get out of Texas, much less reach San Francisco.

"Madam, may I ask where you are from?" Mr. Carruthers inquired. "I believe I detect a Southern accent."

"I'm from New Orleans, sir. The stage from

New Orleans delivered me to Ft. Belknap, where I boarded the Butterfield stage. And there they traded the horses for mules. I thought that rather strange." She glanced at Mr. Rumford. "Why did they do that, sir?"

"This leg of the journey is too hard on horses, Mrs. Hillyard," the agent informed her. "We have found the mules much more dependable in this arid terrain. This is uncivilized territory we're traveling through. You wouldn't want to lose a horse out here and be stranded."

Mr. Carruthers spoke. "Some would call St. Louis the last civilized town until you reach California. I myself was born and raised there." Then he cleared his throat. "Begging your pardon, madam. There is, of course, New Orleans, which has many families of refinement."

Suddenly Makinna had the strangest feeling of being watched. She glanced at the gentleman sitting opposite her, but she decided he still slept because his hat was pulled low over his face. So she was startled when he crossed his long legs and settled back against the seat. Because the stranger was wearing gloves, she couldn't judge his age by his hands.

He shifted again, and his coat fell open to reveal a gun belt. She pressed her back against the seat to get as far away as possible. He must be an outlaw! She'd heard about gunfighters who dressed like gentlemen but had black hearts.

She turned her face away and closed her eyes. Then, immersed in her own troubles, she forgot about the man across from her as well as the conversation between Mr. Carruthers and Mr. Rumford.

Makinna desperately missed her mother and her brother, William. Her mother had died slowly after a long, lingering illness, confined to her bed for nearly three years. Although it had been difficult to lose her, Makinna had at least been somewhat prepared for her death. But her brother had lost his life in a sudden, senseless accident. How could anyone with William's knowledge of horses fall and break his neck?

And as if that was not enough, a month after her brother had died, the bank foreclosed on their small house. She had been in despair when her sister, Adelaide, had written to invite Makinna to come live with her and her husband in California. When Adelaide married a miner and merchant ten years earlier and moved west, Makinna had missed her dreadfully. Their only contact had been through letters. But upon receiving Makinna's details of their mother's and brother's deaths, Adelaide had insisted Makinna come to California.

Makinna had had to sell her mother's jewelry

to have money for the trip, but she couldn't part with the wedding ring that her father had given her mother. She gazed down at the wide gold band on her finger. At the last moment, she'd decided to wear it. If people thought she was a widow it might make her traveling alone more acceptable.

Would she find a life for herself in California? she wondered for the hundredth time. Her sister's last letter had been filled with plans. Pretty, with their father's brown hair and gray eyes, Adelaide was older than she by six years, and Makinna tried to imagine what her sister would look like now.

Makinna sighed. Whatever promise California did or did not hold for her future, she'd had nothing to keep her in New Orleans, except sadness and memories. She hadn't had a social life in years. Even though her mother had pressed her to attend parties, she had been reluctant to leave her helpless and alone and had refused every invitation until the invitations had stopped coming. Maybe her venture into the unknown would prove exciting.

She stared out at the swirling dust and frowned, remembering something. As a young girl, she had dreamed of adventure and of sharing it with the perfect man who would love her as passionately as she loved him. She was older now, twenty, and so tired that she no longer dreamed of adventure or the perfect man. Or

any man, for that matter. At her age it was highly
unlikely that she would find a suitable mate.

Makinna was jerked out of her musing by the
sound of Mr. Rumford's voice. "If you're interested in the history of this area, it's really quite
colorful. There are legends of hidden gold and
Indian curses and a tribe no white man has
ever met and lived to tell about."

"Now, there you have me intrigued," Mr. Carruthers admitted, leaning forward, his eyes
aglow with interest. "I need a few fierce stories
to tell the missus when I get back to St. Louis.
She envisioned dangers lurking all along the
way, with outlaws and Indians waiting in
ambush behind every cactus to hold up the
stage."

"Well, the Indian tribe I was speaking of is
called the Perdenelas, and it is said that they
are fiercer even than the Apache. It isn't that
they come looking to do you harm, like the
Apache, but that if you invade their sacred
land or try to tamper with their hidden treasure, you will simply disappear, never to be
heard of again."

Mr. Carruthers blinked excitedly. "Tell me
more about the Perdenelas and the treasure."

Mr. Rumford knew he'd found an avid audience as he usually did when he spoke of the
gold of the Perdenelas. "No one knows exactly
where their land is located. A few misguided
souls with gold fever have ventured into the

desert, seeking their treasure. Most of them never returned, and those who did were half-starved and ranting about evil spirits. Don't know what they encountered out there, but evidently something drives them out of their minds."

Alvin Carruthers laughed nervously. "You're trying to lead me down a fool's path, aren't you?"

"Judge for yourself. The word lately is that the old chief of the Perdenelas has died and that his chosen son will be taking his place. No one seems to know much about the son, but they say he may be far more ruthless than his father."

The man across from Makinna shifted his position, and his knee bumped hers. She drew back, tucking her legs away from him.

She didn't want to believe there was a tribe in these parts that was even more ruthless than the Apache. But what if Mr. Rumford spoke the truth? She shivered and glanced out the window at the vast desert, thinking few could survive in that wasteland.

What kind of man would it take to live out there?

Chapter Two

Makinna relaxed a bit when Mr. Carruthers smiled and said, "I believe you're trying to pull a ruse on me, Mr. Rumford. I've heard about some of the tales you Westerners spin to ensnare us city folk."

"I won't deny that I've been guilty of weaving a little trickery with tenderfoots in the past, but what I tell you now is not a sham. At least, I believe there's some validity to the story, since it's spoken of among the other Indian tribes."

Mr. Carruthers still looked skeptical. "Very well, then. Why don't you tell me more about your mysterious Indian tribe and their hidden gold? Who knows? I may decide to take up a shovel and go looking myself."

"This is as much as I know," Mr. Rumford

continued. "The legend says that the Perdenelas live in a secret oasis in the desert called Valle de la Luna, which means Moon Valley. Their sacred mountain is called the Mountain of the Moon. Hidden somewhere in that mountain is a vast treasure, its exact location known only to the chief. The secret is supposedly passed down only from father to son."

Excitement flashed in Mr. Carruthers's eyes. "Where'd the treasure come from?"

Mr. Rumford shrugged. "Perhaps a mine, maybe lost Spanish gold. No one knows for sure."

"It's just as I thought. What you're saying is that no one knows anything for a fact."

"Well, there's no tangible proof, if that's what you're asking, but there's evidence enough to make me consider that there might be some truth in the tale."

"No, no. I will not go along with you on this unless you can give me something substantial," Mr. Carruthers challenged.

Mr. Rumford shook his head. "I, too, am a bit skeptical, but bear in mind that this is a legend that will not die." He turned to the window, suddenly pensive. "I personally witnessed a man crawling out of the desert, raving like a lunatic, swearing he'd seen a lush, green valley hidden by twin peaks in the middle of the desert, and that he'd entered the face of the mountain."

"Nonsense!" Carruthers said scornfully. "The man had probably been too long in the sun, and it had addled his brain."

"Maybe, maybe not," Mr. Rumford replied. "But that man had a nugget clutched in his hand that was the purest gold I've ever seen. Explain that if you can." He shifted his weight. "I'll tell you something else. I met up with an Indian who scouted for the army over at Ft. Bliss. He was a Mescalero Apache, and he swore the Perdenelas do exist. Told me there was bad blood between them and the Chiricahua Apache—something about trouble between the old chief and his second wife. It seems she was from the Chiricahua tribe and was jealous of the chief's son by his first wife. Apparently she and her son were forced to go back to her tribe in shame. He said the young chief would appear when the tribe needed him. If the old chief is dead, I reckon they'll be needing him now."

"Unquestionably a yarn made up by someone with a superstitious mind," Mr. Carruthers stated emphatically. "But it makes a good tale."

"I don't know. That Apache was mighty fidgety and nervous, looking around to see if anyone was listening as he told me the story. And I've learned over the years that it takes a lot to scare an Apache."

"You will never make me believe these yarns of hidden treasures and mysterious Indian tribes. This is the nineteenth century, not the Dark Ages," Mr. Carruthers said firmly.

Horace Rumford turned to Makinna and asked, "Does my tale tap into your sense of adventure, Mrs. Hillyard? Aren't you just a little captivated by the thought of a secret Indian tribe and hidden treasure?"

She shuddered. "I'm afraid I'll have to go along with Mr. Carruthers on this. I saw my first Indians at the way station at Manora, Texas, and they were certainly not mysterious or captivating but wretched and pitiable. They looked lean and hungry and desperate for a crust of bread. One of them looked at me with those dark, piercing eyes, and I was terrified."

"But you defended the Indians just a while ago," he reminded her.

"To defend their right to this land is not the same as being eager to keep company with them on it. No, I want nothing to do with any Indians, least of all your dangerous, feuding Perdenelas and Apaches."

The man sitting across from Makinna chose that moment to remove his hat and place it on his lap. And Makinna looked into the darkest, most contemptuous eyes she'd ever seen. The man's face was bronzed, his cheekbones high, and his hair even blacker than his eyes.

In spite of his manner of dress, there was no mistaking the fact that he was an Indian.

Fear clutched her heart, and Makinna

pressed her back against the seat to gain as much distance as she could in such a limited space. She quickly glanced at the other two men, who appeared to be as shocked as she was.

After a heavy silence, Mr. Rumford was the first to speak. "Sir, we have not been introduced, since you were asleep when we boarded. Name's Rumford, and this is Mr. Carruthers." He chose not to introduce Makinna.

The Indian did not offer his name or acknowledge the introduction except with the slightest nod of his head.

This did not deter Mr. Rumford. "You from these parts?"

The Indian nodded.

Mr. Rumford prodded further. "El Paso?"

"That general vicinty."

Makinna had averted her eyes from the Indian, but she now looked at him. His voice was deep, but what mystified her was that he'd spoken with a decided English accent.

"You been abroad?" Mr. Carruthers asked, eyeing the Indian's fine clothes. He, too, had detected the English accent.

"Yes. I have."

Mr. Rumford continued his questioning. "Sounds like you spent a good deal of time in England—is that right?"

The Indian drew in a long-suffering breath. "Yes." It was obvious he did not want to make conversation with his traveling companions.

Mr. Rumford ventured still further. "I was just telling Mr. Carruthers about the legends of the Perdenelas tribe. Do *you* know if they really exist or if they're merely mythical?"

"I can tell you nothing."

"You're an Indian, aren't you?" Mr. Carruthers asked. "Mr. Rumford here said that other Indians know something about these Perdenelas stories. Why don't you tell us what you know?" he added with a somewhat superior, condescending air.

The Indian's eyes were piercing as he gazed at the man from St. Louis, and his voice held a hint of irritation. "I said that I can tell you nothing about the Perdenelas."

Mr. Rumford was clearly annoyed with the arrogance of the Indian and decided to put him in his place. "I'm a Butterfield Stage Line representative, and it's our usual policy that Indians ride topside if they are allowed to board the Butterfield Line at all."

The stranger's gaze and voice hardened. "Your agent took my gold, and I will ride here."

"Well, uh, you seem civilized, so I'm sure there's no harm in your riding here as far as the way station," Mr. Rumford blustered in irritation.

The Indian turned to look out the window.

Makinna studied his profile. She had seen handsome men before, but none as handsome as this one. His cheekbones were high and pronounced, his jaw square and strong, and altogether his face was as beautiful as any chiseled in stone. She was ashamed of her own comments and of the way Mr. Rumford and Mr. Carruthers had treated him. She wondered what he must be thinking about his fellow travelers. There was a guarded tension in him, and she sensed something powerful and dangerous about him. Once again, she was grateful for her veil so the Indian would not know that she was studying him so intently.

Then, as if he sensed her gaze on him, the Indian turned his head to look at her, and she had the sensation that he could see right through the veil. Her heart began to beat so fast that she could hardly breathe. Her hand instinctively went to the door handle and she gripped it tightly. For a fleeting moment, she thought she detected something haunted in his expression, but it was quickly replaced by a look of sardonic amusement. Finally he looked away and turned his gaze out the window.

The rest of the afternoon was spent in uncomfortable silence, even Mr. Rumford having ceased trying to make conversation.

Makinna was relieved when the coach ultimately came to a rocking halt. They had arrived at Adobe Springs. Mr. Rumford helped her from the stage, and when she entered the station house, she was greeted by a thin pinched-looking woman who introduced herself as Mrs. Browning. The woman instantly began to chat, but Makinna pleaded weariness and asked to be shown directly to her room.

Mrs. Browning looked disappointed as she led the way. "We hardly ever get any female travelers out here. I'd be pleased to sit and talk a spell with you."

"I beg you to forgive me, but I am tired, and I have a headache. I want no more than to lie down for a while."

Mrs. Browning's mouth tightened. "Well, if that's the way you want it. I'll have my husband bring in your grip."

"Thank you." After the tense hours with the Indian on the stage, she didn't want to talk to anyone; she just wanted to be left alone.

When Mrs. Browning departed, Makinna looked about the small chamber off the back of the main room. It was cramped, the only furniture a narrow cot and a washstand with a pitcher of water. She sat on the lumpy mattress and leaned back against the adobe wall. The bedding was surprisingly clean, smelling of lye soap.

But the room was so hot that her hair was plastered to her forehead. With a sigh, Makinna stood to remove her veil. Stepping to the open window, she hoped for a breath of fresh air. But a dry wind parched her throat, and suddenly tears blurred her vision.

Life as she'd known it was over. She was left with only sorrow and an uncertain future. She tried to push her troubled thoughts aside and instead study the landscape. But this stark country appeared to have no color—it looked lifeless, empty. The adobe way station and its outbuildings were the same dull tone as the ground and the distant hills. The only growing things seemed to be an occasional cactus and scraggly stalks of straw-colored grass poking through the hard, cracked ground.

In that moment, Makinna longed for the lushness of New Orleans. Could any place this side of hell be as hot and dry and miserable as Adobe Springs? She thought of green Louisiana fields, where horses frolicked, and the Mississippi, where paddlewheel boats floated lazily along the current.

A shadow fell across her view, and she quickly pulled away from the window. It was the Indian walking past. He was tall, and his stride was long, but she caught a quick glimpse of his face before he moved away. She gasped at the singular impression of a man tortured in mind and soul.

Did Indians have the same feelings as white people? She had always thought of them as completely alien, needing no one, raiding and marauding, killing and scalping their enemies just for the sport of it.

The Indian had removed his coat and unbuttoned the collar of his white shirt, which opened to reveal a smooth, bronze chest. Again, she was struck by his handsomeness and the power he exuded.

She watched as he released his hair from a black cord, and it fell dark and heavy to his shoulders. Makinna's heart began beating wildly. Never had she seen such a man. There was something thrilling about him that captured her attention, yet at the same time something dangerous and frightening. More than mere handsomeness, there was a wild, savage beauty about him, a strength of spirit that seemed to reach out to her.

She closed her eyes to steady her heartbeat. She wondered about his life. He was unlike anything she imagined an Indian to be. His diction was aristocratic, and he had a superior manner about him. His expensively cut suit would have been at home on the finest plantation in Louisiana.

It seemed strange that he chose to dress like a white man, and stranger still that he was traveling on the Butterfield stage.

Feeling guilty for watching him, Makinna moved away from the window and prepared to wash the dust from her face. But her thoughts kept returning to the Indian.

What, exactly, was his story?

Chapter Three

Makinna recognized the voices of the station manager and his wife just outside her window. Mrs. Browning's voice was high-pitched with indignation. "I don't care if he is a Butterfield passenger. I told him, and I'm telling you, I ain't gonna serve no Injun. It's too much for anyone to expect. Land sakes, Jack, we could all be scalped in our sleep!"

Her husband replied in an irritated tone. "Nonetheless, he gets hungry like everyone else, and he deserves to be fed. He seems harmless enough, Edna. Almost civilized."

"He'll not eat at my table, and that's that! You didn't see the way he looked at me when I told him where we stood—I swear, Jack, he's think-

45

ing up something terrible to do to us during the night."

"It does seem kinda strange to see a savage pretendin' like he was a white man. What the hell kind of Indian is he, anyway? I've never seen one so tall, or with his sharp, clear features. I wouldn't mind askin' him a few questions to find out what he's about."

"Well, if you ask me, he's up to no good. You tell him he's to sleep in the barn, and I want him gone tomorrow."

Makinna approached her window in time to watch Mr. and Mrs. Browning walk toward the barn. Her gaze went to the Indian, who had melted into the shadows, almost becoming a part of them. She realized he'd heard every word the Brownings had uttered, and she felt a rush of pity for him.

Without pausing to think, she headed out of her bedchamber. The main room was crudely furnished with a long wooden table, a potbellied stove, and dirt floors. Mr. Rumford and Mr. Carruthers were sitting at the table talking amiably, their empty plates in front of them.

They both looked up when she approached. Makinna realized she had forgotten to put on her veil, but she was too angry to care about that at the moment.

She went directly to the table, found an empty tin plate, and begin spooning beans into it. She speared a chunk of meat and plopped it onto the plate, then added a slice of cornbread to the mound.

Mr. Carruthers nodded at the heaping plate. "You must be hungry, Mrs. Hillyard."

"It's not for me," she answered sharply.

"Didn't think a young, pretty thing like you could eat that much in one sitting," Mr. Rumford observed in a jovial if patronizing way. "If you don't mind an old man's compliments," he added.

"I am in no mood for compliments, Mr. Rumford. As a representative of the Butterfield Stage Line, how could you allow that man and woman to work for you? Aren't they supposed to see that your passengers are fed and sheltered?"

He looked taken aback. "Are you speaking of Jack and Edna Browning?"

"I am."

He assumed an official-sounding tone. "Obviously, they have done something to offend you. Tell me what it is, and I'll speak to them about it immediately."

"I'll tell you what they did, if you don't already know. They refused to feed the Indian," she said angrily. "What is he to do, starve to death?"

Mr. Rumford looked uncomfortable. "Well, he should have known what might happen when he boarded our stage. My only obligation is to my legal passengers."

"That's right," Mr. Carruthers spoke up. "If you let one Indian ride the stage, they'll all want the privilege."

Mr. Rumford nodded. "No need to worry about that possibility. I've already informed him that he won't be leaving with the stage in the morning. Can't think how he got aboard in the first place. In spite of his fine attire, he's still a savage."

Makinna glared from one man to the other. "I wonder who among us are the uncivilized ones. I am ashamed to be in a room when he is consigned to a barn. Even if he is an Indian, he's a human being, and he gets hungry and needs rest just like we do. You treat your mules better than you do him. At least you see that they are fed and watered."

She turned away, heading for the front door. Seldom had she been so angry. No person, not even that Indian, was going to go hungry if she could help it. She brushed past Mr. and Mrs. Browning at the door and kept going without acknowledging them.

Edna Browning stared after her. "Humph. What bee's stirring in her bonnet? That high-and-mighty passenger of yours, Mr. Rumford, seems to think she's too good for the likes of us." She huffed toward the kitchen, her husband tagging behind.

Makinna didn't see the Indian at first. Then he silently emerged from the shadows and stood directly before her. She flinched and instantly stepped back, wondering if she should have asked one of the gentlemen inside to accompany her. A cloud was covering the moon, and she couldn't see the Indian's face clearly, but she knew he would be frowning.

"I am sorry if I startled you, Mrs. Hillyard," he said, moving away from her and turning his head up as if contemplating the heavens.

She stepped hesitantly closer to him. "I . . . brought you . . . I thought you might like something to eat," Makinna said, daring to hold the tin plate out to him.

He didn't look at her. "You could have saved yourself the trouble. I am not hungry."

She took a step closer. "You should eat anyway."

He swung his head in her direction and said in a biting tone, "Why should you concern yourself with my dining habits?"

She was silent for a moment, trying to think of the right words to say. "I am sorry about the others."

His tone was cynical as he asked, "Are you?"

"Yes, I am. Otherwise, I wouldn't be here now."

"Yet you are just as frightened of me as they are, Mrs. Hillyard. Do you think of me as a savage ready to pounce on you?"

She didn't bother to deny her nervousness about being around him. "I doubt you would be that desperate."

She was amazed when she heard him laugh. "You are right. I have no desire to pounce on a married woman, one who is in mourning. And a white woman at that."

"Please," she urged, holding the food out to him again. "Take this. You haven't eaten all day."

"I think not." He turned his face back to the quarter moon now emerging from the clouds. Again she sensed in him a sadness, a wound of the spirit, and it troubled her.

She placed the food on a nearby wooden bench. "I'll just leave it here, should you change your mind. It may not be very good, but it will be nourishing."

He said nothing.

Makinna noticed that he had suddenly tensed, as if he were listening to something in the distance. All she heard was the howl of some nocturnal animal. Although she was unfamiliar with them, she suspected it must be a coyote or even a wolf. As she listened, she heard an answering howl, and then another and another until the creatures seemed to be all around them.

"You had better go inside now, Mrs. Hillyard," the Indian said, turning his head in the direction of the barn and staring into the darkness.

Makinna was only too happy to get away from him. She had offered him food. If he didn't want to eat, it was no concern of hers. At least now she could sleep with a slightly clearer conscience. "Good night . . . sir."

He didn't reply but simply moved silently and quickly toward the barn. Something was bothering him, and Makinna didn't think it was the Brownings' rudeness.

She went back inside, passing through the main room without speaking to the people gathered there. She was still too angry. Entering her chamber, she closed the door, noting it had no lock. Neither did the window. She felt uneasy. If the Indian did take it into his head to enter her room, she had no way to stop him.

After removing her cumbersome bustle, she lay down on the bed fully clothed, too weary even to undo her stays or remove her shoes. She would just rest a bit and later undress and put on her nightgown.

She could still hear the animals howling. They seemed to be getting closer. Or was that only her imagination?

Soon her eyes drifted shut, and she fell into a deep, dreamless sleep.

Makinna awoke in a suffocating darkness, gasping for breath. She lay still, listening, her heart pounding as some unknown fear coursed through her veins. It was quiet—too quiet. The never-ceasing wind had died down, the howling animals that had frightened her earlier in the evening were now silent, and she couldn't even hear any crickets chirping. She pressed a hand against her thundering heart. She wanted a sound—anything but this ominous silence, like the inside of a tomb.

Abruptly, fearfully, Makinna sensed that she was not alone. It wasn't a sound or a movement that alerted her, but a feeling. She sat up and swung her feet to the floor, peering into the darkness, but discerned no shape or movement or sound.

She started violently when a hand clamped over her mouth, and a strong arm wrapped around her, pulling her to her feet.

A harsh whisper came to her out of the darkness. "Be still, and listen to me. Your life depends on it."

Chapter Four

It was the Indian's voice! What did he want with her?

"Do exactly as I say, and you might stay alive. Now, I am going to remove my hand from your mouth, but first you must promise that you will not make a sound. Can you do that?" he insisted.

Hearing the threat in his voice, she nodded. It was doubtful that she could make a sound anyway, because fear had closed her throat. Was he there because he wanted to ravish her? Oh, why had she attempted to be kind to him? The others had been right about him all along. Why hadn't she listened to them?

The Indian gripped her arm and led her to the window. He quietly lifted her through, then quickly joined her before she could react or call for help. He again clasped her arm and stood still for a moment, listening.

Makinna knew that the others were asleep, so no one would come to her immediate rescue. "Why are you—"

His clamped a hand over her mouth, cutting off both her speech and her breathing. He dipped his head and whispered harshly in her ear. "Do not make a sound, woman. If you do, it may be your last."

Before she realized what was happening, he was tugging her deeper into the night shadows, silently, ominously.

Makinna closed her eyes, trying to gather her courage so she could contend with the terror that was paralyzing her reasoning.

Was he taking her to the barn to ravish her there?

No. He moved around the barn and away from the way station, toward the desert. He dragged her up the side of a sand dune and glanced back briefly as if he feared being followed.

Dear God, he was taking her farther away from the station and any help.

He walked with an easy stride while she struggled along beside him. He was a powerful man, and she knew she had no chance of fighting him off.

After they had been walking for some time,

he paused and glanced back in the direction of the way station. Then he pushed her to the ground with such force that her face went into the sand. When he dropped down beside her, a scream built in her throat, but she dared not let it pass her lips.

For a long, tense moment she waited, fearing what he would do. His hand was on her shoulder, keeping her in place, but so far he seemed more interested in the way station than in her. Maybe he was making sure that no one was following them before he ripped her clothing off.

At last she found her voice, and it trembled with fear when she pleaded, "Please don't hurt me."

"Do not speak," he said, angrily pushing her face back down. "Be silent!"

Suddenly a bloodcurdling yell broke the stillness, and Makinna raised her head to follow the Indian's gaze. The night was so black that it was difficult to see anything, but her eyes widened when she spotted what appeared to be torches. She felt hope flare in her heart. Someone must have discovered that she was missing, and they were searching for her!

But her hope died when another bloodcurdling yell split the night, and she saw men mounted on horses. Dear God, Indians were attacking the station!

"We have to go help the others!" she cried,

scrambling to get to her feet, but the Indian pushed her down again.

"Do not speak, and do not move," he commanded. "There is nothing we can do to help."

"But—"

"I will not tell you again to be quiet," he said ominously.

She clamped her lips together, forced to watch helplessly while the Indians intensified their attack. She heard sporadic gunfire, and again hope flamed within her. Someone was firing at the Indians; perhaps they would chase away the attackers.

But again her hope died hard when she saw more Indians joining those already circling the way station.

"You should have warned the others," she whimpered. "Why can't we go back and help them now?"

He gripped her arm and pulled her to her feet. "Silence! We must get away from here at once."

She jerked her arm out of his grasp and said angrily, "You aren't even going to try to help them, are you?"

He said nothing as he grasped her hand and pulled her forward. She tried to free herself, but his grip only tightened, and in one swift move, he swung her in his arms and carried her down the other side of the sand dune. Makinna had never seen a night so dark, with only the pale moon's feeble light.

The Indian carried her for some time before he roughly set her on her feet. She stumbled and fell, and he did not attempt to help her up.

She dusted sand from her arms and face. "You are a monster."

He either didn't hear her or chose to ignore her, his attention focused on the way they had come.

"Did you hear me?" she asked, wanting to pound her fists against his chest. "I said you are a monster. You wanted the others dead because of the way they treated you. For all I know, those Indians might be from your tribe, and you might have put them up to attacking the Adobe Springs station."

She cringed when he reached for her. But he merely grabbed her hand and pulled her along. "We must leave."

She drew back, reluctant to be led still farther away from potential help. "What will the Indians do to them?"

"They will all be killed," he said with no emotion in his voice. "And if they find you, they will do far worse than that."

"Are they your tribe members? Can't you stop them?"

"They are Apache," he informed her, pulling her forward so swiftly that she was forced to run to keep up with him.

"Apache! Dear God, we must do something!"

"We cannot help them." His powerful grip

57

pulled her along with such a force that she almost lost her footing. She had no choice but to go where he led.

The Indian set a punishing pace for what seemed like hours, and Makinna, tired and gasping for breath, was sure she could not take another step. Her soft leather slippers had filled with sand that cut into her skin with each step. But the Indian urged her forward mercilessly.

Finally Makinna could not move another inch. She fell to her knees. "Leave me here," she said between gasps of breath. "I can't go any farther."

He yanked her up and turned her to face the direction from which they'd come. "The Apache has a keen eye. If the sun comes up before they have finished at the station, they will discover our tracks leading into the desert, and they will follow. Look for yourself what they are capable of."

In the distance she saw crimson flames leap toward the sky. The station buildings were all on fire. She felt sick and clamped a hand over her mouth. "What did they do to—"

"Do not ask," he broke in. "You would not like the answer."

"You are just like those savages, heartless and unfeeling. Why would they kill people they don't even know?"

He pulled her forward. "We must reach the lava hills before daylight."

She kept glancing back until Adobe Springs was no more than a dim red glow against the darkened sky. Tormented by the thought that everyone was dead, she gradually realized that if the Indian hadn't spirited her away, she would be dead, too. She should feel grateful to him, but she still didn't know his intentions for her, and that fear still tightened her throat.

But her fear that the Apache were pursuing them even now gave her the strength to keep moving.

Over and over she forced one aching foot in front of the other, repeating silently to herself, *This, too, shall pass.* The desert was a huge wasteland that seemed to go on forever. When would this night end, and what would happen to her when it did?

She was overcome with relief when they finally reached the lava hills. But the ground was hard and uneven, and the jagged lava rocks cut into the flimsy soles of her shoes. When they reached the top, the Indian released her arm, and she collapsed, exhausted. She lowered her head, gasping for every breath she could drag into her lungs. The hot wind seemed to scorch her throat and felt like a blast of fire against her skin.

Tears blurred her vision as she watched the

Indian, standing in a narrow patch of moonlight, turn to stare back the way they'd come.

"Do you know where we are?" she asked weakly between gulps of air.

"Yes."

"Are we going to die out here?"

He returned to loom over her, silent for a moment. When he finally spoke, it was a grim whisper. "Do you want the truth?"

"Yes."

He knelt down beside her, and she pulled back, frightened. "We have little chance of coming out of the desert alive, unless you listen to me and do everything I tell you to.

Makinna sat up straight, wondering if he might ravish her now that he had turned his attention to her. As exhausted as she was, she wished they hadn't stopped. She had felt safer while they had been moving.

"No," she protested. "I certainly will not do everything you ask of me. You can't expect me to—to submit to you. Never!"

An agitated breath hissed through his teeth. "You seem to prize yourself very highly, Mrs. Hillyard. I can assure you that, as a female, you hold no interest for me. In truth, you are an encumbrance I can ill afford. While I have no desire to touch you, if you fall behind, I *will* leave you to die."

She was glad for the darkness so he would not see her blushing in shame. She had assumed the worst of him when she should have been thanking him for saving her life. But why had he not warned the others about the Apache attack? She abruptly remembered him listening attentively to the animal howls when she'd taken him a plate of food. "You knew that those animal calls earlier this evening were Apache, didn't you?"

"I suspected it. But I was not certain."

"Yet you did nothing to warn the others. Did you happily leave them to die? Do you hate the white race so much?"

"Do you suppose those fine gentlefolk would have heeded the suspicions of a 'savage'?" he challenged. Then he seemed to grow weary. "In truth, Mrs. Hillyard, lately I give very little thought to your race."

But she would not let the subject go. "You could have saved the others, too."

"If I had tried to, *you* would now be dead."

A sob caught in her throat, but she did not give it voice. Instead she ventured a frail hope. "Perhaps they were able to fight the Apache off."

"There were too many. Fifty, maybe more."

She fought back tears. Mr. Rumford and Mr. Carruthers, massacred? Even the Brownings didn't deserve to die that way. Then there was the stage driver, and the men who'd ridden shotgun, and several Mexicans who worked for the station. Surely they were not all dead.

She glanced at the Indian, wishing there was light so she could see his face. She still wasn't sure she could trust him. For all she knew, he might be an Apache and had known about the raid.

"What are you going to do with me?" she finally asked.

He let out a breath. "God only knows. It was never my intention to be saddled with a difficult, stubbornly inquisitive female."

"I am not your responsibility. You can just leave, and I'll make my way back to Adobe Springs when it's light enough."

He stood up, laughing sardonically. "You would not even know in which direction to start out. You would be hopelessly lost within minutes."

Makinna opened her mouth to deny his accusations but clamped her lips together. After all, he was right. "When the sun rises, you can point me in the right direction, and I'll just walk back."

His hand dropped to her shoulder. "You don't understand, Miss Hillyard. There is nothing for you to go back to. The station has been burned, and everyone is dead."

"But—"

"They're dead," he said harshly, his grip tightening on her shoulder. "You have to accept the truth of that. And if you go back, the Apache will find and kill you. Do I make myself understood? You had better pray that they don't come looking for us as it is."

She shrugged off his hand and lowered her head as sadness enveloped her. She knew he was right, but it hurt to think about Mr. Rumford and Mr. Carruthers being senselessly slaughtered. Still, she knew the Indian was right again. The truth was, she could do nothing to change what had already happened, no matter how tragic, and pretending otherwise only muddled her thinking. She sent up a silent prayer for their souls and tried to focus on what she *could* do. "What do we do now?"

He turned away, grumbling, "We stay alive. Avoid the Apache if we can."

"But you are an Indian. What have you to fear from them?"

"The Apache have no love for me or my kind. Indeed, they may have attacked Adobe Springs because they had heard I would be there."

"You! But why?"

"Get some sleep if you can, Mrs. Hillyard."

"How can I possibly sleep with so many questions left unanswered?"

"You had better sleep. Tomorrow will test your strength far beyond its limits. We will be traveling fast, and we cannot leave any footprints behind. When the Apache discover I was not among the dead, they will probably come looking for me. And make no mistake, Mrs.

Hillyard, the Chiricahua Apache are among the fiercest warriors of any tribe. They can cover forty miles a day on foot and seventy-five miles on horseback. Can you?"

"No human can do that!"

"I assure you, the Apache can."

"Why do they hate you so much that they would commit such atrocities against innocent people?"

He thrust a canteen at her. "Take only one swallow. We have a lot of desert to cross before we reach water."

Makinna raised the canteen to her lips and took a sip, wishing she could drink the whole thing. She felt as if she'd swallowed half the sand in the desert. She handed him back the canteen and leaned against a boulder, cradling her head on her arms. "Suppose the Apache come upon us in our sleep?"

"I will be watching for them. Now no more questions."

She closed her eyes. She was so weary. *Why were the Apache after him?* Why had they slain the people at Adobe Springs? Could she trust *this* Indian?

Her eyes popped open. "Just one more question," she insisted.

"What is it now, Mrs. Hillyard?" he asked wearily.

"Mr. Rumford said your name was something like Silverhorn. Is that correct?"

He sighed. "That's one of my names."

"Oh," she said. "What's the other?"

"Tykota. My name is Tykota."

Chapter Five

Tykota sat with his back braced against a boulder, his gaze sweeping the darkened countryside, his ears attuned to the night sounds. If the Apache had known he had returned, who else knew?

He glanced to where the woman lay sleeping. She was going to slow him down. He should have left her behind. Why hadn't he? Because of her kindness to him? Something in her spirit that called out to him? Whatever it was, he'd had time to save only one person, and she'd been his choice.

Tykota hadn't even seen her face yet. She'd been swaddled in a black veil on the coach, and when she had brought him the food, it had been too dark to make out her features.

He wasn't even sure of her age. Maybe mid-thirties? She had told Mr. Rumford that she would be living with her sister in San Francisco. Odd, she'd made no mention of her husband. And somehow she seemed very alone in the world.

He stared back into the darkness. He knew about aloneness. Both of his fathers, Indian and white, had died within a year of each other, leaving an enormous void in his life. He thought about the letter he'd received from his white mother just before he'd left England, after burying George Silverhorn. It had carried a warning from Mangas, his long-time mentor and aide to his Indian father, Valatar. His old teacher had wanted him to know that his half brother, Sinica, had become the leader of a renegade band of Apaches and had boasted that Tykota would never return to Valle de la Luna alive. Tykota breathed deeply, hoping Mangas was wrong. He hadn't seen any of his Indian family since the night George Silverhorn had spirited him away. But would Sinica truly turn against him in violence? Perhaps he was still bitter because his mother had been shamed by their father, and their father had not named him the future chief of the Perdenelas.

Tykota sighed wearily. He had never wanted to be chief. He was sure he was unworthy of the honor. He was not ready to make all the decisions for the tribe.

Perhaps the Apache attack on Adobe Springs had been random, he mused. But if it had been Sinica, he'd come for Tykota. And he would keep coming.

Tykota had thought often of that night when his father had renounced Sinica and Coloradous and placed shame on them and their mother. And as he'd grown older he'd still thought that his father had been too harsh with his other two sons. They were of his blood, yet he had banished them from his life. And Sinica, hot-blooded as he was, would probably settle for nothing less than Tykota's death to settle the wrong.

Tykota glanced back at the woman. It might have been kinder to her if he'd let her die with the others back at the way station. If Sinica did catch them, she would meet a much worse fate.

He closed his eyes, feeling tired and heartsick. He would just have to outwit Sinica, and that was not going to be easy. Although Tykota knew this desert well, Sinica knew it better. His half brother had been living with the Apache, and they were the ultimate rulers of the Guadalupe mountains and surrounding countryside. If it was Sinica that was following them, it wouldn't be long until he picked up their trail.

Tykota had to get the woman to safety and

then go as quickly as possible to the Mountain of the Moon. Unrest must be stirring among his people. They would expect him to be a strong leader, and he could only pray he was equal to the task his father had entrusted to him.

The sun was no more than a golden glow in the east when Tykota bent over the woman. In the dawn light he was startled to see how young she was. Probably somewhere in her twenties. He stared at the golden hair curling around her shoulders, her long lashes lying softly against her rosy cheeks. Her lips were full, her face very lovely. He was so overwhelmed by her delicate beauty that a lump formed in his throat. At last he touched her shoulder gently to awaken her.

Her eyes opened, and they were bluer than the desert sky. Tykota watched as the confusion in those eyes was replaced with fear. She sat up quickly and moved away from his touch.

"Here," he said, holding food out to her. "Eat quickly. We must leave right away."

Makinna stared at the concoction he'd handed her. "It looks like . . . like raw plants. I can't eat this."

"Then you will go hungry, Mrs. Hillyard, because there is nothing else to eat."

She brushed her hair from her face. "What is it?"

"The beans are from the mesquite tree and do not taste so bad. The other is from the mescal cactus. It would taste better roasted, but I dare not light a fire, even if we did have the time."

She shook her head. "I am not hungry enough to eat this."

"As you wish. But you will be," he warned. "And, as I told you last night, I will not wait for you if you lag behind."

She glared at him. "No one asked you to." She stood slowly, stretching to relieve muscles cramped from sleeping on the hard ground.

Her movement was inadvertently provocative, making her breasts bulge against her gown, and Tykota quickly glanced away. A primitive stirring inside him heated his blood. This stubborn, spirited, outspoken woman was different from other females he had known. And he didn't want to feel this way about her. He didn't even want to like her.

"You are not in a genteel Southern town out here, Mrs. Hillyard. At the height of the noon sun it will be so hot that you could cook meat without a campfire. We may encounter rattlesnakes and scorpions and, at the higher elevations, bears, wolves, or pumas. Can you face all that, Mrs. Hillyard?"

She eyed the canteen slung over his shoulder. "Ask me again after I have a sip of water."

His mouth curved into a small smile. "You may have two sips. But no more."

When he handed her the canteen, she raised it to her lips, savoring the two sips he allowed her. Then, wiping her hand across her mouth, she handed it back. "Can you tell me where we're going?"

She watched him, puzzled, as he bent down, and poured some of their precious water into the dirt, mixing it into mud. "If I told you, you still would not know. But, I will say this much: after today, we will rest in the heat of the day and travel only by night. It will not be easy."

"Because of the heat?"

"Mostly, yes."

She watched him as he cupped his hands and scooped up the mud. "What are you doing?"

"You will need this on your face so your skin will not blister."

"What! Oh, no! You aren't putting mud on my face."

"Close your eyes," he commanded.

She wanted to defy him, but she could see by his hard expression that to do so would be futile. She reluctantly closed her eyes in submission. After all, he did know about the desert, and she didn't. When he finished daubing her face, she asked, "Does it look as awful as it feels?"

Tykota nearly chuckled but quickly became serious. "If your face baked in the sun, you would feel much worse." He looked her over carefully to make sure he'd covered all the exposed skin. "We will be moving fast, and you must keep up."

"You didn't put mud on your face," she objected.

"I do not need it."

"May I ask you one more question, Mr. Silverhorn?" she persisted.

He cast her a look of impatience and turned and walked away.

She hurried to catch up with him. "Will you explain to me about your names?" she asked, practically running to keep pace with him.

"Ty Silverhorn is what I am called in your white world."

"And Tykota?" she pronounced carefully, thinking the name suited him because it sounded powerful and masculine. "What does it mean?"

He glanced sideways at her. "Do you always talk this much?"

"No, Mr. Silverhorn. But I have been very much on my own lately, with no one to talk to."

He was quiet for a time, and just when she thought he wasn't going to answer her, he said softly, "Tykota means 'the chosen one.'"

Since he didn't seem inclined to talk, she lapsed into silence. Besides, it took all her strength just to keep up with him. After a while, she lagged behind, and she found herself observing the way his white shirt was plastered to his skin with sweat. She could see the muscles ripple across his back, and the black hair falling over his shoulders fascinated her. Her gaze dropped to the gun belt strapped about his narrow waist. No bow and arrow for this Indian, she mused.

As the morning wore on, Makinna found herself falling farther and farther behind. At last, she could not take another step, and the sun was so hot, she could hardly draw a breath. She was hungry and wished she had eaten the plants Tykota had offered her that morning.

She was grateful when he stopped and turned back toward her, waiting for her to catch up with him.

"I told you I would not wait for you. I mean it." His dark eyes were stormy.

"I know," she gasped. "I am trying my best to keep up."

His gaze seemed to soften, and he slowed his pace a bit to allow her to catch her breath. She did not complain, but the day was young and she was already struggling just to breathe.

Tykota halted again. "Take off those contraptions that hold you in."

Her eyes rounded in horror at the very

thought of removing her undergarments. "Surely you aren't suggesting that I—" She shook her head, utterly shocked. "Sir, that I will not do."

Tykota glared at her. "You will either take them off, or I will do it for you."

She spun away from him and took several hurried steps away. "You wouldn't dare!"

The look he gave her implied that he would.

"I . . . will do it," she said, giving in with ill grace. "But you will have to turn your back."

"I am going to scout ahead. When I return, I will expect you to be ready."

She watched him leave, wishing she could hit him with one of the many stones that littered the ground. He was insufferable.

Waiting until he was out of sight, she unhooked her gown and struggled out of her corset. Holding the device in front of her, she wondered what to do with it. Finally she refastened her gown and and carefully hid the offending garment under some rocks and shrubbery, mindful of Tykota's warnings that they might be followed. She had to admit that she could breathe easier, but she felt positively indecent.

When Tykota returned later, he asked what she had done with the discarded undergarment. When she showed him, he nodded in approval and began walking. She fell into step beside him, and after a while she smiled to herself, feeling far freer without the tight corset, although she would not admit it to him.

He glanced down at her, and she thought for a moment that he, too, was smiling. But his jaw tightened, and she realized she must be mistaken.

Then he said, "Admit you feel better."

She was glad for the mud on her face, or he would have seen her blush. She lowered her gaze so he couldn't read her eyes. "My mother would have been horrified to see me abandon my . . . my . . ."

"Undergarment," he finished for her.

"A gentleman would never make mention of anything so delicate in front of a lady, sir."

"You may be a lady, Mrs. Hillyard, but if I were a gentleman, we'd both be dead back at Adobe Springs," he reminded her. "You might want to think about that."

Insufferable man, she thought heatedly, wishing he'd fall off a cliff.

Chapter Six

The heat was so intense that Makinna could actually see waves rising from the desert floor. She tried not to think of the lush greenery of New Orleans or the coolness of the evenings when she had sat on the porch with her mother. At the moment, she wished for a downpour, anything but this infernal heat. She was glad now of the mud on her face; otherwise, she'd be in anguish.

"We will stop here until the cool of the evening," Tykota told her.

An overhanging cliff created a narrow stretch of shade, and Makinna sought refuge there. But she found no relief from the heat that burned through her clothing when she leaned back against the rock.

Tykota stood so still, peering out over the valley, that he could have passed for a statue. But his eyes were alive, and his gaze moved keenly over the countryside. Makinna could feel the tension in him until he was satisfied that they were not being followed.

Makinna began emptying the sand from her slippers. When she glanced back at Tykota, she saw him remove his shirt and tear a long strip from it. Blushing at the sight of his broad bronze chest bared to her gaze, she watched him twist the strip of cloth and tie it about his brow, like a headband to match the leather bands circling both of his muscled arms. Even from her vantage point she saw what looked like gleaming golden eagles set into each armband. Surely the carvings couldn't be real gold, could they?

Makinna quickly slipped into her shoes. Tykota now looked even more like the Indian he was. She had never seen a man in such a state of undress, not even her brother. She meant to lower her gaze, but she could not keep from looking at him. She realized that the farther they got from her world, the more any semblance of civilization was stripped away from Tykota. Layer by layer he became more primitive, untamed, with a dangerous, tightly leashed aura about him. Despite his tall boots and tailored black trousers, he was every inch an Indian.

Clearly Tykota was a complex man, but Makinna was slowly beginning to trust him. She sensed in her heart that he would never willfully harm her. Although he might very well leave her behind as he'd threatened if she didn't keep up with his pace.

"I am hungry now," she said nervously. "May I have some of those plants you offered me this morning?"

He turned to her with a fierce expression. But the fierceness evaporated when he looked into her sincere blue eyes and saw that she had moved aside to allow him room to sit in the shade.

He reached into his pouch and walked toward her, then held the food out to her.

"Tell me about this plant," she said before taking a bite of the softened mescal. The taste was not offensive, but neither could she say it was good.

"The mescal is excellent food for traveling because it keeps well dried. The blossoms taste quite good, but the sap can be an intoxicating drink. The root can be used for soap. The mescal plant is as essential to the survival of the Apache as the buffalo is to the Comanche."

"And to your people?"

"No. Not my people. Although we will eat the plant when forced to, we have other resources."

She finished another bite of the mescal. "Who are your people? From what tribe do you come?"

Tykota's gaze slid away from hers. "You would not know of them."

She smiled. "Perhaps you come from the mysterious tribe Mr. Rumford was talking about on the coach—the one that no white man has ever seen and lived to tell about."

Makinna had spoken whimsically, but the memory of Mr. Rumford made her close her eyes against the sudden pressure of tears. When she opened them again, she saw the tightening of Tykota's jaw. When he did not answer her question, she tried to move on to less painful thoughts.

"It is so hot," she said. "I have never known such heat."

"Is not New Orleans hot? What is your city like?"

So he had been listening to her conversation with Mr. Rumford and Mr. Carruthers in the coach. She sighed. "Louisiana is as different from this desert as two places can be. It is green and teeming with life. Rivers and streams meander through dense swamps, and the Mississippi River dominates everything around it."

Tykota watched her carefully. "Why did you leave New Orleans? Surely you set out on a journey difficult for a woman alone."

"I am certain you heard much of my conversation on the stage, even though you pretended to be asleep. You probably know that my mother and brother both recently died."

"Tell me more about them."

"Mother had been an invalid for many years, but she was so sweet-natured and uncomplaining that it was a joy to be with her. I wanted to make her life comfortable and ease her suffering as much as I could. It was hard to watch her become weaker and weaker over time. My brother was, I imagine, like most big brothers: protective, kind, and loving."

Tykota looked suddenly thoughtful but did not speak, so she concluded, "William died in a horseback riding accident."

"What about your husband?"

She averted her eyes. "I have allowed you and the others to form a misconception about me. I have never been married. I just thought it was safer to pretend to be a married woman while traveling alone."

"I see." Tykota found that that revelation brought him an odd satisfaction. "So, did your family do business in New Orleans?"

She studied her hands, noticing the nails were chipped and dirty. "Yes. At one time, my family owned storage warehouses and shipping barges. But the war came, and we lost everything, as many of our friends did. My father died soon thereafter. My sister married and moved out West."

"And then you lost your mother and brother?"

The thought of what she had suffered touched him. But then again, perhaps she was on her way west to join not only her sister but the man she would marry. "I suppose you had a full social life in New Orleans."

"No. None at all. My mother needed constant care."

He could hear the loneliness in her voice. "There is a man now, perhaps, who wants you for his wife?"

She shook her head. "No one."

He smiled, and it transformed his face. "Then the men in New Orleans are either blind or fools."

She looked at him, stunned. "Was that a compliment?"

"You do not know you are pleasing to look at?"

She smiled ruefully. "I am too tall for a woman, and I have a terrible temper, besides. But I thank you all the same."

So, she did not know she was a beauty. How unlike many other women, who were forever fishing for compliments. "Makinna is your first name, is it not? How did you come by it?"

"It was my mother's maiden name." She

clasped her hands and looked at him intently. "Now I have told you about myself. So what about you? I want to know why you speak English like an Englishman, not an American."

A veil seemed to descend over his face, and he leaned back against the cliff. "When I was very young, my father sent me to live with an Englishman who was his trusted friend. I came to know George Silverhorn better than I knew my own father. He took me to England with him, and I lived with him and his wife, Hannah, on a country estate. Since he had no children, he raised me like his own. In my eleventh year, he bought a ranch in Texas, so I could be nearer my own land and people."

"You grew up in Texas?"

"I grew up in many places, but Biquera Ranch is the home I remember the most fondly. It is very near the Mexican border."

"You must have missed your real family."

"Yes. But I saw much of the world I would otherwise never have known. And I was sent back to England to be fully educated."

"That explains the accent, among other things. And now you are going home to your family? But which one—your Indian or your English family?"

He closed his eyes and let out a long, slow breath. "You should sleep if you can, Miss

Hillyard. We will be walking most of the night."

She realized he did not want to say any more about himself, so she closed her eyes and did indeed feel tiredness enveloped her. She was hot, hungry, and thirsty, but she had a feeling that with Tykota as her guide, she would live through this terrible ordeal.

Makinna turned her head to look at him. He appeared to be sleeping, but she knew that at the slightest sign of danger, he would be alert. And she knew that no matter where she went after this, or what turn her life took, she would never forget this tall, beautiful Indian so shrouded in mystery.

Makinna awoke with a start, and at first she could not remember where she was. It was almost dark, and she could smell meat cooking.

She came to her feet and followed the wonderful aroma to where Tykota was cooking something over a campfire.

"Have you ever eaten rabbit?" he asked, watching her carefully.

Makinna dropped down beside him. "No," she replied, hungrily watching the drippings from the meat splatter into the fire. "But it smells wonderful, and I'm willing to eat anything at the moment."

Tykota removed the meat from the skewer

he'd fashioned from a mesquite branch. On a flat stone he carved the meat with expertise.

He offered her the first piece. "Be careful. It's very hot. Don't burn your fingers."

Makinna handled the meat gingerly and blew on it until it cooled. She closed her eyes with the first bite. "Mmm, this is delicious." She opened her eyes. "But I would have thought a rabbit would be meatier and have bones."

Tykota bent his head so she did not see him smile. "Oh, that isn't rabbit. It's rattlesnake."

She paused with a piece of meat halfway to her mouth. She knew he was waiting for her to reject it, but she would not give him the satisfaction. She hoped her voice sounded casual. "Oh, really? You said it was rabbit."

"That is not what I said, Miss Hillyard. I merely asked you if you had ever eaten rabbit."

"Well, it's delicious, anyway."

He gave her another rare look of approval. "You are a most unusual woman, Miss Hillyard."

"So you've implied, though not always in the most flattering terms."

He handed her the canteen, knowing she was having sudden trouble swallowing the remaining snake meat. "Here, wash it down." He watched her take a drink before he spoke again. "You are also a brave woman. I wonder if there are many more like you back in New Orleans."

"Of course. We women of Louisiana spring from hearty stock." She glanced out at the desert, watching the sun splash gold across the land. "I thought it was too dangerous to have a campfire."

"At this time of day, anyone who might be tracking us would not see the fire in the sunset, and the smoke will blend with the twilight."

"Tykota, will you not tell me something about your life before you went to England? I have told you about my youth."

"I left my people when I was very young. Nothing happened that would be of interest to you."

She turned away, realizing he still refused to talk about himself. She dropped the subject for the time being.

Absently running her fingers through her hair, she came across endless tangles. Finally, in moment of brazenness, she lifted her skirt hem, ripped the bottom ruffle from her petticoat, and tied her hair away from her face. "There," she said, pleased. My hair won't get in my way now."

"I could cut it for you. It would be cooler. Besides, you will never get those tangles out now."

She glanced down at his knife. "I don't think so. I'll manage the way it is."

He shrugged. "If you should change your mind . . ." He flashed the knife.

"I won't." She rose to walk away from him. No, she would not allow him to cut her hair.

"Miss Hillyard?"

"I said no," she replied, without breaking her stride.

"It's not that. You are walking in the wrong direction. If you keep going, you will soon fall off a cliff."

She stopped and turned back to him. "How can you expect me to know that? I wasn't born here."

"All I expect from you is that you obey me, that you do what I tell you to. That way you will come to no harm."

She raised her chin in proud defiance, looking almost comical with the streaked mud on her face. "I will do what you say as long as it's what *I* want to do. I already warned you that I have a temper. And you are testing its limits."

"Ah, yes, your temper. Still, what is important is that you do not test mine."

She wisely made no reply.

He put out the fire and scattered the ashes, and she watched as he wiped away all traces that they had been there. Then he glanced up at her.

"Walk to that higher ledge and wait for me."

She nodded, and when she reached the spot, she watched him brush away their footprints with a spiny branch of a scrub bush. He was leaving nothing behind for the Apache to find.

Tykota joined Makinna and guided her up a steep slope. She gritted her teeth, hoping she wouldn't fall and break her neck. Through her thin-soled shoes she could feel every pebble and stone. It had been bad earlier; now it was agony. Once she tripped and almost lost her footing, managing to stay upright only by grabbing a scraggly bush.

Tykota turned back to her with a scowl on his face. "Try to step where I step."

"I can't. Your strides are too long for me."

He put his hands on his hips and glanced upward, as if seeking patience. "Then walk in front of me so I can cover our trail."

She swept past him without meeting his eyes. He could be the most insufferable man.

Chapter Seven

Makinna's chest tightened as she stood on the cliff, the evening breeze stirring her hair. She could smell the sweet perfume of the desert in bloom. Why had she not seen the beauty before?

She was probably as guilty as everyone else on seeing the desert for the first time and looking past a beauty so subtle that it was woven into the tapestry of this land. Could there be more brilliant sunrises and sunsets anywhere in the world? The land was certainly not colorless, as she had thought at first. The colors were of the earth and sky, with blooming cacti and brilliantly hued birds that soared on the breath of the wind. Also, the desert was teeming with life if one took the time to look. Just then, she watched a hawk dive toward the ground, probably in pursuit of some unfortunate prey that had caught its keen eye.

There was life *and* death here. And renewal.

Makinna hadn't heard Tykota approach her until he spoke. "Do you find beauty in the desert?" he asked.

"Yes, I do. It's unlike anywhere else in the world." She turned her head and looked up at him. "I admit I didn't see it at first, and had I gone on with my journey on the stage, I would probably have been left with the impression that this land was utterly desolate."

He looked pleased for a moment. "Most people do not see with the eye but with the mind. This land offers constant contrasts, a heaven for some and harsh, as well. If a man lets down his guard, the land can easily claim him for its victim."

"You never let your guard down, do you?"

Tykota looked past her at the glowing sunset, knowing he dare not let his guard down around Makinna. Even standing near her was painful. He had never felt this way about a woman before, so he could not put a name to what he was feeling. She was brave and spirited and rarely complained about how hard he was pushing her. It seemed to be in her nature to see the good in any situation. And though she did have a temper, he found he liked that about her as well.

"No," he said at last. "I never let my guard down."

"Why not? Surely *sometimes* it is safe to do so."

He chose to ignore her question. "Do you think you can continue until the sun reaches its zenith?"

Makinna was bone weary. They had walked and climbed hills most of the night, stopping only occasionally to rest. She wanted to cry out that she could not go another step, but she wouldn't let him see that weakness in her. He expected her to complain, maybe even wanted her to. She stiffened her spine. "I can walk as long as you can."

His lips thinned. "Then let us go on."

She stumbled twice, fell once, and was slow to get to her feet. She glowered at Tykota's back as he walked effortlessly ahead of her.

He wasn't human! Didn't he ever get tired? She looked over the steep edge of the cliff, half wanting to shove him off.

He drove on mercilessly, until at last he halted, pointing at a high ridge. "We will spend the day there."

She drew in an exhausted breath, wondering how she would gather the strength to climb to the top.

He motioned for her to go ahead of him. "I will come behind and cover our tracks."

She set her eyes on the summit and her feet

in motion. "This can be endured," she mumbled to herself. "This can be endured." How many times had she spoken those words to keep up her courage in the months her mother had been slowly dying? If she had endured the pain of losing her beloved mother and brother, she could surely get through this.

Makinna sat with her back pressed against a boulder, trying to shade her face against the sun. The mud had long since worn off, and they couldn't use their precious water to make more. Her skin felt as if it were on fire, and she wanted to cry from the pain of it. Her throat was so parched that she could hardly swallow. Her hair was hopelessly tangled, and she was hungry.

But, thanks to Tykota, she was still alive.

Makinna glanced about, searching for him. He'd gone back down the hill some time ago and hadn't returned. Where was he? What if he'd deserted her? What if he'd left her here to die?

She scrambled to her feet and glanced about frantically. She could think of nothing worse than to be left out here to die alone.

She didn't even hear him come up behind her, and she screamed when he placed a hand on her shoulder.

He pulled her to the ground with such a force that the rocks cut painfully into her skin. "Do not make a sound," he warned.

"But what—"

He clamped a hand over her mouth and whispered next to her ear. "Unless you want to meet Apaches face-to-face, remain silent."

She nodded, and he removed his hand but kept his arm about her, holding her still. She heard the sound of horses below and turned a fearful gaze on Tykota. He looked into her eyes, as though willing her to be strong.

The sun was hot on her face, her black gown was plastered to her body with perspiration, and the sharp stones were cutting into her, but she didn't move or make a sound.

It was quiet now, and she feared that the Apaches had dismounted and were making their way up the hill. Tense moments passed, but soon she heard voices and then the sound of them riding away.

Still Tykota held her there, and she wanted to lay her head against his shoulder and have him tell her that everything would be all right. But she knew he would not welcome such womanly weakness from her.

"Are they really gone?" she whispered, fearing their departure might be a trick. "Will they come back?"

"They are gone," he assured her. "They do not know we are here. They will search elsewhere."

Tykota felt himself responding to the softness of Makinna's body against his. He wanted to crush her tightly to him so that he could feel her every breath. Knowing what her reaction would be if she could read his thoughts, he rolled to his feet, trying not to think of how desirable she was. He had wanted women before, had been with many, but none had ever stirred his blood as she did. He wanted to press his lips to hers and feel her arms go around his shoulders. He wanted her body to become a part of his—

"Will they stop pursuing us now, Tykota?" There was fear in her blue eyes.

"They will not come back here," he said, extending a hand to her. "But they have not given up their search."

"What do we do?" she asked wearily.

"We outthink them," he answered, turning away.

She flipped a tangled curl from her face and said softly, "I am so tired. And I feel sure that I could drink a river dry."

"If we can make our water last through this day and tomorrow, you can have all the water you want by tomorrow night."

She brushed gravel from her hands and noticed that her palms were bleeding. "I can do it," she replied with staunch determination.

Makinna did not see the softness in Tykota's dark eyes or his hand reach out to her, then drop to his side. "You must get out of this sun. Already your face is burned."

She glanced about. "I see no shade."

"Remove your petticoat and give it to me."

She was shocked by his suggestion. Taking a hasty step backward, she exclaimed, "I will do no such thing!"

"Remove it, or I will do it for you, Miss Hillyard."

She saw the look in his eyes and knew he meant what he said. She moved away from him a few paces. "Turn your back."

He did as she asked, a small smile on his lips. How could she worry about modesty when she faced death from hunger, thirst, and the Apache? But that was Makinna.

She blushed as she stepped out of her petticoat and held it out to him. "You can turn around now."

Tykota took it and ripped out a seam. "I wonder who decided that a white woman should wear so many undergarments."

She watched as he erected a shelter by stretching the petticoat across two branches that he'd buried in the sand, securing the other end with stones.

"Now I advise you to get out of the sun."

"What about you?"

He reached out and touched her face that was still smudged with faint traces of mud. "I told you, I do not burn."

She was transfixed by his gentle touch and the expression in his dark eyes. In that moment, something primitive called to her that this was the man she had been waiting for all her life. Something about him kept pulling at her, and she wanted to give in to the feeling. She wanted to be in his arms, to feel him hold her close, to never let her go. And that frightened her more than anything else.

Tykota abruptly looked away and dropped his hand, ending the moment of closeness.

Makinna scrambled beneath the shelter, wondering why her heart was drumming against her ribs and why she felt as if she might faint at any moment. Probably the heat, she convinced herself. Hadn't Mr. Carruthers implied that the desert sun could play tricks with a person's mind? Yes, that was probably it.

She watched Tykota walk away and disappear over the rise. She wanted to know where they were going. She would demand an answer from him as soon as the moment presented itself. She had to get away from him, because something was happening to her that she didn't understand. Something powerful and unexpected and frightening.

She closed her eyes and could almost feel his fingers on her face.

"No," she cried, burying her face in her hands. Oh, if only she had remained in New Orleans. If only she had never started out on this ill-fated journey.

Chapter Eight

Makinna jerked awake, disoriented, her eyes wide with fear, her heart pounding. As she got her bearings, she crawled from beneath the shelter Tykota had cunningly erected to protect her from the punishing sun, then stood, stretching her cramped muscles. It was almost sundown, and there was no sign of Tykota.

Again, she feared he'd left her there to die. She turned in every direction, searching for any sign of him. But he had not left even a footprint for her to follow.

"It is time for us to leave."

At the sound of his voice Makinna whirled around to find him standing right behind her. Her stomach tightened in a knot of fear.

Beneath the dying sun, Tykota gazed into

Makinna's eyes and saw more than he wanted to see. He saw pain, uncertainty, and fear. She didn't trust him. It was him she feared.

She stepped quickly away from him, hiding her trembling hands behind her back. "I thought you had left me."

He glowered at her, then turned away to gaze at the sky. "Why would I bring you this far, only to leave you?"

She had no answer. "I'm thirsty."

"I am sorry, Makinna, but you drank the last of the water this morning. There is a water hole nearby, but it is unfit for drinking. You will have to wait until we reach the springs." He gauged the position of the sun and then turned his gaze to the distant hills. "We should reach the springs by full sunrise."

Makinna's footsteps lagged as she rounded a huge sandstone rock and glanced out over the endless dry desert plains. She could not go on. The sun was barely up, but already the heat was as punishing as the inside of an oven. She stumbled and fell and simply didn't have enough strength to regain her footing. She stayed there, with a sob building in her parched throat.

"What kind of a man are you?" she cried out. "You aren't even human. Don't you ever falter or suffer any kind of weakness? Don't you ever get tired, hungry, or thirsty?"

She raised her head and watched him disappear. Would he leave her here to die? She was just too exhausted to go any farther.

She lay her head on the sand, her body and spirits drained. She would never leave this spot. She would die here, and someone, years from now, would find her bleached bones. She closed her eyes, waiting, almost welcoming death to take her.

But that was not to be. A shadow fell across her face, and she glanced up to see Tykota standing over her. Why didn't he just go away and allow her to die in peace?

Instead of rebuking her, as she expected he bent down and gathered her into his strong arms. Limply, she laid her head against his shoulder, too tired to protest or even care.

The sun was so hot, she could hardly breathe. She felt she was being consumed by flames. And she was so weak.

"Do not go to sleep on me, Makinna. There is water just over that next hill. Look, you can see it in the distance. You have to stay awake until we get there."

If she had the strength, she'd defy him and throw his demands back in his face, she thought wearily. He could not order her to stay awake no matter how many times he demanded it of her. She was only vaguely aware that he was walking very fast, and she wondered where he found the energy.

Tykota could barely feel Makinna's breath against his neck. If he didn't get her to water soon, she would die. His strength must not fail him now; he could not lose her. She had trudged along, uncomplaining; even when she was weary unto death. He had sensed by her defense of him at Adobe Springs that she was an extraordinary woman. Now he knew it to be true. What was more, she had feared him then, and she feared him now. But that night at Adobe Springs, her kindness had been stronger than her fear. And her courage had carried her farther than most women could have managed.

No, he could not let her die.

Makinna thought she must be dreaming when she felt cool water wash over her. Opening her eyes, she met Tykota's gaze. The water was real! Tykota had waded into a spring with her in his arms.

He gently set her on her feet, supporting her with one hand while he cupped the other, filled it with water, then held it up to her mouth. She dipped her head and drank thirstily.

"Not too much at first. Take small sips," he instructed. He dipped his hand into the water once more and offered her another drink.

In no time Makinna felt revived enough to duck down and allow the water to wash over her head. Laughing weakly, she came up for air. "I wish this was deep enough to swim in."

Tykota watched her in fascination as she shook water from her hair and pushed wet strands out of her face. "Do you swim?"

"Of course. My brother taught me one summer." She smiled. "But I could never tell my mother that he had. Ladies don't swim," she said, laughing.

"Then a *lady* could drown."

"Ladies do not do many of the things I have done since I left New Orleans."

Tykota found himself fascinated by the water sliding off her soft skin, and he felt an ache begin deep inside. She was so innocent and beautiful, and he was becoming too attached to her. He had to put some distance between them.

She went under and came up again. "I never thought anything could feel so good."

He knew other things that could—his lips touching her neck, then sliding up to her lips. "You remind me of a child given her first toy."

Her laughter was musical. Her happiness gladdened his heart. Beads of water clung to her face, and he wanted to reach out and touch them, touch her hair, her lips.

"Oh, this is better than any toy. I never thought water could taste so good," she said gleefully. "Being raised in a place where there is water in abundance, I have always taken it for granted."

"There are many things that we do not treasure, Makinna, until we lose them."

The way he said her name warned her. She averted her eyes and dipped her hands in the water, sifting it between her fingers. "Have you lost something you treasured?" she asked. When she looked up again, she saw sadness in his eyes. Then his gaze hardened, and he glanced at the horizon.

Clearly, he was not going to answer her question. Already his thoughts were far away, and she sensed that if she spoke at that moment, he wouldn't even hear her. She felt an iron control at work within him, and again she wondered what it would take to ever make that control slip. He dipped his hands in the water and raised them to his lips. He was naked to the waist, and she had to ball her fists to keep from reaching out and touching his bronzed skin.

Makinna turned away, horrified by her improper thoughts and reactions to Tykota. She waded slowly toward the shore and found shelter in the shade of a prickly shrub. But her gaze went back to Tykota, and she watched him emerge from the spring. As he moved toward her, the water became shallower, revealing more of his body with each step he took. His ebony hair hung thickly past his shoulders, and his wet trousers molded to his muscular thighs like a second skin.

She averted her gaze, glancing at the thin ribbon of greenery growing alongside the spring. But again her eyes sought out Tykota. He was such a marvelous-looking man. She blushed and ducked her head, hoping he wouldn't realize what she was feeling as she saw the clear outline of his disturbing masculinity.

Against her will, she watched again as he removed his boots, pouring the water out of them. Then she gasped when he began to remove his trousers. She tensed, fearing he would have nothing on underneath. But he wore a skimpy breechcloth that did little to cover his rippling muscles. Blushing, she lowered her gaze, again ashamed of her improper thoughts.

She lay back, closed her eyes, and tried to still her beating heart. She would not look in his direction again, she told herself.

Makinna lay still, listening to the wind and trying to recall happier days in New Orleans. But suddenly she could only remember the sad times. Her father being forced to sell their home and move them to a smaller house near the docks. She hadn't minded so much, but her brother and father had. Her father had died a broken man a year after the move. She remembered her sister moving away. Her mother and brother dying. Makinna couldn't bear to think about her family—the pain was too deep, the loneliness too sharp.

She cushioned her head on her folded arms and tried to sleep.

Makinna awoke to the most delicious aroma she'd ever smelled—meat roasting over a campfire. She sat up and stretched her arms over her head, smiling at Tykota, who was bent over the spit turning the meat.

"I don't care if that is rattlesnake, I'm ravenous."

He stood up to his full height, and she was relieved to see that he had put on his trousers and boots. "We dine on rabbit tonight."

She rose to join him at the fire, watching the drippings sizzle on hot stones. "Isn't it dangerous to have a fire at night? Do you no longer fear the Apache?"

"The Apache do not know of this place."

"Oh."

She watched the meat with hungry eyes. "When will it be ready?"

"Now."

She stepped to the spring to wash her hands and take a deep drink before returning to Tykota. "I didn't hear you fire your gun. How did you kill the rabbit?"

"I used my knife."

"Oh. Of course." She could not imagine anyone hunting with just a knife. "Is that your usual hunting method?"

"Sometimes."

Makinna was becoming annoyed with his vague answers—or no answers at all. "You never talk unless it's to give me an order, Tykota."

He met her gaze. "I talk when there is something important to say." He smiled at her. "While you, Makinna, chatter like a magpie."

She knew it was rather forward to use each other's given names, but dire circumstances had taken them past conventional etiquette. "That's true." She settled on the ground and spread her tattered gown about her. "I do. So it's your turn. Tell me more about yourself, Tykota. I know so little about you."

He sliced off a chunk of meat and handed it to her. "I told you before. I left my family, to spend most of my life in England."

She was intrigued. "But *why* did you leave your family? Have you got a mother and father, brothers or sisters?"

"I thought you said you were hungry."

"I am, but—"

"Then eat."

She looked pensive. "Tell me more about the ranch near the Mexican border."

His strong white teeth tore into the meat. He said nothing.

"You don't want to talk about it?"

"I do not feel so inclined, no."

She took a bite of the meat and lowered her head. "I'm sorry. I know it's none of my affair."

He stood up abruptly, and before she could say anything further, he walked away, swallowed up by the darkness.

Makinna was becoming accustomed to his moody silences, his abrupt departures, and his unwillingness to talk about himself. But she wanted to know more about him.

She finished eating and went back to the spring to wash her hands. She tried to work the tangles out of her hair, but it was useless. Tomorrow maybe, she would give in and ask Tykota to cut her hair.

She lay back on the soft grass that grew beside the spring and closed her eyes. It was so peaceful there after traveling across the harsh desert. Weariness overtook her and drew her into sleep.

When Makinna awoke the next morning, she found Tykota hollowing out three gourds with his knife. She pushed her hair out of her face and watched him. "What are you doing?"

"We can carry extra water with these. It is a long way until the next water."

Dread settled over her. "If we get out of this alive, I never want to see the desert again."

He glanced up at her. "You were meant for the easy life, sitting in parlors gossiping with the ladies, talking about the latest fashion or what so-and-so had on at the dance the night before."

That was the longest speech she'd ever known him to give, and instead of being angry with his unflattering suppositions about her character, she was amused. "You do not know me at all if you believe that."

"But I have met women like you."

She hid a smile. "Have you? Yet you so often point out that I am a bit unusual. But do tell me about these woman you now compare me to."

He glanced at her. "You tell me. You have lived among society ladies, who wear silly undergarments and do not swim."

"I refuse to say anything more about myself." She watched him deftly thread cloth strips through holes he'd made in the top of a gourd. "Not until you tell me about yourself."

He dipped the gourds in the water, filled them, and stood, slipping them over his shoulder. "After you have eaten, fill the canteen and bring it with you. We should be leaving very soon."

She stood up and placed a hand on his arm. He looked down at her hand and then into her face questioningly.

"I have a favor to ask, Tykota."

He silently waited for her to go on.

"I have decided to let you cut my hair."

She could tell nothing from his expression, but he laid the gourds on the ground and unsheathed his knife. Then he looked from her hair to the knife and back. To Makinna's surprise, he begun to prowl back and forth with the grace of a mountain lion and the intensity of a man with a heavy decision to make.

"Why do you worry so? It's my hair, not yours. And it was your idea to cut it."

At last he stopped in front of her and grasped her shoulders, turning her back to him.

Makinna squeezed her eyes tightly shut.

Tykota lifted some strands of her golden hair and raised his knife, but when the tendril curled around his finger, he hesitated. The texture was like silk. Something within him resisted the thought of cutting off anything so beautiful. He raised the strand to his lips and closed his eyes.

"Do it quickly," she said, her eyes still squeezed shut.

His hand actually trembled as he sliced through the curls. Then he sliced another and another, cutting it to the top of her shoulders. When the ground about them was littered with gold, he retrieved one of the curls and slipped it into his pocket.

Makinna turned slowly to face him. "Do I look awful?"

Tykota's gaze went from her hair to her startlingly blue eyes, which held an almost childlike expression.

"Do I?"

She must know she was beautiful; she did not need him to tell her. "You will be more comfortable this way. The tangles can now be easily worked out with your fingers."

Makinna looked worried, and her bottom lip trembled a bit. "And in time it will grow back," she reassured herself.

Tykota swept away the cut hair to leave no evidence of their passage. Then he lifted the water gourds and moved away. "You will want to eat quickly and make yourself ready for a long trek. Tomorrow night we cross the worst of the desert."

She began working the worst tangles out of her hair. "I wish we could stay here."

He didn't answer.

Makinna bent to gathering the pouch of meat and the canteen. She sighed heavily. Tykota was the most complicated man she'd ever known. It must be because he was an Indian. They came from different worlds, and she didn't understand him any more than he understood her.

But what did it matter? When this was over,

if it ever was, their paths would never cross again.

So why did that thought bring such a pain to her heart that tears sprang to her eyes? What was happening to her?

Chapter Nine

As Makinna stumbled forward, the scorching wind that blistered her face seemed to be borne on the wings of hell. Only the hardiest plants clung to life here in this wasteland, and they were dry and brittle, creeping through the baked cracks of the hardened earth.

Makinna shaded her eyes against the intense afternoon sun. She squinted toward the sky and counted five buzzards circling above them, waiting for them to die so they could feast on their flesh. She shivered, thinking the birds might just get their meal. The earth burned through the thin soles of her shoes, which now had countless holes in them. But she trudged onward, her eyes on Tykota's back as she wondered again where his strength came from.

At last she fell to her knees. She felt water on her parched lips and knew that Tykota had lifted her head and was offering her a drink. She drank deeply of the life-giving nectar, but it did little to ease her torment. She felt something cool against her face, and she realized that he had used some of their precious water to make mud to protect her from the sun.

"You must go on, Makinna. If you do not, you will die."

She barely had the strength to shake her head. "I can't. You must go on without me."

He lifted her to her feet and supported her weight. "I will not go on without you. If you insist on staying here, we will both die."

She pressed her head against his shoulder and knew he was supporting most of her weight. "I know what you are trying to do," she said weakly.

"And that is?"

"You are trying to give me energy by making me feel responsible for your life."

She heard him laugh. "At the moment, it feels as if I am responsible for yours."

"How much farther?"

"Do you see those mountains?"

With effort, she raised her head and stared across the waves of heat to the high mountains more than a mile away. "Please, not those in the far distance?"

"We will stop when we reach their base."

111

If she hadn't been too proud, she would have cried. Each step was agony as the hot ground seared the soles of her feet. She was beyond the limits of her strength and she just wanted to lie down and sleep. "I can't, Tykota. I can't go on."

"I never expected you to make it this far." His voice sounded suddenly harsh. "An Indian maiden would not complain when the going was rough. But you are a weakling, a white woman who wants to give up at the least hardship."

His words cut into her soul. She knew that she had slowed him down, that she'd been a burden to him, but he was the one who'd brought her with him. "I did not ask to come with you."

He closed his eyes; his harsh words had wounded his own heart. She had been braver and had endured more than most men he knew, but he could not let her lose her courage now, or she would perish. He had long watched her struggling with her stubborn pride, and he'd hoped that if he challenged that pride, he might just might keep her alive.

He'd judged her correctly. He saw her spine straighten, and she rose to her feet. He felt pride in her courage, and he felt humbled by her power to endure when most women would have quit.

In defiance, Makinna pushed away his arm and stood on her own. "Just don't *you* lag behind, or I'll leave you to the buzzards." She glared up at him. "I may even personally feed you to them." And she began to walk.

Behind her back, Tykota smiled. Oh, yes. No woman he'd ever met could stand toe-to-toe with this one. She might look fragile, but she had strength of heart and mind.

After they had walked for over an hour, Tykota stopped and glanced back the way they'd come. Their footprints were clearly visible if the Apache were still searching for him, and he knew they would be.

"Are you sure we aren't lost and you just don't want to tell me, Tykota?" Makinna asked, bending over to catch her breath. "No one could find their way across this desert with nothing to guide them."

He glanced down at her. "This land speaks to me. It is in my blood and in every fiber of my being. It would speak to you if you would listen."

"Well, it does speaks to me," she said, drawing in a scorched breath. "It shouts that if thirst, heat, or the Apache don't get us, those buzzards surely will."

"You are not in good cheer today."

She moved across the crusted ground. "So you noticed. I would be perfectly happy," she answered bitingly, nodding upward, "if I could personally feed you to one of those circling devils."

She heard him laugh aloud. "I probably deserve that. I will bargain with you, Makinna."

She gave him a suspicious glance. "What?"

"If you will conserve your strength by remaining quiet until we reach the foothills, I will allow you to ask me some questions, and I will answer them."

She was silent.

"Do we have a bargain?"

Still she said nothing.

"Makinna?"

"You asked me not to speak, so I'm not."

He laughed deeply. "You are quite a woman, Makinna Hillyard."

She mumbled to herself. Earlier, he'd implied that she was a weakling. Now he offered praise. Still, she was endlessly curious about him. There were so many things she wanted to know that she spent the next hour thinking about just what to ask him.

She did not see his smile grow wider or the softening of his dark eyes.

It was almost sundown when the mountain loomed before them. Tykota was exhausted, and he could only wonder how Makinna had made it this far. Today had been the worst. The desert had claimed many lives in the past, and he'd had to make her angry to force her to keep going.

When they reached the foothills, he dared to hold out another challenge to her, although he wouldn't blame her if she refused. "Makinna, if you can climb up past that rock face, there is a cave. No one knows about it but myself, my father, and one of my brothers. We will be safe there tonight."

She glanced at the steep mountain as if it were the enemy. "I can make it."

He handed her the gourd of water. "You can have as much water as you want. You earned it today, and we are almost within reach of a stream."

She raised the water to her lips. It was so hot it burned a trail down her throat, but she didn't care. It revived her, and she set her foot forward. "Do you climb, Tykota, or linger to rest?"

He was just about to take a sip of water, and he paused to look at her. "I climb," he said hurriedly, because she'd already started to ascend the mountain.

The cave didn't seem deep, but it was cool inside. Makinna leaned her face against the stone and dragged air into her lungs. That's when she noticed the ceiling. Crystal prisms formed strange formations. "This is beautiful," she said, allowing her gaze to roam the cavern.

"I was just a boy when my father brought me here," Tykota told her, looking around reflectively. "I had the same reaction as you that day."

"Where is your father now? And the brothers you mentioned?"

His lips curved into smile. "Do the questions start already?"

"No." She shook her head. "I will choose a time when there is nothing to distract us." Her gaze locked with his. "I can ask as many questions as I choose, can't I?"

He nodded. "That was the bargain." He moved across the cave to a dark corner and rolled away a huge stone. "Follow me."

Makinna scrambled after him through a narrow passage and then a tiny opening to another chamber. She could see a light ahead, and speechlessly, she stepped into a huge, dome-shaped room with a tiny opening at the top that let in sunlight. She gasped at the beauty of what she was seeing. There were more magnificent crystals, but these reflected the sunlight and sent rainbows dancing across the walls. Some of the crystals were shaped like palaces, while others were lacy, and still others looked like huge icicles. A small stream splashed over the rocks and emptied into an emerald-colored pool that had been carved into the stone over hundreds of years.

Her gaze met Tykota's. "Surely this is the treasure mountain Mr. Rumford spoke of." She reached out and laid her cheek against one of the prisms. "Do you suppose this could be the sacred mountain of the legendary Perdenelas Indians?"

He stared up at the opening and was quiet for a moment. Finally he spoke. "You will find nothing of earthly value here. No gold, no treasure. If you carried away everything in this particular cavern, it would not be worth your trouble. And, yet, some would consider this cavern itself more valuable than treasure, for in its beauty is food for the soul."

Her eyes grew misty. "Yes, I understand what you mean. I could spend the rest of my days here and be happy."

He shook his head. "I do not think so, Makinna. You were not meant to be hidden away in a cave."

"Perhaps not. But I am so glad you showed this to me. I will never forget it."

Makinna knelt down beside the pool and drank. The water was sweet and cool and revived her spirits. How could such a place as this exist in the burning desert? God must have placed it here as a heaven for the weary traveler.

Tykota drank, too, and then moved away from her. "I will leave you alone. If you would like to bathe, you will not be disturbed. When you are ready, come back to the outer cavern."

Once Tykota had gone, Makinna began to unhook her gown. Soon she waded naked into the pool. It was deep enough for her to submerge her whole body, which she did, allowing the water to cleanse away her exhaustion.

She washed her tattered black gown, and when she climbed out of the pool and was fastening the hooks, she suddenly found herself wishing Tykota Silverhorn could see her in a silk creation, wearing flowers in her hair. She paused, feeling uneasy, and chided herself for being foolish. Tykota would not care what she looked like in rags or silk. And, besides, why should she want him to think she was pretty?

Makinna finally went back through the narrow passage to find Tykota. He had built a fire and was roasting meat. She sat down near him and ran her hands through her hair to untangle it—a task that was indeed much easier since she'd allowed Tykota to cut it.

"What do we dine on tonight?" she asked, smiling. "Is it snake, scorpion, wolf, or bear?

"Rabbit."

"I like rabbit," she said, frowning at a stubborn tangle.

Tykota held out something to her. "Here. Use this. I carved it for you after I hunted, while you were still bathing."

Her face lit up happily when she saw the crude wooden comb. "How wonderful!" she

118

said, taking it from him and running it through her hair. "Thank you so much!"

Tykota watched her, and her happiness with his simple gift gladdened his heart. This was not a woman who would idle away her days at parties and dances as he'd once thought. She was young and innocent, kind and generous, and very genuine. And he hoped nothing would ever change her.

He stood, smiling down at her. "You may eat when you wish. It is my turn to bathe."

Makinna watched him walk toward the narrow passage, wanting to call him back. She wanted to tell him so many things. She wanted to thank him for all he'd done for her. She knew now why he'd goaded her that afternoon—it had been to keep her going, to keep her alive.

She drew her knees up and rested her head on them. For the first time, she wondered if Tykota had a wife somewhere. Or even several wives. She'd heard that some Indians took more than one. Or perhaps there was a girl he loved, one he was coming home to.

She felt a heaviness in her heart, and she didn't know why. Reaching for the meat, she tore off a leg and ate hungrily.

Where would she be now if Tykota Silverhorn hadn't come into her life? She'd be charred bones back at Adobe Springs with the others who had died there. As it was, she would probably die here, with no burial and only those buzzards to pick her bones clean.

Makinna was tired. With the half-eaten rabbit leg in her hand, she leaned back against the cave wall and fell asleep.

Chapter Ten

When Makinna awoke, the campfire was cold, and the only light in the cave came from the moon filtering through the entrance. She sat up, searching for Tykota, but he wasn't there. She always felt uneasy when he wasn't with her.

She slipped into her shoes and found, to her surprise, that Tykota had sewn thick leather strips across the worn soles. It seemed nothing escaped his notice, not even holes on the bottom of her shoes.

"Tykota?"

Silence.

Standing up, Makinna hurried outside and stood on the overhanging ledge, her gaze roaming over the valley below, but she couldn't see him anywhere.

She went back inside and made her way through the narrow passage to the crystal room.

He was standing so still that she didn't see him at first. His head was raised to the opening, and silver moonlight streamed around him. When she saw that he wore nothing but his breechcloth, she started to leave.

"You don't have to go, Makinna. I was merely remembering the last time I was here, with my father and my brother, Coloradous. Then there was the time my father brought me here alone. That was many years ago."

She ventured a step closer to him. "You were very young at the time?"

"Yes, I was." He glanced down at her and saw that she appeared uncomfortable. He'd forgotten that he wore only his breechcloth. "Very young."

"And you have not been here since then?"

He smiled. "Have the questions begun?"

She didn't know whether to appease her curiosity or leave because he was not properly dressed. "I am not—I don't—"

He addressed her apprehension. "Makinna, this is the way my people dress. We are a desert tribe. But if it makes you uncomfortable, I will put something on."

She moved forward several steps to show him that she respected and accepted his custom. "Please, don't trouble yourself on my account. It is as you say, the way your people dress."

He indicated that she should be seated. "Why not make yourself comfortable?"

Tykota watched as Makinna sat down and commenced to nervously smooth impossible wrinkles out of her tattered gown. He moved out of the stream of moonlight and sat down some distance from her to ease her nerves.

"Thank you for mending my shoes, Tykota." She glanced at him and then quickly averted her eyes. "How ever did you manage it?"

"I am an Indian, remember?" A smile curved his lips. "We are good at making things out of leather."

She nodded.

"What would you like to know about me, Makinna?"

She raised troubled eyes to him. "First of all, I would like to say how ashamed I am for not thanking you for saving my life. There have been times when I am sure you would have liked to abandon me, and I thank you for your forbearance."

"You have not been a burden, Makinna. And there are still troubled times ahead of us. Before this is over, you may very well wish you had stayed behind with the others."

"Do you foresee great danger?"

"Yes, I do. The closer I get to my destination, the more aggressively the Apache will pursue me."

"We have managed to avoided them thus far. You have outsmarted them at every turn, and I believe you will continue to do so." Makinna said loyally.

"I wish that were true. But you see, Makinna, one particular Apache knows exactly where I am going. He is smart, and he can always place himself between me and my destination."

"Do you know him?"

"Yes."

She frowned. "Does he hate you so much?"

"Yes, he does. He has waited a long time for our meeting. He will find me, Makinna."

"You will know what to do if that should happen."

"I wish I was as sure of that as you are."

"What does he mean to do to you?"

His expression seemed pained. "He wants to see me dead."

"Why would anyone hate you that much?"

"There are many customs among the Indian, Makinna, that are difficult for the white world to grasp. This particular Indian and I share a bond that can only be severed if one of us is dead." His gaze met hers, and he saw the puzzlement on her face. "You cannot be expected to understand. Do not try. Now, what else do you what to know, Makinna?"

She leaned forward. "I want to know about your boyhood. Why did you leave your home? Why were you educated in England?"

He nodded. "My father, my Indian father, sent me away because . . . It was for the good of the people. On that, I can tell you nothing more."

"You were raised by a white man, yet you seem to have little love for our race."

"You are mistaken, Makinna. There are good and bad people in every race. I have found that many white men are not to be trusted, but the same can be said for many Indians."

"I have not found that to be true. I believe most people are honest and care about their fellow man."

"Do you?"

"Yes, I do. Tell me about Mr. Silverhorn."

Tykota raised his head and stared at the dome opening as if he were remembering something from long ago. "I told you before that George Silverhorn became like a second father to me, and his wife, Hannah, was the mother I never had. But in the first two years I was with them, I was very rebellious and ran away three times. Of course, since I was in England, I could not get back to my people without boarding a ship."

"So you stopped running away?"

"My father, George, made me a promise that he would buy land in Texas, so I could be nearer my people, if I would not attempt to run away again."

"And he kept his promise."

"Yes, Makinna, he kept his promise."

"And you loved being here again?"

"I did, yes. When we moved to Biquera Ranch, I was happy because they allowed me to spend summers with my boyhood friend, Santo, and my old teacher, Mangas. Sometimes my white friend, John Kincaid, who lived on the neighboring ranch, would join us. But after a while, there was some kind of trouble between John and Santo—I never learned what it was."

"Are you still friends with John?"

"I would like to be. For a time we were almost like brothers. He went to school in England with me. But I do not see much of him now."

"Tell me more about your early treks into the desert." She wrinkled her nose. "I can't imagine anyone doing it for fun."

"It was for me. I always looked forward to those months when the three of us would go into the desert and live off the land with only our knives."

"That is why you know this area so well."

"Yes." He glanced at the trickling waterfall. "But I never brought either of them here. This was a private place I had shared only with my father and brother."

"Yet you brought me."

Tykota turned to look at her. "I had little choice in the matter. If I had not brought you here, you would have died."

Makinna smiled. "Your secret is safe with me. Anyway, I could never find this place again if my life depended on it."

Tykota's gaze roamed the ceiling. "Within this cavern live boyhood memories, nothing more."

"When I came in a moment ago, you were trying to recapture something you'd lost," she stated softly.

Tykota was surprised that she was so perceptive. "That is so. But one cannot step back into the shoes of a child."

"Did you never see your father again?"

"No. But I received messages from him through Mangas and Santo."

"Were you . . . was there a time when you became contented with your life with the Silverhorns?"

"It is strange that you should choose the word *contented*, because that is what it was— never complete acceptance or happiness, but a restless contentment. George Silverhorn adopted me and gave me his last name. He taught me many things, and after my father, he was the most important influence in my life."

"You walked a hard road, Tykota—not white, not Indian. It must have been difficult."

Again he was surprised by how perceptive she was. "Less and less as time passed. When George told me that I was to go to school in England, I rebelled against the idea. But word came from my own father that I must go, so I had to obey. I learned later, from Santo, the reason my father wanted me out of this country."

"Why?"

"There had been a few mishaps when I was small—one nearly fatal. My father believed someone still wanted me dead."

Makinna gasped. "Do you believe that?"

"Yes, I do."

"But you were just a child. Why would anyone want to harm a child? Perhaps that was why your father sent you to Mr. Silverhorn in the first place."

"Yes." He stood up. "Have I answered all your questions?"

"One more? Were they kind to you in England—I mean, the others at the school?"

"Not at first. But once I proved myself, they were more accepting, and I made many lasting friendships there. But know this about me, Makinna. Though I have a very fine education—I speak French, Spanish, and Italian—inside I am an Indian, and no amount of education will change that. It's what I am."

She stood. "Now I understand you a little better."

He towered over her.

"Do not deceive yourself, Makinna. When you scratch my skin, I may bleed like a white man, but underneath, I am still an Indian. I have the heart of a warrior. No white woman can understand that. So do not think that you know me."

She was startled by the change in his demeanor. "I am *trying* to understand, if only you would help me. Do you now go back to your tribe and turn away from the life you have known with the Silverhorns?"

"George Silverhorn is dead. I had just come from burying him in England."

"So now you go back to your real father?"

"I go back to my people. My real father is dead."

How much he must have suffered! "I am so sorry. What of the rest of your family?"

"I have a sister, Inea." He paused, as if pondering something. "And I have two half brothers by my father's second wife."

"And you have no wife?"

His gaze touched her face. "There has been little room for a woman in my life. He smiled. "At least none that left a lasting impression." He could have added, *until now*, but he didn't. "It would not be wise for a woman to love me, Makinna," he warned, as if he knew her heart was turning to his. "I have something to do that

129

may—" He broke off and looked into her eyes. "I have no time for a woman."

She suddenly wanted to put her arms about him and comfort him. She wondered how many women in El Paso and England had felt the same way about Tykota. No woman would be able to ignore him, he had such a strong presence, capable of drawing others to him.

"I feel there is much more to your story than you are willing to share with me. You are going home for some purpose. I believe that you are in danger, from the Apache but maybe also from someone in your own tribe?"

He nodded slightly but did not respond.

She looked into his dark eyes, touched by the torment she saw in their shimmering depths. There was danger for her, too. Not that Tykota would harm her. The danger was that she was losing her heart to him, and he would not welcome her affection.

"I have decided we should remain here for a time," Tykota said. "We have food and water in abundance, the Apache do not know of this place, and you need the rest. It will give your skin and your feet time to heal."

She frowned. "I can go on if you must get to your destination to be safe."

His eyes glistened. "I knew you would say that. But I want you to rest, Makinna."

"I don't want you to stay here and be in danger because of me."

He smiled. "You have known hunger, thirst, and pain, and it did not break your spirit. I wonder if anything could."

She smiled. "Just think of the adventures I can tell my grandchildren."

"You will tell them how one time an Indian suddenly crossed through your life and left it, just as quickly, Makinna Hillyard."

She felt saddened by his words. That was what would happen. He would soon pass out of her life. But she would never forget him. She sighed deeply. "I would welcome a rest." What she wanted to say was that she would treasure every moment she spent with him. "Perhaps the Apache will give up when they can't find you."

"No. They will not give up. I want you to understand that there is still danger. They could even have tracked us here." He turned away. "Get some rest, Makinna. It is still hours until daylight. I am tired now."

She wanted to stay with him, but he had clearly dismissed her. Already his mind was on other things, and she doubted that he even heard her leave.

Tykota turned his face up to the stars and whispered, "Why did this woman come into my life at this time? Why does my heart want to bind with hers, to live out my days with her at my side?

"Why at this time in my life, when I shall surely die?"

Five days passed, and in that time Tykota hunted and dried meat for the last leg of their journey. Makinna rested, soaking in the healing powers of the inner cavern and its pool, dipping her feet into the cooling water. Sometimes, she simply lay on her back gazing up through the opening in the domed ceiling at the blue sky and wishing they never had to leave. She had never known life could be so magical.

This was her paradise, here in this beautiful place with Tykota.

Chapter Eleven

Tykota had been gone for hours, and Makinna was beginning to worry. He'd left early that morning, and it was now almost sundown. He'd never stayed away this long. A wave of despair hit her as she imagined the Apache finding him, or any number of other hazards he might have fallen prey to. Danger lurked everywhere in this scorching, hostile land.

Moving out of the cave, she stood atop the ledge that gave her a wide view of the countryside. She shaded her eyes against the glaring sun and looked for any movement.

A dust devil danced in the distance, and the ever-present vultures circled in the sky, but beyond that there was nothing—no sign of life, just the brittle heat and the never-ceasing wind.

Where could Tykota be? she wondered. Why had he been gone so long?

She couldn't just stay in the cave waiting for him to return. If he was in some kind of danger, she needed to find him.

She discovered that climbing down the mountain was more difficult than climbing up. Once she lost her footing and slid toward the edge, her feet dangling over the side. She was able to save herself only by grabbing hold of a plant that clung to life in the rock surface. Inch by inch she eased herself away from the edge, then collapsed, trembling. After she'd caught her breath and gathered her courage, she continued her descent.

It took her the better part of an hour to reach the bottom. When she stood on level ground, she still saw no sign of Tykota. Of course, he'd leave no tracks behind, nothing that would attract attention. He was much too intelligent for that. She ripped a scrub bush up by the roots and brushed her own tracks away as she'd seen him do, thinking he'd be proud of her for being so cautious.

Makinna tried to decide which direction he would have taken. She reasoned that he wouldn't head into the desert but might have gone hunting in the foothills to the west. She settled on exploring those. As she walked along, she paused often to search for any sign of his presence.

She felt every stone under her still tender feet, and she soon grew thirsty and wondered why she hadn't brought the canteen with her. Weary, she tripped and fell.

She rose slowly, glancing toward the west. The sun was low on the horizon. She would never be able to make her way up the mountain in the dark, but she couldn't return without finding Tykota. She studied the ground but saw nothing to indicate that he'd come this way.

Her leg was throbbing; she must have injured it in the fall. Raising her skirt, she saw the cut on her knee. It was bleeding, and she wished she had a strip of her petticoat to tie around it.

Suddenly Makinna saw Tykota leap toward her, and she was shocked when he propelled her backward with such a force that he knocked her to the ground. Gripping her tightly, he fell with her, and they tumbled and rolled down a slight embankment into thick, gnarled foliage.

Thorns jabbed into her, but she was more aware of Tykota's body on top of hers, her fingers clutching his hard, muscled shoulders. When she caught her breath, she asked, "Why did you—"

Tykota clamped a hand over her mouth and nodded toward the top of the embankment. She heard the sound of horses, heard voices speaking a guttural language she did not understand.

It was the Apache!

Makinna lay trembling with fear, hoping they hadn't seen her. She was dimly conscious of sharp rocks digging into her skin, and the weight of Tykota's body cutting off her breathing. But when she shifted the merest bit, and he raised his head to look at her, like lightning striking, like a hammer against an anvil, she became aware of his body in an entirely new way. She felt the formidability of his strength, the swell of him against her thigh, and she was excruciatingly aware of his manliness. She could scarcely breathe when he rested his brow against hers, and his hand went up to tangle in her hair. Raw emotions tore through her body, and she knew he could feel it, too.

He stared at her, his eyes penetrating and fierce, as if she was the one woman he dare not love. Yet they might be mere moments away from death.

Makinna daringly placed a kiss on his bronze cheek.

Tykota's eyes flamed as if the sun was shining through them. His mouth was only a breath away from hers, and Makinna wanted to move that fraction of an inch that would bring their lips together. Even the threat of the Apaches seemed to fade from her mind. All she was aware of were the new feelings splintering through her body, and the man who had aroused those feelings in her.

Tykota's brow furrowed, and he tried to ease himself off her, but the movement tugged up her gown, exposing the smoothness of her thighs.

Makinna gasped, her eyes round with bewilderment, as wave after wave of heat surged through her. And she could tell by the way Tykota suddenly went rigid that he was fighting whatever feelings were stirring inside of him. He trembled with the tight restraint he tried to keep on his emotions.

Tykota gazed down at Makinna, ran a hand through her silken hair, and his heart raced. Like a man in a dream, he could not stop himself, could not control his own actions. He lowered his head, his mouth almost on hers. "Makinna," he whispered, his breath gently touching her lips. "Makinna."

She reached up, her fingers sliding though his thick hair. "Kiss me," she whispered.

A raw urgency built in the pit of his stomach and spread through his veins, his mind, his whole being. It didn't seem to matter that the Apache were nearby, or that they might die at any time. In that moment, she became his woman, his to protect, to love, to take. Just a kiss was all he wanted, or so he thought. But when his lips touched hers, he knew that would never be enough. His mouth ground against hers. His tongue explored the recesses of her mouth, darting in and out, stirring the heat in his belly. He wanted to know her in every way a man can know a woman. He wanted to explore her hidden beauty and kiss every part of her body. Wild, primitive emotions tore through him, and he was on fire. He needed her more than the air he breathed.

Makinna smothered a groan as Tykota's mouth continued to plunder hers. She felt him harden against her thigh, and she trembled. His body seemed to shelter her, and she thought she would die from his nearness. Oh, what was this weakness she felt, this awakening of her body and spirit? Why did she wish the Apache would stay for a very long time so she could absorb the feel of Tykota Silverhorn into her mind and body?

Suddenly, Tykota tore his mouth away from hers and stared at her lips, which were swollen from his kiss. "Makinna, I—"

He suddenly froze. Two of the Apache were moving down the ravine, and they were talking excitedly. Tykota glanced quickly at the ground where he had tackled with Makinna before rolling her into the bushes. He'd had no time to erase their footprints, which would be very apparent to the Apaches' experienced eyes.

Tykota knew that their only hope was the encroaching darkness. The sun had almost dropped behind the mountain, and that would make it more difficult to see the evidence of their presence.

By now, Makinna realized that the Apache

were moving in their direction. Her eyes widened when Tykota reached down and clasped the handle of his knife.

She lay quietly, his body pressing against hers, his face only inches away, listening to the Apaches. The two warriors stopped so near them that Makinna could have reached out and touched one of them. She felt the bitter taste of fear in her mouth. She closed her eyes, sure that the Indians had discovered their hiding place.

Tense moments passed as the Indians continued to talk. Then, Makinna's fear seemed to melt away as she felt Tykota's body soften into hers. She felt his every intake of breath against her breasts, and somehow she felt he was breathing for them both. She had such faith in Tykota's power that she believed the two warriors would not have a chance against him. Tykota would keep her safe.

Silently, she waited, knowing he could not move off her or the sound would attract the Apaches' attention. She could still feel the touch of his lips on hers. The sweetness of it was almost unendurable. It was as though he had kissed her good-bye.

Tykota raised his head when one of the Apaches moved closer. He tightened his grip on his knife. With a look of profound sorrow, he placed the tip of the knife to Makinna's breast. Her eyes widened as she realized the significance of his action. If the Apache found them, he would plunge the knife into her heart to spare her an even more hideous fate.

His lips silently shaped the words, "Do not move."

She licked her dry lips and nodded, wanting him to know that he must not hesitate to kill her if their hiding place was discovered.

Tykota gazed deeply into Makinna's sky-blue eyes. She seemed to understand and trust him to do what he must. He dipped his head, pressing his lips once more against hers. Her lips trembled beneath his, but she did not pull away. He wanted to save her, wanted to have her with him until the day he closed his eyes in death, but if they were found by the Apache, this moment was all they would ever have. He would never know the sweetness of her body.

He laid the knife at his side where he could grab it if he had to. Afraid he would never have the chance again, he moved his hand across the breasts straining against her bodice. Silently, he opened the neck of her gown and lowered his head, his mouth touching one rosy tip gently, almost reverently.

Her arms slid around him, and she bit her lips to keep from crying out as a flood of feelings rocked her body. She realized that he was distracting her from the danger and taking her mind off the knife he might have to use.

His tongue aroused her nipple, and her

hands clenched in his dark hair. The sensation that moved through her was liquid and hot, and she arched her body to fit snugly against his.

Even while Tykota was tasting the sweetness of Makinna's breasts, he was aware of every movement the Apaches made. He knew when one warrior knelt down to examine the ground, and he also knew that the sun had dropped behind the mountain by now, casting the land in shadows.

The Apache called to his companion, and Tykota raised his head, pulling Makinna's gown together. What was he doing? He had to keep a clear mind if they were to escape detection. He gripped the knife anew. If the Apache discovered their hiding place, he must not let them take Makinna alive.

Makinna felt the breath of death brush her. Strangely, she was no longer afraid, only deeply sad because Tykota's death at the hand of his enemy would be much worse than hers at his hand.

The Indian poked at the bush with the butt of his rifle, and Tykota gripped the knife and placed the point against her breast once more.

Minutes passed with the slowness of hours. Then, to Makinna's surprise, the two Apaches walked away and climbed back up the hill, where they joined their companions. But Tykota did not move the knife until he heard them riding away.

Makinna closed her eyes as relief washed over her. "Have they really gone, Tykota?"

"Come," he said, rising and taking her hand. "It is safe to return to the cave. It is too dark for them to search further tonight."

He led her up the steep hill and into the cavern. There in the darkness he turned her to him. She hoped he would take her into his arms and kiss her as he had earlier, but his voice was cold and distant when he spoke.

"You know I would have killed you if they had found us?"

"I know that."

"We were fortunate this time—next time we may not be."

She felt like crying, because he had stepped away from her. "I know that, too."

"You should not have come out of the cave without me. You were aware of the dangers."

She nodded, even, knowing he could not see her in this darkness. Or could he?

Makinna slid down to her knees and leaned back against the rock wall. It was clear to her that Tykota had only kissed her to keep her from being so frightened of the Apache. He had used his sensuality, and it had worked only too well.

Makinna silently waited for him to continue. She didn't have to wait long.

"We have to talk," he said, moving away from her and standing at the entrance to the cave.

142

She stood up and walked over to him. "I know."

"First, I will ask you to forgive me for what happened between us."

She came up beside him. "There is nothing to forgive. I know why you . . . kissed me."

He turned around and took her hands. "I should never have touched you with such intimacy. No one should be that familiar with your body but the man you will one day marry."

She pulled her hands free of his, feeling cold and empty in the depths of her heart. "I know you were only trying to distract me from the danger. It worked as well as when you goaded me to anger to get me across the desert. You are very good at ruling people, Tykota."

"I am sorry." His voice sounded devoid of emotion.

A lump formed in her throat. "As I said, there is nothing to apologize for."

Makinna just wanted him to leave before the tears that were in her heart reached her eyes. He must not know that she loved him, that if he wanted her, she would go anywhere with him, brave any hardship, just to be with him.

"Please," she said, turning away. "I am weary. I want to be alone now."

She heard him walk away, and she held her back straight until the sound of his footsteps disappeared.

It was a long time before Makinna fell

asleep, and when she did, it was with the memory of his lips on hers.

Tykota paced the floor of the inner cavern, paused to splash water over his face, and fought against going to Makinna and finishing what he had started earlier. But he mustn't. Their lives were never meant to join. She had family waiting for her in California, and he had to honor the promise he'd made to his father.

He had watched the proud tilt of Makinna's head and knew that he'd hurt her tonight. But it was better to hurt her a little now than to hurt her much more later on. In the ravine, he had awakened emotions in her that should have been left for her husband. She was young and inexperienced and had mistaken desire for love. When she returned to her world, she would meet a man who would—

He stopped himself, unwilling to think about another man touching her as he'd done. In his heart, she would always be his. But in the real world, she could never belong to him.

He did not sleep, and when the sunlight filtered through cave's ceiling, he was still awake. But he knew what he must do.

Chapter Twelve

Makinna stood on the ledge, looking out at the desert. She didn't hear Tykota came up beside her, and she jumped when he spoke to her.

"Makinna, I have to leave you here for a day or two. You will have plenty of food and water." He had his gun belt slung over his shoulder, and he placed it beside her. "I am leaving this with you. You will be safe if you do not wander out of the cave as you did yesterday. Will you promise me that you will remain here until I return?"

Unable to find her voice, she nodded.

He stared into her eyes for a moment, as if there was something he wanted to say, but finally he turned away. She watched him descend the mountain and disappear below the ridge. Frantically, she searched for him, but he had already melted into the landscape.

Never had she felt such an emptiness. Not even with the death of her mother and brother had she felt so alone.

She walked to the inner chamber, stripped off her gown, and waded into the pool. She remained there for over an hour, allowing the cool water to soothe her aching body.

But nothing could soothe her aching heart.

The hunted had now become the hunter. Tykota knew that he had to have horses if he was going to get Makinna out of this desert alive. The Apache would know by now that he was traveling with a woman, and that that made him even more vulnerable to them.

It didn't take him long to come upon their trail. They were making no effort to cover their tracks, since they had no fear of just one man and a female. He slipped behind a boulder and watched as they set up camp. All he had to do now was wait to catch one of them alone.

There was an urgency within him. He would need two horses if he was going to outrun and outsmart his enemy.

The dying sun cast jagged shadows across the desert as Makinna watched for Tykota. He had been gone for three days, and she was certain that something had happened to him. He was dead, or he'd be back by now.

Apprehensively, she looked at a bank of clouds forming in the west: heavy, dark, ominous clouds that arched above the horizon like black smoke. Thunderstorms had terrified Makinna ever since she'd gotten lost in the woods when she was five years old. She could still remember the terror she'd felt as she had huddled beneath a tree while thunder boomed and lightning struck all around her. She had been panic-stricken when lightning had hit a nearby tree, splintering it and causing it to burst into flames. With the dark terror known only to a child, she had been certain she would be struck by those jagged spears and burn just like the tree.

Somehow her father had found her, cold and wet and huddled in the darkness. That night she had trembled beneath a warm blanket and basked in the affection of her family, but she never recovered from her fear of thunderstorms.

She rushed back into the cave and went to the inner cavern, thinking it would be safe there and perhaps she wouldn't be able to hear the thunder. She stared through the opening at the top, watching as the sky grew darker and darker. Soon the blackness became so deep, so frightening, that she welcomed the intermittent flashes of lightning that gave her a moment's reprieve from the black void.

Makinna clung to the walls of the cave, her fear becoming like a living thing that could pounce on her at any moment. She was sobbing as she dropped to her knees, so frightened that she couldn't stop shaking. Just when she thought she could stand it no longer, strong arms came around her, and she was pulled against a hard chest.

"Makinna, it's all right," Tykota said, holding her tightly. Her fear struck at his very soul. "The storm will not harm you. You are safe in here."

She buried her face against his chest, trembling. "I have ... always feared storms," she gasped between sobs.

Tykota had never seen her cry, so he knew her fear must be unspeakable. "It will not harm you in this cave. The lightning cannot penetrate solid rock."

That thought calmed her. Or was it being in Tykota's arms that made her feel safe? She drew on his strength and was comforted by it.

"I thought you weren't ever coming back."

He brushed tumbled hair out of her face and spoke as a father might to a frightened child. "I would never desert you, Makinna."

She looked up at him just as a flash of lightning illuminated his face. She was stunned by the softness she saw in his expression. Or was it a trick of the shadows?

The emotions between them were as electrifying as the lightning that tore the sky. But now, instead of fear, desire rippled through her in waves. "Hold me. Hold me tight," she pleaded.

Tykota's arms tightened about Makinna, and he felt her melt against him. She trusted him, and he was waging a war within himself, trying not to think of her softness, her curves, her lips pressed against his neck.

He took her hand and pulled her to her feet. Gently, he guided her through the narrow opening to the outer cave. "Do you trust me?"

"Yes."

"Then let me show you and tell you about the storm you are frightened of. An Indian learns at an early age that if he understands his enemy's strength, it diminishes his fear."

He led her out into the rain and turned her toward the valley. Her heart was still pounding furiously.

"Take a deep breath, Makinna. Feel the rain. Smell the rain. Become part of the storm. Feel its power. Respect its strength, and do not try to ignore it or take it lightly. Become as one with the storm. Then there is nothing in the storm that will harm you."

She did smell the rain being absorbed by the dry earth, and that scent somehow reminded her of home. It was the same cleansing smell that came right after an April shower.

149

Tykota gazed down at her. "Do you feel the force of the storm bringing the earth renewal, Makinna? Listen. Listen to the song of the earth as it responds to the storm. Where there was desolation, the rain brings life."

She felt the heat of his body, and it was definitely bringing hers to life. "Yes," she whispered through trembling lips. "I feel it."

His gaze went beyond her to the rumbling sky. "Think of the storm like a man giving life into the body of a woman. The land would die without the storm." His gaze fastened on her lips, and he felt as if his soul was on fire. "And a man will die inside without the love of his woman."

Rain pelted against her, plastering her hair to her face and her gown to her body. "I don't believe I shall ever fear a storm again," she said, as he turned and led them back into the cave. "I don't know if it is because you are with me, or because of what you said, but the fear is gone now."

He wanted to pull her against him. He wanted to ask her to be his woman and to walk through life with him. But where he must go, she could not follow. Where he went, she did not belong.

"Fear, like every other emotion, can be conquered, Makinna. It takes only the will and the need."

"Can love be conquered as easily, Tykota?"

Tears began mixing with the wetness already on her cheeks. "Can love be cast aside like something unwelcome and unwanted?"

He stared at her for a long moment and then said harshly, "Love is the easiest of all emotions to conquer." He glanced away, since he couldn't look into her eyes, knowing he was wounding her, wounding himself. "Make ready to leave. We ride out tonight."

"Ride?"

"That is right. We ride."

Her eyes widened. It occurred to her that the only way he could have acquired horses in this desert was to take them from the Apache warriors. "They are Apache horses, aren't they?"

"Not anymore." He shoved the dried meat into a leather pouch and handed it to her. "It will be better to leave while it is storming so the rain will wash away any tracks we might leave behind."

"Yes, I can see the sense of that. Can I also assume that the Apaches whose horses you took will want them back?"

He looked at her. "No," he replied. "They will not be needing them anymore."

The significance of his words hit her hard. She shivered at the knowledge that Tykota could be as ruthless as the Apaches tracking them. He would do whatever it took to survive. "You killed them, didn't you, Tykota?"

"Makinna," he said impatiently, "when your enemy is riding and you are on foot, you have little chance of evading him."

She felt little sorrow for the men he'd killed. After all, they had attacked Adobe Springs and killed everyone. Would have killed Tykota and her, had they remained. She nodded. "I will be glad for the horses."

"Can you ride?"

"Of course."

"Sidesaddle, I assume."

"Yes, I—"

"You will be riding bareback." His gaze was hard. "All I ask of you is that you stay on the horse and keep up with me." He moved away from her and through the narrow passage to the crystal cavern, where he would fill the water skins he'd taken from the dead Apaches.

When he rejoined her, his tone was abrupt, and he didn't even look at her. "We must leave now."

She shouldered the leather pouch and walked out of the cavern. She tried to shake off the sadness she felt at leaving this magical place. But she knew they could not stay here forever.

His voice cut through her musings. "You will have to be careful as we make our way down to the ravine where I tied the horses. The slopes are slick in places."

It was a difficult descent, and when they finally reached the bottom, Makinna was trembling with fatigue, drenched, and muddy. But she told herself this was not as hard to endure as the scorching sun and the thirst that had plagued them on the first part of their journey.

Makinna approached the horses with trepidation, glad, at least, that the lightning had moved farther to the east.

Tykota took the food bag from her and secured it to his horse. He then gripped Makinna's waist and lifted her onto her horse.

At first riding bareback felt awkward, but in time she adjusted to it. She tried not to think about the man who had died so that she could ride.

It was raining harder now, and although she was soaked to the skin, she was grateful for the coolness. When the sun rose and the rain stopped, it would be sweltering, and they would once again have to contend with the Apaches tracking them, likely angrier and more determined than ever.

Tykota urged his horse into a gallop, and Makinna gripped the sides of her mount with her legs, praying that she would not be unseated. The Indian pinto was smaller than the horses she was accustomed to, but after they had been riding for over an hour, she gained a new respect for the sturdy animal. It was responsive and surefooted as it raced across the rugged terrain with tireless energy.

They rode through the night to put as much distance as they could between themselves and the Apaches.

Chapter Thirteen

Makinna led her weary mount down a muddy gully as she watched the sun rise over the distant mountains. She was enchanted by the transformation that had come to the land washed clean by the storm. The desert had sprung to life overnight, the flowering cacti exuding a sweet perfume.

She was observing the brilliant crimson blooms on a prickly pear when Tykota slowed beside her. "This is as good a place as any to rest the horses. We can see for miles in any direction."

To Makinna, he looked like he belonged on the back of the sturdy Indian pony. His dark hair rippled in the wind, and his eyes were fierce and unfathomable.

She dismounted, lay her head against the horse's neck, and closed her eyes. "This is the finest horseflesh I've ever seen. He carried me through the night without once faltering."

Tykota patted his horse. "The Indian's pinto has to be of sturdy stock, for reasons you can well imagine."

"I certainly can. A lesser breed would never survive in this desert." She laughed and tossed her head back. "Perhaps I'm a bit like them. After all, a lesser breed could not have made it this far."

Tykota looked at her for a moment, then took the reins and led both horses back to a patch of dried grass, where they began to graze.

He turned his gaze westward as Makinna joined him. "What happens now?" she asked.

He stared into the distance as if he'd forgotten her.

"Where are we going, Tykota?"

Finally he looked down at her. "We are but a few days from my home."

Pushing a tumbled curl behind her ear, she asked, "Aren't we going to El Paso?"

He looked into her eyes. "There is something important I must do."

"Something that concerns your tribe?"

"Yes."

"Will you . . . will . . . I . . . continue my journey to California?"

He appeared startled by her question. "Of course. You are not now, nor have you ever been, my prisoner. As soon as I can arrange it, you will board the Butterfield Stage in El Paso. Then, before you know it, you will reach your destination in California."

Makinna glanced back the way they'd come. The trek had been hard and dangerous. It was a miracle that they had made it this far. But somehow she could not imagine it ending. What would she do when she could no longer hear the sound of Tykota's voice, feel him by her side? "Thank you. I would appreciate that," was all she said.

"Soon this will all seem like a bad dream," Tykota said.

Makinna knew their time together would be something she would always cherish. She tried to keep her voice from trembling. "Do you think the Apaches are still trailing us?"

"Doubtless, more fiercely than ever, because they know that I am getting close to my people and destination. During the night we crossed the Rio Grande into Mexico. I hoped by going the long way to confuse them and slow their search."

"We are not in the United States?" she asked in amazement.

"Indians recognize no boundaries and owe no allegiance to any country other than their own tribe."

"I understand."

He looked doubtful. "Do you?"

He walked away from her. "The horses have rested and fed, so we must ride on. Are you up to it?"

"I can ride as far as we have to."

She approached her horse, then turned back to him. "But without stirrups, I can't mount by myself."

Tykota's hands spanned her waist, and he lifted her onto the animal's back. Makinna rode up the ravine and waited for him there. He frowned down at the tracks left in the mud. He could do nothing to cover them. He would double back into Texas in the hope of throwing the Apaches off their trail. Perhaps gain them a little time.

The sun was at its hottest when the weary travelers stopped again to rest the horses. Makinna dropped down to the ground in the thin strip of shade cast by a yucca tree. She uncapped her canteen and took small sips as Tykota had taught her. Through drooping eyelids she watched while he tended to the horses. Then she slumped over and drifted off to sleep, dreaming of a soft bed and a cool breeze.

Makinna came awake quickly when Tykota called her name. "Come," he said, offering her a hand. "We must ride hard. That dust cloud to the south is the Apaches."

That was the only prodding Makinna needed. They hurried to the horses and rode at a full gallop, the sturdy pintos giving their all. Tykota slowed them to an easier gait when he was sure that they had left their pursuers behind.

"Will they not follow?" she asked.

"Perhaps, but they will not catch us today, and tomorrow we will be out of their reach."

Night had fallen when Tykota drew his mount to a halt and motioned for Makinna to do the same. On the edge of a mesa, together they gazed down at twinkling lights below.

"Are those campfires, Tykota?"

"No. It is a ranch."

"It must be huge. There are so many lights."

"It covers over a hundred square miles." He nudged his horse forward. "You will find a warm welcome there."

Makinna felt relief spread through her. They had made it out of the desert and eluded the Apaches. They were going to live!

But when they rode past a corral, a man stepped out in front of them, his rifle cocked and aimed at Tykota. Makinna's heart stopped. The man was an Indian.

"If you have weapons, throw them down and then dismount," he commanded.

Tykota's laughter stunned Makinna, who remained frozen in fear.

"Have I been away so long that your keen eyes do not know me, Mangas?" Tykota said.

The old man stepped beyond the light spilling from the barn. "Tykota?"

"It is I, my friend." He slid off his horse, and the two men embraced one another. "Do you shoot me or welcome me?"

After that, Makinna did not know what they said, because they lapsed into another language.

Finally Tykota turned to lift Makinna from her horse, and the old Indian gazed at the white woman.

"Makinna, this old warrior who tried to shoot us is my teacher and friend, Mangas."

The Indian's gray-streaked hair hung to his shoulders, and he stood tall and straight. Makinna did not know quite what to say to the man who stared at her with open curiosity. "I have heard of you from Tykota."

The old man suddenly grinned. "I have heard of you, as well. The Apache drums spoke of a white woman traveling with Tykota, and their talk reached my ears."

Tykota spoke at length to Mangas in their language, then led Makinna toward the huge ranch house.

"What did you say to him?" she asked.

"I told him to be alert because the Apaches

may track us here. And I asked him to take our horses into the barn for a good rubdown and extra feed."

As they walked toward the ranch house, the clouds moved away from the moon, bathing the dwelling in light. "This house could easily be in New Orleans, Tykota," Makinna exclaimed. "It's so lovely." The house had wide galleries on both the upper and lower floors. There were wide pillars on the veranda, and wrought-iron railings on the balcony. "I never thought to see anything so grand in this rustic setting."

"The house was modeled after a French chateau," Tykota explained. He led her up the steps to the front door. "You will find many things here that might surprise you."

"Do you know the people who live here well?"

"Yes. Very well."

Without knocking, he opened the door and ushered Makinna inside. A small, white-haired woman was bent over her sewing. She glanced up, and her face brightened with joy. In her excitement, she dropped her needle-work, propelled herself out of the chair, and met Tykota in the middle of the room. "Ty, my son, you are safe! I was so afraid when Mangas told me that the Apache drums talked of you."

She spoke with a soft English accent, and Makinna realized she must be Mrs. Silverhorn,

Tykota's adoptive mother. And this was Biquera Ranch.

"I've been so worried about you, Ty!"

His arms engulfed the tiny woman, and he kissed her cheek. "Mother, it has been too long since I saw your face. But Father now rests in peace in his native land."

She placed a trembling hand lovingly against his cheek. "You have been away so long, Ty."

"I had to see that everything was done properly, and there were much I had to settle for you."

Remembering her manners, Mrs. Silverhorn turned her attention to Makinna. "And this is?" she asked, smiling.

"Mother, meet Makinna Hillyard. She was with me when the Apaches attacked Adobe Spring. She was on her way to her sister's home in San Francisco."

The woman took Makinna's hand. "My dear, I can only imagine what hardships you have suffered! But you are here now. Your ordeal is over."

Makinna smiled, almost forgetting her exhaustion and bedraggled state in the face of Mrs. Silverhorn's warmth. "I am happy to meet you, Mrs. Silverhorn, and glad to be here. And please accept my condolences on the loss of your husband. Tykota has spoken so highly of him."

"Thank you, dear."

"I am sure Makinna would welcome a bath and a soft bed, Mother."

"And so she shall have them. Immediately. Come with me, my dear." She began to lead Makinna away but glanced back at her son. "And you could do with a bath and a change of clothing, too." The smile on her lips softened her words. "You seemed to have misplaced your shirt. Do hurry to put yourself to right. I want to hear all about your awful adventure."

It was quiet except for the squeaking of the rocking chair that Hannah Silverhorn kept in motion. Seeing her son now safe and sitting in her husband's chair filled her with happiness. She knew that even though he seemed to be resting, he was aware of every sound around him.

"Will you stay this time, Ty?" she asked with hope in her voice.

"Mother, you know I cannot. I have duties that call to me."

"But this is your ranch, your home. Your father wanted you to have it when he died. I am old, Ty, and I cannot run a ranch as big as Biquera for long."

He leaned forward and put a hand on hers. "Mother, you know an Indian cannot own land in the state of Texas."

"I know that, but there are ways around it."

"Please understand that I must go to my people. I am obliged to do so by my promise to my Indian father. And the tribe has been without leadership since Valatar died."

She nodded, knowing he would attend to his duty as he had been raised to do. "It will be difficult for you, Ty. You have lived so long away from the tribe. And Mangas told me that you still have enemies, those who have been pursuing you and Makinna."

"Yes, I know." His eyes grew hard. "My brother will live long enough to regret his actions. I do not know why he still hates me after all these years."

"Mangas says it is because of the shame. And his ambition."

"That is so. I always thought that Valatar was too harsh with my half brothers. I had hoped to see Sinica and Coloradous back with the tribe and their honor restored."

"Ty, you know I could not love you more if I had given you life, and that is why I feel I must say this to you." She grasped his hand in both of hers, and her eyes sought his. "You have called two fine men Father."

"And I loved and honored them both."

"I know you did, Ty. But both of them asked too much of you while they were alive. When you were but a child and uncertain of your own goals, Valatar made you feel responsible for the Perdenelas. And George brought you into his world with all its expectations and had you walk a path that was both rigorous and unfamiliar to you. Neither afforded you many choices." Her eyes filled with tears. "Ty, I love you, and I would rather see you walk away from this ranch *and* the Perdenelas if it meant you would find happiness and peace for your restless soul."

His gaze softened with affection. "No one could have had a better, more loving mother than you. But you must understand my life is *not* mine. It never has been. As Valatar taught me, I was born to lead my tribe, to walk in his shoes."

She shook her head, touching his cheek softly. "I suspected you would still feel that way. But I want you to know that if your path gets too hard, and you find you cannot go on, Biquera Ranch will be here waiting for you."

"Thank you, Mother."

She leaned back and watched his face. "Tell me about the woman."

"There is nothing to tell."

"I see the way your eyes follow her, Ty. She is a very beautiful woman, and it would be difficult to . . . be with her as long as you have and not feel something for her. You care for her, don't you?"

He drew in a deep breath. "It would not matter what my feelings were, Mother. She has her life, and I have mine."

"How does she feel about you?"

"I believe she may fancy herself in love with me. But when she returns to her world she will realize it was not love. . . ."

Hannah looked into Tykota's eyes. "The two of you were alone together for a long, difficult time."

He met her gaze. "I did not act dishonorably with her, Mother. She is still chaste."

Hannah shook her head. "I was not questioning your honor, son. I was asking how you feel about Makinna."

He was thoughtful for a moment before he answered. "I never knew love could be so deep or hurt so much."

Hannah felt tears burn behind her eyes, and her heart went out to her son. "Because you think you must let her go?"

"We cannot have a life together. I am chief of the Perdenelas, and the law says that the chief cannot marry outside his tribe."

"Your father made that law because of the betrayal by his Apache wife. You are a chief now. You can change the law."

"It is law meant to protect the tribe. I cannot change the law to suit my own needs. The tribe's welfare is what matters."

Hannah knew Tykota would always deny his needs and desires if he thought it was for the good of the Perdenelas. "When the time comes, can you walk away from her?"

Tykota stood and begin to pace. "I must. What choice have I?"

She placed a hand on his arm. "Oh, my dear son, with all our good intentions, what have we done to you?"

Tykota went to the door. "I must speak to Mangas."

Hannah nodded. "That dear man has waited patiently for your return. But he is old, Ty, so see that he gets his rest."

Tykota moved out of the house, reflecting that within its walls he had known much happiness. But he would soon need to leave this part of his life behind forever.

Makinna sank into the soft mattress and sighed contentedly. She had bathed and eaten and now wore one of Mrs. Silverhorn's soft cotton nightgowns. A cool breeze filtered through the open window, and she closed her eyes, welcoming sleep. She dreamed that she and Tykota walked together; she belonged to him, and he belonged to her. Then she fell into a deeper sleep and did not dream at all.

Chapter Fourteen

Makinna awoke to the sound of voices filtering into her room. She nestled deeper into the soft pillow and smiled. No more running from danger or going thirsty. The long ordeal was over. She and Tykota were safe.

She stretched her arms over her head and watched a warm breeze stir the lace curtains at the window. It felt good just to rest her tired body.

Suddenly she sat up, her heart pounding. Suppose Tykota had left her there without saying good-bye?

Makinna shook her head. Tykota would not leave without telling her.

She slid quickly out of bed and looked

around for her tattered dress. It was gone, and so were her shoes. Draped across a chair was a pink gown and soft leather shoes to match. At the foot of her bed, she found undergarments, and she smiled with delight when she saw a comb and brush on the bed-side table.

After fastening the corset, she slipped the dress over her head and found to her delight that it fit. She brushed her hair until it crack-led, then ventured out of the room.

As she descended the shiny wooden stairs, she met Mrs. Silverhorn coming in the front door, a basket of wildflowers hooked over her arm.

"I hope you slept well, my dear."

"Yes, I did. Thank you very much." She smoothed her dress and smiled. "Thank you for the gown. It fits perfectly."

"It's not new, but I thought the color would suit you nicely. I took it in a bit at the waist and let out the hem. You're taller and slimmer than I am."

"How very kind of you. But how did you guess my size?"

Makinna watched Mrs. Silverhorn's eyes crinkle into a smile. "I used your old gown as a pattern. Are you hungry, Miss Hillyard?"

"Starved. And, please call me Makinna."

"Makinna it is." She ushered Makinna into

the kitchen and seated her at the table. "It's cozier here than in the formal dining room," she said, placing the basket of flowers in the center of the table.

Everything was neat and clean, just like the woman Tykota called mother. "It must be lonely for you out here, Mrs. Silverhorn." Makinna said as her hostess scooped scrambled eggs onto a blue china plate.

Mrs. Silverhorn turned to remove biscuits from the oven and placed them on the table before she answered. "There's never enough time to be lonesome on a ranch, Makinna. There's so much to do; the work is never done."

Makinna spread honey on a steaming biscuit and bit into it. "Have you ever thought about going back to England?"

Mrs. Silverhorn poured coffee for herself and Makinna and sat down across from her. "This is my home now. Tykota just got back from England, where he took my husband's body to be buried in his family crypt in Cumberland."

"He didn't want to be buried here?"

"Although George learned to love this land, he only settled here for Tykota's sake. It was his wish that his body be returned to England. I shall be buried beside him when my time comes."

"So that was the reason Tykota was traveling on the stage."

"Yes. He sailed to Galvenstan where he took the stage. My son . . . Well, I keep hoping that Ty will one day decide to make Biquera his home."

"Do you think he will?"

Mrs. Silverhorn shook her head. "I don't know what will happen in the future. If only— I wish—" She made a helpless gesture and changed the subject. "My son told me you were on your way to live with your sister in California when Adobe Springs was attacked."

"Have you ever been to California Mrs. Silverhorn?"

"No, I haven't. When my husband bought this ranch and we moved here, we talked about traveling, but we never seemed to have the time." She took a sip of coffee. "Now I don't really care to leave. I only go to El Paso when we need supplies."

"I suppose Tykota was up early this morning."

"That's right. Ty's always been an early riser. He went to the Kincaid ranch to see his old friend, John. They were once very close."

"I recall Tykota's mentioning John Kincaid. They went to school together in England, didn't they?"

"That's right. We were glad Ty could have an

171

American friend with him there. John is a very fine young man, and I know he misses Ty."

"When . . . when will Tykota return?"

Mrs. Silverhorn laughed. "Oh, he's already back. He's in the office going over the ledgers for me. I'm hopeless when it comes to tallying figures." Hannah gazed at Makinna for a moment. "Do you mind if I ask you what happened to your hair?"

Makinna's hand went to her shorn curls. "It got so tangled, Tykota cut it with his knife."

"Say no more. If you want me to, I'll straighten it out for you later on. I cut my own hair." She patted the neat bun at the back of her head. "And I'm pretty good at it."

"I'd appreciate that."

She patted Makinna's hand. "You have beautiful hair. It just needs a snip here and there."

Makinna took another bite of the mouthwatering biscuit and honey. "Perhaps Tykota will decide to remain on the ranch and help you out now that you are alone."

The little Englishwoman shook her head. "He has too many people depending on him. Always has. I will not add to that burden." She propped her elbows on the table and studied the petal of a delicate primrose thoughtfully. "As the new chief of the Perdenelas tribe, Tykota feels his first obligation is to his people."

Makinna gasped and paled, and Mrs. Silverhorn patted her hand again.

"I see that my son didn't tell you about the Perdenelas. He can be very secretive at times."

"I . . . I wasn't sure the Perdenelas really existed. One of the men on the stage spoke of them, but even he wasn't sure if they were real or just a legend."

"Oh, they exist all right. But I will trust you to keep their secret."

"I will say nothing about them. But I am amazed that an entire culture can exist in secret."

"As far as I know, my husband was the only white men ever invited to their hidden village." She leaned back, remembering what her husband had told her about his first meeting with the chief of the Perdenelas. "My George once saved Chief Valatar's life. Many years ago my husband came to Texas with some of his friends on a hunting expedition. On their third day out, he became separated from the rest of his party, and that was when he encountered a man being attacked by several Apaches. Later, my husband learned that the man was chief of the Perdenelas. When George came upon him, all of Valatar's braves had been killed, and the chief was pinned down in a gully, gravely wounded. My husband came at the Apaches with both guns firing. The Indians must have

173

thought George crazed, because they promptly rode away."

"How amazing!"

Hannah's eyes softened. "My husband was an amazing man. He bandaged Valatar as best he could and made camp for the night.

Hannah took a sip of her coffee, wrinkled her nose at the taste, and added more cream before she spoke. "George remained with the chief for several days, tending to his wounds and nursing him back to health. When Valatar was well enough, he rode away during the night without a word to George."

"That seems a bit ungrateful. Did Valatar ever come back?"

"No. But when George finally made his way back to his friends, who had given him up for dead, and told them about his adventure, they were a bit skeptical until, one day, an Indian came riding into their base camp. He was tall like Valatar, and George knew he was from the same tribe."

"What did the Indian say?"

"With sign language and arm motions, he indicated that George was to go with him. He took him to the hidden village of the Perdenelas, in the sacred Valley of the Moon. Valatar wanted to reward him, and he also wanted George to teach him English."

"And did he?"

"Indeed. George remained with the tribe for

over a year, learning the Perdenelas language as well, and when he was ready to leave, Valatar loaded him down with gold."

"It must have come from the legendary treasure!"

"You will not tell this to anyone?"

"Never." Makinna shook her head.

"George didn't want to take the gold, but Valatar insisted. And as it happened it allowed us to take even better care of Ty—buying this ranch and educating him in England. Valatar was a stubborn man. His son has that same trait."

"I know all too well about that side of Tykota," Makinna admitted. Then she hesitated. "He told me that you and your husband took him into your home because someone was trying to kill him."

Mrs. Silverhorn lowered her gaze. "And I fear there are those who still want him dead."

"Do you know who?"

"I have always suspected his half brothers and his stepmother."

Saber could better understand why Tykota was so secretive about his life. "I can only imagine how pained Tykota must feel, wanting to be your son and care for you, yet knowing he owes his loyalty to his tribe."

"My son walks in two worlds, belonging to neither. I pray every day that he will find peace within himself." Mrs. Silverhorn stood and began clearing the table. "Ty wanted to see you after you had eaten. He's in the study off the entry."

"May I help you with the dishes?"

Mrs. Silverhorn smiled. "You have not met our cook, Frances, since she has gone to El Paso for supplies. She barely allows *me* in her kitchen. But let's go into my sewing room first, and I will straighten you hair, and then you can go to my son."

As Makinna walked beside Hannah, the older woman placed a hand on her arm. "You won't tell anyone what we talked about this morning, will you?"

Makinna shook her head. "I would never betray your trust. Or Tykota's."

Tykota had just closed the ledger when a soft rap came on the door. He stood. "Come in, Makinna."

She opened the door and stepped inside. His long hair neatly tied back, Tykota was dressed in buff-colored trousers, highly polished boots, and a snow-white shirt that provided a sharp contrast to his bronzed skin. He was so handsome her heart raced at the sight of him. "Your mother said you wanted to see me."

He pulled out a chair for her. "Please be seated."

Tykota seemed so different in this setting, somehow at peace with himself.

"I like your mother, Tykota," was all she could think to say."

"Thank you. Everyone does."

He seated himself and studied her for a long moment. The pink gown made her skin glow and enhanced her delicate beauty. "Your skin is nicely tanned, Makinna."

She winced. "My sister will probably be horrified. It will take months to get rid of it."

"I forget that your race favors light skin." He rearranged some papers on his desk, and if Makinna hadn't known better, she would have thought he was nervous.

"You had something to tell me?" Sensing what it was, she dreaded hearing it. He was going to send her away.

Tykota met her gaze. "After you have rested and recovered completely from your ordeal, I will have some of the ranch hands escort you to El Paso where you can board a stage for California." He hesitated. "No one need ever know what happened, Makinna. I know your reputation would suffer if anyone found out that you spent days in the desert alone with an Indian."

She stared at him. "Do you think I care about that? I am proud of what we did, proud to know you." She fought against the tears that were gathering in her eyes, but one trailed down her cheek anyway. "I . . . I will miss you."

His throat tightened. "You knew the day would come when we would have to part."

She closed her eyes, trying to regain control over her emotions. "There were times, Tykota, when I didn't think we would live from one day to the next." Finally she was able to smile. "Yet you never gave up. You pushed me on when I wanted to quit. If you hadn't, I would have died. I want you to know that I will always be grateful to you. Always be proud to have known you."

"To speak truthfully to you, Makinna, I wrongly supposed that, being a woman, you would hinder our chances of survival. But I was wrong. I underestimated your strength and determination. I have been proud of you, too, Makinna. You did better in a dangerous situation than most men would have."

She beamed under his praise. "Even Mangas?" she teased.

He smiled. "Mangas, I believe, has special powers from the Great Spirit. No one could best him."

"Admit, Tykota, there were times you wished me back in New Orleans, or anywhere but at your side."

Again he smiled. "And there were times when you wanted to push me off a cliff."

"True," she said with a laugh. Then she sobered. "When will you leave to join your tribe, Tykota?"

"There are a number of things that need my attention here before I can leave. I would say at the beginning of next week."

Her heart felt shredded. "And when do I leave?"

He took a deep breath. "As soon as you feel up to it. Though I know my mother would love your company and would like to keep you here as long as possible."

She almost shook her head, almost said she would stay forever, if only he would not leave her. Instead she said, "Thank you but I must resume my journey to California."

He stood, suddenly distant and aloof, and Makinna realized that she was being dismissed.

"If you would care to, I can have one of the hands show you the ranch. That is, as soon as you are ready to ride again."

She smiled slightly, although her heart was breaking. "I'm ready now, if I can use a real saddle."

"We don't have a sidesaddle. Mother does not ride."

"Well, then, just give me any kind of cushion between me and the horse, and I'll welcome it. It'll be a while before I want to get quite so close to a horse again."

He answered her in an austere tone. "I will see you at dinner, Makinna."

She held her back straight as she walked to

the door. She tried repeating to herself, *This too shall pass*, but she doubted that her broken heart would ever mend. Tykota must never know she loved him.

After Makinna closed the door, Tykota wanted to go after her. But he didn't. He sat pensively, reliving the time they had spent together: their closeness, their kiss, touching her body, his spirit blending with hers. Makinna had broken the reins he'd always kept on his emotions, and he wanted to hold and cares her until she submitted to him.

Makinna was in his heart, and he doubted he would ever get her out.

He glanced upward, wondering in agony why he must give up the only woman for him. The woman who would always be in his heart, in his blood.

He did not want to think about what her life would be like once she was gone. With her beauty and sweetness, she would be surrounded by gentlemen ready to lay their hearts and their fortunes at her feet.

"Damn!" he swore, going to the window and jerking the curtain aside. Perhaps he should leave sooner than he had planned. Maybe it would be easier to ride away now than to stay and watch her go from his life forever.

He lowered his head. His father had placed a heavy burden on him. But he was bound by honor to fulfill that promise he had made as a boy. A promise that was calling him back to the Perdenelas. And he would have to make the ultimate sacrifice to fulfill that promise— the woman he loved.

Chapter Fifteen

Tykota rode beside Mangas, his heart growing lighter as he surveyed his beloved Biquera Ranch. They rode to the top of a mesa, and Tykota looked down upon a fertile valley where a thousand head of cattle grazed. He had almost forgotten just how beautiful and tranquil this part of Texas could be. It was fed by two rivers—the Rio Concho, flowing from Mexico, and the Rio Grande, which formed the border between Texas and Mexico.

This ranch had been his home for so long. But once he returned to his people, he would never return.

"Tykota," Mangas said, "I can see that your

heart is troubled, and I wish I could offer words to comfort you."

Tykota's hand tightened on the reins. "What I must do, no one can help me with, old friend."

"But the burden weighs heavily on you. You love this land, and yet you return to a way of life you can hardly remember. It is true that the Perdenelas need guidance, because evil walks among them. Many of the young men have been stirred up by Sinica, and some of them have joined him in raids."

"How is it that Sinica's influence can reach inside the valley?" Tykota asked angrily.

"When Chief Valatar died, and the Old Ones waited for you, many of our young warriors lost direction, and they answered Sinica's call to join his renegade Apaches. Sinica is still so eaten up with hate that I fear only your death will satisfy him."

"You know what he did at Adobe Springs. I will always have to live with the thought that people died there that night because of me."

"I heard the drums talking, and I know what happened. Sinica shows mercy to no man, red or white. You cannot blame yourself for his ruthlessness."

"What about Coloradous? Does he hate me also?"

"I believe that Coloradous is a good man, but he has been unable to curtail his brother's raids. And he lives alone in the mountains since your father sent him from the village. Leaderless, the Perdenelas do not attempt to stop Sinica. It will be up to you to put an end to his marauding."

Tykota looked into the faded brown eyes that were still alive with intelligence. "It is a sad thing, Mangas, when a man must spill the blood of his brother."

"It is. But if you do not stop Sinica, he will slay you. There is no knife sharp enough to cut the poison from his heart."

"I know. Perhaps I have always known, though I have wished it otherwise."

The old man waved a hand, gesturing across the land. "You grieve to leave this which has been your life for so long."

"It will be difficult to turn away and never look back. But I know that I must. I cannot fail my father."

"I will walk with you wherever you go. I will stand beside you, and you will not be alone."

The young chief's brow furrowed, and he glanced at the ranch house, where Makinna was. "I must leave tomorrow."

"You do not want to leave the woman."

Tykota looked into his mentor's face. Denying his feelings would not fool the old man. "You see too much, Mangas."

"Your feelings for her are in your eyes. I see pain in them when you look at her."

"My father told me to always put the good of the people before my own needs. And in my new life, there is no place for Makinna."

Makinna found her situation strange. She had shared hunger and thirst and danger with Tykota, and they had barely managed to stay one step ahead of the Apaches pursuing them. Now they sat at table laden with food and drink, she wore a lovely blue silk gown Mrs. Silverhorn had given her, and Tykota was dressed in a black dress coat and tailored white shirt.

He was seated at the head of the long dining table, his mother on his right, Makinna on his left. She met his glance and judged from his pensive expression that he was also remembering the past.

"This is an occasion," Hannah Silverhorn announced, filling two glasses with wine and handing one to Makinna. "I toast the safe return of my son."

Makinna noticed that Tykota's glass was filled with water. Her inquiring gaze met his.

"I am an Indian, Makinna. I do not partake of spirits."

"What has being an Indian to do with drinking a glass of wine?"

He looked amused. "Let us just say that, as an Indian, I do not handle wine as well as you do."

Makinna took a sip and started coughing, red with embarrassment. "It seems I can't drink wine either. That was my first taste, and clearly I wasn't very successful with it."

"Well, perhaps the wine was a mistake since this is both a happy *and* a sad occasion," Mrs. Silverhorn said. "My son has returned safely, but he will be leaving tomorrow." She turned to Tykota. "I will miss you my son."

Makinna looked at Tykota. "You are leaving so soon? I thought that you would . . ."

Tykota took a moment before answering. "I must. My people need me."

Makinna lapsed into silence. It was torture for her to be so near Tykota and pretend they were mere acquaintances. When his bronzed hand rested on the white tablecloth, she remembered the strength and the gentleness in those hands.

She wanted to cry. She wanted to go down on her knees and beg him to take her with him. But she would do neither. She held her back straight and tried to make polite conversation. "Everything is delicious, Mrs. Silverhorn. I especially like the soup. It's not unlike the gumbo my mother used to make."

Hannah thanked her and began chatting to cover her sadness that her son would be leaving the next day.

After a while, Makinna withdrew from the conversation, concentrating on her misery. To never see Tykota again—how would she bear it?

"What do you think, Makinna?" she dimly heard him say. Belatedly, she realized that Mrs. Silverhorn had been speaking to her.

"I beg your pardon, I didn't hear what you said."

"My mother asked if you would consider remaining here on the ranch with her for a few weeks. She would love to have you. It is seldom she has another woman to talk to, apart from Frances, the cook."

Makinna would like nothing better than to stay at Biquera Ranch, where she could at least be near Tykota. But her mother's long illness had taught her to face painful truths, and she did so now: impossible as it seemed, she had to move on, resume her journey to California without Tykota.

"You are most kind, Mrs. Silverhorn, but my sister will worry if I do not arrive soon. Even now she must be wondering what has happened to me."

"You could write to her and explain that you are going to remain with us for a time," Hannah said hopefully.

"I'm sorry, but I must decline. My sister has surely made plans for us."

Somehow, Makinna managed to get through

the meal, although she scarcely tasted the food that had been carefully prepared for the occasion. She was about to excuse herself and go to her room, when Tykota stood and spoke to Mrs. Silverhorn.

"Mother, will you excuse us? I wish to speak to Makinna."

"But I should help your mother clear away the dishes."

"Nonsense," Hannah said. "Frances has returned, and she will not welcome help from either of us. Go along with Ty."

Tykota indicated that Makinna should precede him, and when they were out of the dining room, he escorted her out the front door. They stood on the veranda, both with so much to say, yet neither willing to speak.

Makinna moved to the porch railing and gazed out at the ranch. The full moon was so bright, it looked almost like daytime. "It's so peaceful here," she said at last.

He came up beside her, resting one hand on the ornate post. "Yes. Yes, it is."

They were so close and yet not touching, but Makinna could feel his presence as strongly as if he were pressed against her. "So," she said, hoping her voice did not tremble, "you are going away tomorrow."

"I must."

"Your mother will miss you."

He seemed to be struggling to say something.

At last he said in a harsh tone, "My life does not belong to me, Makinna."

He broke off and moved away from her. He gripped the railing with both hands, fearing he would take her in his arms if he didn't hold on to something. "My life was ordained for me the day I was born. The path I must follow leads away from here."

"Your mother told me that you are the new chief of the Perdenelas." She turned to him. "Why didn't you tell me? Didn't you trust me to keep your secret?"

"I do trust you, Makinna." He gazed toward the corral where the pintos, not accustomed to being fenced in, were trotting about restlessly. "I would trust you with my life. But I have never told anyone about my people."

"You must have heard what Mr. Rumford said about the Perdenelas that day in the stagecoach."

"I did."

"When he asked you if you knew anything about the tribe, you told him you didn't."

He let out a breath. "That is not what I said, Makinna. I told him I could tell him nothing. Which is not the same thing. . . ."

"Yes, I see."

A long silence followed until Tykota turned to her.

"I just wanted to say that it has been an honor to know you, Makinna." He swallowed quickly before he continued. "I want to wish you happiness. I want . . . I want . . ."

She had never known him to be this uncertain. She stepped closer to him. "What do you want, Tykota?"

The words seemed ripped from his throat. "When you leave, you will take my . . . best wishes with you."

"Is that all?"

He reached out to her, pulling her against him. He rested his chin on top of her head. "Take my heart with you, Makinna, because no other woman will ever have it. But understand this: there is no place in my life or heart for a woman—any woman."

She was afraid she might cry. He had just admitted he cared for her, but not enough to take her with him. Her heart yearned for so much more. She could not speak.

He held her in silence. "I will never love a woman as I—" He broke off. "I do not want to hurt you, Makinna."

She raised her head and looked into his dark eyes. "Tykota." She touched his face. Her lips quivered, and pain she could hardly bear tore at her heart. "How can I endure it when you go?"

His arms tightened around her, and he held her without saying a word. At last he raised her chin and bent his head, touching his lips to hers.

Makinna surrendered to him, her eager lips opening to his. He deepened the kiss, expressing his emotions in the only way he could. His hands slid down her back, pressing her tightly against his swelling hardness, needing this small intimacy between them, yet hating himself for the weakness.

Makinna pressed her hips against him, feeling almost faint. She wanted . . . she wanted more from him than a kiss. She wanted to feel his heart beat against her aching breasts, and—

Tykota broke off the kiss and quickly stepped away from her. How could he have given in to his desire? He turned away from the confusion in her eyes. "I didn't mean for that to happen, Makinna. But when I am with you, I cannot seem to stop myself. Will you forgive me?"

She wanted to scream at him that she would never forgive him for throwing her love away. If he didn't love her, at least he desired her. How could he walk away from what they had? "I want to be with you, Tykota."

His voice was husky, and he still did not look at her. "What do you mean, Makinna?"

She went to him, slid her arms around his waist, and rested her head against his back, listening to the drumming of his heart. "I don't know what I mean, Tykota. How could I, since I have never known a man? I want you to teach me, because I don't want anyone else."

She felt him tense. "One day your husband

will teach you." She felt him tremble. "Some day a man will touch you." He dislodged her hands and turned to face her, touching her lips with one finger. "He will kiss those lips until they swell with longing." One trembling hand went up to her breasts. "He will know the sweetness of these and make you moan with pleasure." He lowered his head and kissed her through the material of her gown, and she could feel that kiss burn through her.

Then he pressed her back against the house, deep in the shadows, and his hand went between her thighs, and his breath came out in a groan. "One day, a man will know the joy of deflowering you, Makinna." He caressed her until she threw back her head and bit her lip to keep from crying out.

"Tykota. Oh, Tykota," she whispered, her body quaking with desire.

Tykota wrestled with his own desire and felt himself losing the battle. He hadn't meant things to go this far, but he could not seem to stop himself. He dropped to one knee and kissed her between her thighs through the skirt of her gown. He felt her tremble, and tears blinded him as he too, quaked with desire. "One day a man will enter that paradise and know the sweetness of your soul."

Makinna wanted to rip off her gown so there would be nothing between her and the wonderful hands playing such havoc with her body.

"Tykota, please," she begged, her virginal body on fire for him.

He stood to his full height and moved away from her, pausing on the steps to gain control over his emotions. "I could take you right now, have all of you, Makinna. But I am not willing to sacrifice your future to satisfy my desires." Her eyes were shining with passion, and he wanted her so badly it hurt. "I cannot. You would always suffer for it if I did."

Her lips parted. "But I want you to."

He groaned. "You do not know what you ask."

When she moved forward and pressed her lips to his, his resolve almost snapped.

"I know what I ask. I want to be with you." She must make him understand how she felt, that she would never want any man to touch her but him.

His voice was deep and trembled when he spoke. "Someday you will be loved by a man, Makinna. But that man will not be me."

Shattered, she turned away and ran into the house. She hurried up the stairs and into her bedroom. Throwing herself onto the bed, she sobbed with the pain of loving a man who was utterly unobtainable.

Why had he made her want him? He had awakened her to desire, then left her feverish and unfulfilled. She would never again be the same innocent girl who had begun her journey from New Orleans. And she would never forget the tall, dark-eyed Indian who had stolen her heart.

When Makinna finally stopped crying, the house was dark and quiet. Needing a breath of air, and seeking release, she made her way carefully down the stairs and out the front door. Shards of moonlight struck the landscape, making it seem almost enchanted. She headed for the corral and put a bit between the pinto's teeth, then hoisted herself onto its back and she raced away from the ranch, into the darkness.

Lost in her misery, she did not see the dark angry eyes that watched her gallop away. She did not know she was being followed.

Chapter Sixteen

When Makinna heard the sound of a rider behind her, she urged the surefooted pinto into a faster gallop across the flat land, scattering cattle as she rode past. She was afraid it was Tykota chasing her, and she couldn't face him yet. If she did, she might crumble into a thousand pieces.

Suddenly, the river loomed in front of Makinna, blocking her path. She reined in her mount with such force that the animal reared up on its hind legs, and she tightened her grip to keep from sliding off.

She whirled her horse around to face the inevitable. In the bright moonlight she saw not one rider but six bearing down on her. She gasped in horror. Indians!

She wheeled the pinto, ready to risk being drowned rather than taken by the Apache. But it was too late. Already two Indians were beside her, one grabbing the reins from her hands, the other blocking her path.

Dear God, help me, she prayed.

Tykota arose before sunup. He wanted to ride the ranch one last time, to say good-bye to the home of his youth and to a way of life that would soon be ending for him. He also wanted to leave before Makinna awoke; he didn't trust himself to see her again.

After walking around the barn and pausing to glance toward the distant mountains, he walked purposefully toward the corral. The black and white pinto cantered up to him and brushed against his outstretched hand. Tykota glanced around the corral. Where was the second pinto, the one Makinna had ridden?

He climbed over the fence and jumped to the ground. Bending down, he examined the footprints he found in the soft sand. Makinna had been there. He traced her steps until they disappeared, where she had mounted the second pinto.

Uneasiness settled on him, and he quickly headed for Mangas's cabin. Without knocking, he burst inside. The old man was having breakfast, and he looked up at Tykota quizzically.

"Have you come to eat the morning meal with me as you did as a boy?"

"One of the Apache pintos is missing," Tykota announced.

"Why does this concern you?"

"A woman's footprints, made hours ago, probably sometime last night, show that Makinna mounted it and rode out and did not return."

Mangas listened carefully. "I will saddle two horses."

Makinna struggled against the rough hands pulling at her. She spun her pinto around, but she was no match for the Indians. One of them struck her with the butt of his rifle, and she fell forward, unconscious.

When Makinna regained consciousness, her head was aching, and she couldn't move. She remembered being surrounded by Apaches, and then exploding pain. She tried to move her arms and her legs, but they were tied.

Glancing around frantically, she saw that she was lying on the ground. The only light came from a small campfire. After evading them for so long, she had fallen into the hands of the Apache because of her own carelessness.

Stark terror ruled her mind. What were they going to do with her?

Makinna counted six Apaches speaking excitedly, and she wished she knew what they were saying. Or maybe she didn't want to know. She cringed when one of them rose to walk toward her and stared at her with dark, menacing eyes. She lowered her gaze, waiting for death. But he merely bent to make certain her ropes were tight enough, then rejoined his companions.

After a while, two of the Indians took up their rifles and left camp—she supposed to stand guard—while one of the others put out the fire.

Hope flared to life within her. If they sent guards out, they expected Tykota to come after her. Then her hope faded, and she felt a sob building up deep inside. Of course Tykota would come for her. That was what they wanted him to do. And she was the bait to draw him in.

Tears ran down her cheeks. Tykota was going to die, and it was all her fault.

Tykota and Mangas dismounted and crouched by the river, examining the unshod horses' tracks.

With a grim expression, Mangas said, "Apache. At least six of them." The old man traced one of the hoofprints with a bony finger; he could read them like a white man could read the pages of a book. "Chiricahua Apache, but not the warriors of Cochise."

"I know who they are, Mangas," Tykota said grimly. "It could be no one but Sinica or some of his warriors."

The old man nodded. "He will use the woman to trap you."

"I know this."

"He turned renegade and makes war wherever he goes. He has set the white man's hand against all Chiricahua Apache. But he does not care. He thinks only of your death. He has broken the lance and sworn to kill you."

Tykota gazed into the distance. "There should not be such hate between brothers."

"Hear this, Tykota. Sinica would kill the woman to get at you, but more likely he will keep her alive long enough to entrap you and to make you watch her die."

Tykota raised his head to the sky and remembered to keep from yelling out his rage. The last traces of civilization stripped away from him. Then he took a deep breath, and his eyes narrowed. "Sinica's days to walk this earth are small in number. And if he has harmed my woman, I will make sure he begs for death before it welcomes him."

Mangas stood up and looked around, his eyes seeing that which few people could. He pointed to the muddy riverbank. "That is where the woman went into the river, and that is where her horse left with the others. But it was lighter. She was carried away."

"Are you certain?"

"I am."

Tykota knew Mangas was never wrong when it came to tracking. "I must go after her."

"That is what Sinica wants you to do."

"Yes."

"He will be expecting you."

Tykota nodded.

"They will be ready for you."

Tykota swung onto his horse. "I want you to go back to the house and tell my mother what has happened, then see if you can find Cochise. He might be our only hope. He must want Sinica as much as I do."

Mangas's gaze settled on Tykota. "You send me away because you fear we will not come back alive."

"This is my fight. I go alone."

"I am an old man. If I die today, I have lived many years. I have no fear of death."

"I go alone," Tykota said in a tone that brooked no dissent. "They will be expecting me to bring many men with me. I will have a better chance to surprise them if I am alone. Go, Mangas."

Mangas looked with sad pride upon the warrior he had once taught. Tykota was now chief of the Perdenelas tribe, a man who must be obeyed. "I will do as you say."

"I will need your horse. Can you make it back to the house within the hour?"

Mangas nodded and handed over his reins. "Remember all I taught you. Do not rush foolishly into danger."

When Mangas turned to head back toward the ranch house, Tykota glanced down at the tracks of the Apaches. He knew they would be expecting him. The thought of Sinica touching Makinna chilled his blood and stirred his rage.

How would he live if they harmed her?

After riding all day and most of the night, Makinna barely had the strength to stay on her horse. The Apaches stopped only for brief periods to rest the horses, then ride on again. She remembered Tykota telling her that an Apache could ride seventy-five miles a day, and she believed it.

The sun was coming up on the second day when they finally halted to make camp. They chose a high mesa that offered a panoramic view of the countryside.

Makinna had not been given food or water, and she was so thirsty that her tongue stuck to the roof of her mouth, and her lips were cracked and bleeding. There was a gash on her forehead where the Indian had struck her, and it throbbed painfully.

Suddenly, she heard horses approaching, and

ten more Indians rode into camp. One of the newcomers dismounted and walked toward her, his dark gaze sweeping over her menacingly.

Makinna shrank away from him, but he grabbed the rope that bound her hands and yanked her up from the ground. He was different than the other Indians. He had more of a presence. She knew he was the leader.

"You are Tykota's woman?" he asked in stilted English.

She said nothing.

He rammed a knee into her stomach, making her double over in pain. "You will answer me."

"No," she whispered, her eyes on the knife in his hand. "I am not Tykota's woman."

"You lie, white woman. You are my brother's woman."

Brother. She shook her head. This man was nothing like Tykota. He did, however, resemble the other Apaches. But she was almost too weary to think or care. Why didn't he just plunge the knife into her and get it over with?

He dragged her to where two other Indians had been hacking away branches from a slender mesquite tree, leaving only the trunk. She cried out in pain when the Apache slammed her against the rough bark and looped a rope around her several times to secure her to the stake.

The sun beat down on her, and Makinna licked her dry lips. "Water, please," she begged.

But her plea went unanswered, and her head fell forward, her chin resting against her chest.

The Indian grabbed a handful of hair and jerked her head up. "You will die, white woman," he said, peering steadily into her eyes. "And Tykota will cry out in agony when he sees what I do to his woman."

She stared back at him. "I am not his woman."

He smiled with malice. "You were with my brother—you are his woman."

"He will not come after me," she said defiantly. "You can kill me, and he will not care."

He ran a hand down her cheek. "You are good to look at, for a white woman." He ran his hand over her breasts, and when she shuddered, he laughed. "My brother, I think, will grieve much for you, as I have grieved for my shame and that of my mother."

"Do what you will," Makinna challenged weakly.

He motioned one of his men forward and took his canteen. "But you will not die yet. Tykota must see you breathe your last."

Makinna wished she had the willpower to refuse the water, but she drank thirstily, and when he released his grip on her hair, her head fell forward again. She prayed Tykota would not come. The Apaches were armed and waiting for him. Surely he must know that.

* * *

Tykota had already ridden one horse to death, but Mangas's riderless horse was still fresh. He had no trouble following the Apaches' trail, even by moonlight, but that was because Sinica wanted him to find them. His one advantage was that with the fresh horse, he could make better time than they did. Sinica would expect him to be at least a day behind them, while he was now within an hour of them.

A short time later, Tykota reined in his mount and gazed at the distant mesa that stood like a dark shadow against the sky. That was where Sinica would be waiting, with Makinna as his hostage. Sinica hadn't killed her yet, or he would have left her body behind for Tykota to find. Mangas was probably right. Part of Sinica's revenge would be to make him watch Makinna die.

A muscle in Tykota's jaw tightened. He pitied Sinica if he harmed Makinna in any way.

Makinna was barely conscious when the sun rose. She sagged against the stake, and she couldn't feel her arms, which were tied tightly behind her. She tried to clear her mind, but everything was fuzzy. She was dimly aware of men feeding horses, laughing among themselves, and standing guard.

Sometimes one of them would come to her and lift her head to see if she was still breathing.

She was dying, she knew, but it didn't seem

to matter. She closed her eyes, feeling as if she were baking in an oven. It was so hot.

Then suddenly water was being splashed in her face, and some kind of dried meat was being held to her mouth. "Eat, white woman."

If she only had the strength, she would have spit in the Indian's face. She almost wished she would die, just to spite him. But cruel hands forced her to eat and drink. She was not going to die today.

Chapter Seventeen

Tykota chose his time of day carefully. It was almost twilight, and deep shadows crept across the landscape, making it hard to see. That would be to his advantage.

He crept along a ravine that led toward the mesa where Sinica had set up camp. He paused, his gaze running the length of the table rock, locating the guards. He paid particular attention to a sharp slope which was guarded by only one sentry.

Tykota dropped to his stomach and crawled up the slope careful inch by inch, cautious not to cause a single pebble to slide and alert the enemy of his presence.

The sun was almost down and the sky was blood-red as he crept to the top. The Apache guard was no more than a dozen paces from him. He waited patiently as the guard paced back and forth. But the moment the sentry became distracted by taking a drink from his waterskin, Tykota leaped forward. Gripping the man's neck in a choke hold he placed his knife at the Apache's throat, and hissed in his ear, "If you value your life, do exactly what I tell you."

"You will slay me anyway," the man answered, trying to claw Tykota's arm away from his throat.

"Not if you do as I say."

Knowing he was helpless against Tykota's superior strength, the Apache finally stopped struggling and nodded.

With his knife still at the warrior's throat, Tykota forced him forward. "Where is the woman? Take me to her. And make no sound."

"She is tied to a stake fifty feet or so from here."

Tykota's knife pressed against the man's throat as they moved ahead. "Is she alive?"

The Aphache licked his dry lips. "She was when I went on guard."

Finally Tykota could see Makinna. She was tied to the stake. Her head had fallen forward, but she appeared to be alive. Anger shot through him like a burning arrow. He wanted to cut Sinica's heart out and feed it to the wolves while it was still beating. He wanted to run to Makinna, slash through her bonds, and hold her in his arms. She must be so frightened. But that was just what Sinica wanted him to do. He would only have one opportunity to get Makinna out of this alive. And even that was a gamble.

Makinna became aware of frantic activity around her. With effort, she raised her head and blinked the sweat out of her eyes so she could see. "No," she moaned, seeing Tykota walking into the enemy camp his only defense the knife he held at the throat of an Apache.

She blinked again. Perhaps she was only dreaming, or the twilight was deceiving her eyes.

But no. Several Apaches had clutched their rifles and were aiming them at Tykota. Still he moved forward, seemingly unafraid. He even shoved his prisoner aside, with enough force that the man hit the ground and rolled to the edge of the mesa.

Makinna watched Tykota fearlessly approach the leader of the Apaches. She did not understand the language they spoke, but she recognized the threat in Tykota's tone.

Oh, why had he come? He would surely die. What could one man do against so many?

Sinica was shorter by a head than Tykota. He was stockily built, while Tykota was muscled and lean. Still, Sinica was strong, and his hate for Tykota gave him strength. "I have been expecting you, brother."

Tykota's eyes were hard, and a savage expression curved his lips. "I know you have. This day was predestined. This is the day you will die, Sinica."

"Not by your hand," Sinica sneered, laughing and looking at his many warriors. "This is the day *you* walk in the Spirit World with our father."

"I do not think so." Tykota's voice sounded calm, but there was something dangerous about him. "You arranged your own death, Sinica, when you took this woman."

"You have the look and sound of our father. It was because of you that my mother was shamed before the Old Ones. Because of you that my father never saw me as his son. He saw only you. Even my true brother, Coloradous, preferred you to me." Hatred spilled forth from Sinica's lips. "I will take your woman and make you watch. After you are dead, perhaps I will keep her as my woman. Will your spirit rest easy, knowing she belongs to me?"

"That is not the way it will be," Tykota said calmly. "You, my brother, will never leave here alive."

"What can one man do among twenty?" Sinica scoffed. "Even you are not that good a warrior, Tykota."

Tykota smiled, but there was a threat in his smile. "A man who tortures a helpless woman is not a true warrior. And a man who is afraid to accept a challenge of combat from another Indian is not a man."

Sinica snorted. "I see no Indian. I see someone dressed as a white man claiming to be an Indian. If I give the word, my warriors will tear you to pieces!"

"This fight is between us, Sinica. It always has been."

"I will not fight you. Why should I, when I can simply order your death? Those who follow me will do whatever I ask of them. Of you, I ask only one thing before you die: the location of the Perdenelas gold."

"Never. That secret will die with me."

"Are you willing to watch the woman die first, then—after I have given her to the others to enjoy?"

Tykota's lip curled in disgust and rage. "Even then I would not tell you. But this is not about the woman, and it is not about the treasure. It is about you and me, Sinica."

"Why should I fight you when I can order your death?" he repeated.

"Do you tell your warriors, or will I, that you are too afraid of the chief of the Perdenelas to meet me in combat? I have no warriors with me. I came to you alone. You are a coward who surrounds himself with many warriors so you will not have to fight. But when they learn your true nature, the Apache will spit on you and call you dishonorable around the Chiricahua campfires."

Makinna wanted to call out to Tykota, to urge him to save himself, but she didn't have the strength. He would not have heeded her anyway. She saw the rage in his eyes, and she could tell by the tone of his voice that he was goading the other Indian to fight.

She wondered if there had ever been such a man. She knew of no one who would be brave enough to face his enemies in such large number. Truly he had the heart of a lion. She watched the man he called Sinica throw his rifle down and tear his knife from its leather sheath. They were going to fight, and she could not bear to watch. Even if Tykota won, would not the other Apaches kill him?

Like charging bulls, the two warriors came together in a clash of fury.

They both hit the ground from the impact, then both struggled for dominance. The other Indians had gathered in a circle around them, loudly encouraging Sinica.

The two men rolled on the ground until Tykota leaped to his feet, his knife drawn, prepared to kill.

Sinica came to his feet and lunged at Tykota, who artfully sidestepped the thrust, causing Sinica to stumble and fall into a thorn bush.

He flinched in pain and hacked angrily at the bush with his knife.

"I have to admire you," Tykota taunted. "Perhaps the Chiricahua Apache will sing around their campfire about your bravery in fighting thorns."

In his rage Sinica jumped to his feet and charged Tykota, slashing and thrusting with his knife. However, Tykota managed to stay just out of reach of the blade. And the more Tykota evaded him, the more enraged Sinica became, and the more ineffectual his thrusts.

Makinna didn't want to watch, and yet she could not look away, for fear Tykota would be killed. She could see that his opponent was charging in a blind rage, slashing the air.

At last, Sinica lunged forward, shouting in triumph. But Tykota's knife drove into his body. There was a surprised expression on Sinica's face as he slid to the ground, his life's blood soaking into the sand.

Tykota looked at the blood on his hands and dropped to his knees, gathering his half brother in his arms. "Why did you make me do it, Sinica? I did not want to kill you."

Sinica's lips were moving, but he made no sound. Finally, he gasped, "I detest you." Then he stiffened and stared into nothingness. He was dead.

Tykota eased Sinica's head down and stood,

speaking to the Apaches, who seemed frozen with shock. "Who will be next to challenge me for this woman? Who wants to be the next to die?"

Before anyone could react, they were distracted by at least forty Apaches riding up the mesa. When the dust cleared, only one man dismounted, obviously the leader. He carried himself proudly, and his dark eyes took in all that had occurred. Then he turned to Tykota.

Makinna was puzzled to see Mangas with the warriors.

Tykota faced Cochise, chief of the Chiricahua Apaches. "I have slain my brother." He tossed down his knife. "I have no wish to slay anyone else. If you want revenge, you will have no resistance from me."

"There will be no reprisal, Tykota. Sinica has caused the Apaches much trouble. He could not have lived long with his lust for blood. You can take your woman and leave, Chief of the Perdenelas."

Tykota's gaze fell at last on two tall braves in Sinica's band he recognized from his own tribe. "I do not know which path you will travel, but do not return to Valle de la Luna. You will find no welcome there, and every man's hand will be turned against you."

One brave had the good grace to lower his head in shame, but the other glared at Tykota.

"You are both a disgrace to the Perdenelas. Go out and find a better life. Never let me look upon either of your faces again."

Tykota motioned for Mangas to cut Makinna loose while he spoke to Sinica's followers. "If there is any among you who want to challenge me for the death of Sinica, let him step forward now."

He was met by silence.

Cochise spoke in a commanding voice. "If any of you want to come with me, I will take you back into the tribe. But if you come, you will obey me in all things, and you will not war on anyone unless it is my command."

Tykota did not wait to hear more. He lifted Makinna into his arms, and Mangas handed him the reins of his horse. "Take her to our valley. She needs healing. You must hurry."

Tykota nodded. "Follow as soon as you are able, Mangas. I will need you beside me when I take my place as chief."

Makinna leaned her head against Tykota's chest. She wasn't sure just what had happened or why she was free. "You were very brave," she said through cracked, swollen lips.

"Hush. Do not think about it."

"I will always remember your courage."

He knelt down and held a waterskin to her lips. "Drink, Makinna."

She took only a few sips, as he had taught her to do.

He held her to him. "Fear no more, Makinna. I am taking you to someone who can help you."

"I am not dreaming?"

"No, beloved, you are not dreaming." He examined her closely, taking in the severe sunburn, the gash on her forehead, and the bloody wounds from the ropes around her wrists and ankles. "Did they . . . abuse you?" he asked.

"No. They only used me to capture you."

His arms tightened about her. "You are safe now."

"Safe," she whispered, closing her eyes and slumping against him. "As long as I am with you."

Although he would be breaking the tribal law by bringing a white woman to his valley, the medicine woman, Huara, was a great healer. And, besides, he could not let Makinna go. Not yet.

He gently lifted her onto the Indian pony and headed in the direction of Valle de la Luna and the Mountain of the Moon.

Chapter Eighteen

The horse was tired, and Tykota was forced to slow to a walk, although he was impatient to get Makinna to the healer.

After a while he had to stop because the horse could go no farther. He dismounted and lay Makinna down while he tended the pinto.

The moon was still bright, and he gauged it to be early morning. He was still a day's ride from the Mountain of the Moon.

He sat down and took Makinna's head in his lap. She stirred but didn't awaken. Besides the gash, her face also had bad burns from the sun. He only hoped her eyesight had not been damaged. He would have given his life to spare her this anguish.

He gently touched a tangled curl and tucked

it behind her ear. "I know you cannot hear me, but you are the most amazing woman I have ever known, Makinna Hillyard."

She lay motionless, but he was encouraged by the even rise and fall of her chest. Her breathing was good.

At first light, Tykota was again on the move. He was thankful for the sturdy Indian pinto that carried both him and Makinna through the desert with ease. By early afternoon, he saw the twin peaks that looked like clouds banked against the sky. Unless someone accidently happened upon the narrow passage that led to Valle de la Luna, it was so well concealed that they would not know it was there.

He had not traveled that narrow trail since he was a small boy. His heart was thundering in his chest, and he felt he was being yanked back in time. He almost expected his father to ride out to greet him.

On the other side of that passage through the desolate-looking Mountain of the Moon was a wide river feeding a lush, green valley, and an Indian tribe that lived in peace and plenty.

He would soon be reunited with the Perdenelas, would soon be their chief. He had been gone for such a long time, surely the elders who had pledged their loyalty to him that night his father had brought him before them were all dead. How would the other tribe members receive him?

He set his gaze on the seemingly solid mountain, its granite face rising inhospitably toward the heavens. He knew where the entrance was located—the memory was burned into his mind.

He slowed his pace when he entered the narrow gorge that wound for over a mile through the mountainside. He felt the cool breeze that came from the valley, and, gazing down at Makinna lying against his chest, he felt her breath on his neck. The medicine woman, Huara, knew all the healing herbs. Soon Makinna would be safe and well.

When he reached the end of the passage, he reined in the horse and stared at the valley below.

At last, after so many years, Tykota had come home.

When Makinna awoke to sunlight, she tried to move, but she was too weak. She dimly realized she was on horseback, encircled by a strong pair of arms. "Where am I?"

"You are safe, Makinna. No one will hurt you again."

She gazed up into Tykota's dark eyes. "That Indian called you his brother."

"He was my brother. My half brother, Sinica."

Tears came to her eyes. "I am so sorry you

had to fight him. To kill him. It was all my fault. If I hadn't—"

"Say no more," he interrupted her. "Sinica had to die, Makinna, or he would have gone on marauding and killing. Someone had to stop him."

"I am sorry," she said weakly.

He urged the horse forward.

Makinna frowned. She'd thought they were still on the mesa, but this place was different. There were steep inclines on either side of them, and a mountain looming up to the sky. "Are we going back to Biquera?"

He shifted her so she could see ahead. "No, Makinna, we are not. This is my home, Valle de la Luna."

Her first view of the valley was breathtaking, with the sun breaking through a mist. The valley was so green, it almost reminded her of New Orleans, but there the similarities stopped. A wide, serene river cut its way though fields and pastureland, and deer and elk wandered about unafraid. Makinna gasped when she saw that many dwellings had been carved into the stone mountain itself. It was like nothing else she had ever seen. And it seemed only right that Tykota should have come from such a singular place.

"It is beautiful," she said softly.

"Yes. It is just as I remembered it." His gaze moved over every inch of it, as if he were taking account of each bush and tree.

Abruptly they heard riders, and three armed Indians appeared, blocking their path. They aimed rifles at Tykota, and one of them spoke in a language Makinna did not understand, but from the angry tone she gathered that they were not welcome.

"You have crossed into the land of the Perdenelas, and you must die," one of the men said.

"I am here by right. I am Tykota, son of Valatar, and your new chief."

The warrior frowned and cocked his rifle. "I do not believe you. Our chief would not have a white woman with him."

"This woman is injured and in need of Huara's medicine." Tykota had expected to return with Mangas at his side. Now he had to face skepticism from his own people. "Look into my eyes, and see the truth there."

One of the Indians cried out with joy, and his cry was echoed by the other two. "We have waited for this day. Is it really you, my chief?"

"I am Tykota."

There was a commotion behind them, and Mangas came riding up, a reprimand in his voice when he spoke to the three guards. "Is this how you welcome your leader? Go, tell everyone the chief has come home!"

One warrior reluctantly rode back to guard his post, while the other two raced ahead to alert the village. Tykota watched them cross the river, their happy voices carrying as they called for everyone to gather to greet the chief.

"How does it feel to come home after all these years?" Mangas asked.

Tykota wanted to tell his old teacher how unsure he was that he could be responsible for the well-being of the Perdenelas people. He had been born to lead, but had he the wisdom? Had he the desire?

"I do not know how it feels. My father was a wise man. I am not."

Mangas's sagacious eyes settled on his chief. "You are Valatar's true son. His blood runs in your veins; you will know what to do when the time comes."

They moved forward as warriors, women, and children poured out of their homes to hail the chief.

"Let me carry the woman, so you can greet the people properly," Mangas suggested.

"No. She needs to have her wounds tended. I will give her over to Huara myself. Assemble the people, and let them know I want to speak to them."

Tykota rode to the cliff dwellings while the tribe begin to gather near the river. He brought Makinna to the medicine woman and explained to her what had happened.

Huara smiled. "I will take care of the woman. Welcome home, my chief."

Reluctantly, Tykota left Makinna and made his way back to the river.

The crowd opened to let him pass, and he saw joy on each face. He had been gone for so long, he hardly recognized anyone. His old friend, Santo, came up and clasped his arms, welcoming him home, but the rest were as strangers to him. He saw the reverent looks on many of those gathered, and they stared at him as if he was a deity. The thought was unsettling, because he was only a man, and unsure if he could be the leader the Perdenelas needed.

When the crowd fell silent, one of the council spoke. "Perdenelas, we have long waited for this day, since Chief Valatar passed from among us. But the Great Spirit has sent Valatar's son, who will settle all our uncertainties. Here stands Tykota, your chief!"

There was an uproar among the people as Tykota stepped forward. "My people, I have been long away from our valley, but not a day passed that I did not think of you. I will try to lead wisely. I embrace you all."

He saw a beautiful young woman who wore the headband with the golden eagle, and he knew who she was before she spoke.

"I am your sister," she said shyly, searching his eyes to see if he had missed her as much as she'd missed him.

He raised her face and smiled as warmth spread over him. She had been a small, chubby girl when he left. Now her raven-black hair fell to her shoulders, her dark eyes were sparkling with happiness, and her face was so lovely, he imagined she must look like their mother. She was his only pure-blood tie with his deceased father and mother. His family. "I came home expecting to find a child, and instead I find a woman, Inea."

"I have waited long for this day, my brother. My heart sings with joy that you have returned."

"I, too, have wanted our family reunited. I know that while I was in England, you spent a summer at Biquera Ranch."

Inea lapsed into English. "Yes. Your white mother taught me to speak her language."

He embraced her and whispered so only she could hear. "Come to me after the council meeting. We have much to talk about." He rested a hand on her head. "Will you go to the healing woman for me and stay with the white woman there? Her name is Makinna, and she will be frightened, because she is not accustomed to our ways."

Inea bowed her head and smiled, her heart filling with pride that he had asked this of her. "I will do as you say."

"Until later, little sister."

He moved on down the line, talking to as many as he could. At last, he came to Santo once again. "Your sister has grown into a very beautiful woman," his friend said.

223

Tykota smiled. "So she has."

"Can I speak to you about something important?"

"Later tonight," Tykota replied, knowing there were many who would now seek his advice. "Find me after the council meeting."

Santo nodded. "It is good to have you home."

Tykota moved on through the crowd, and when he reached the end, he was still looking for another familiar face. He turned to Mangas and asked, "Where is my brother, Coloradous?"

Mangas bent forward and said in a low voice. "Have you forgotten that your father sent him from the village? Coloradous has not been here since the night you left the valley."

Tykota's jaw clamped tightly. "Then you shall take me to him tomorrow. For now, ask the Old Ones to meet me in the council room."

Makinna awoke in total darkness and felt panic. She heard voices, but she could not understand what they were saying. She reached up to her eyes and found a cloth had been tied about her forehead. She tried to pull it away, but a pair of hands grabbed hers, and she heard a woman speak softly to her. Although Makinna did not understand the words, she responded to the kindness.

"Where is Tykota?" she asked.

A second gentle voice, this one younger,

spoke to her in English. "Tykota said to tell you he would come to you tonight."

"It is not night now?"

"No. The darkness is because the healing woman, Huara, has put herbs on your eyes and bandaged them. You are not blind, but your eyelids were burned from the sun."

"When can I get up?"

The young voice spoke to the older woman, and then to Makinna. "Huara says you may get up tomorrow, if you do not do too much."

"And when can I take the bandages off my eyes?"

Again, the young voice spoke to the older woman. "Huara says that the bandages must remain in place for a while yet."

"Who are you?"

"I am Tykota's sister, Inea."

Makinna felt relief wash over her. "You speak English very well."

"Tykota's white mother taught me."

Makinna relaxed and felt herself getting drowsy. "Mrs. Silverhorn," she said fondly. Then her voice trailed off, and she surrendered to sleep.

Chapter Nineteen

Tykota felt like an imposter as he sat on the sacred white buffalo hide where his father had once sat, and his father's father, and his ancestors for as far back as the history of the Perdenelas was told.

He allowed his gaze to move over the twenty men who waited for him to speak. His expression was grave. "I know that you all grieve with me for the passing of my father from this world to the Spirit World. I see several of you who were in this chamber many moons ago, when you pledged your loyalty to a small boy."

The remaining Old Ones nodded their heads.

Frowning slightly, Tykota continued. "That boy is now a man returned to fulfill his own promise to his father. But first I must say this.

If any one of you feels that another chief would be better than me, that I am not the man to lead our people, let me hear your voice, and I will step aside."

Mangas stood, his eyes sharp and intelligent, his jaw tight. "Before any man speaks, let me say that this young chief who stands before you has never lost sight of his responsibilities to the tribe. His eyes and heart have always turned in the direction of Valle de la Luna, and he would have come home sooner had his father allowed it. By birth, he is your rightful leader, and let no man say differently."

Batera, the most senior of the Old Ones, stood, his back curved and his hair white but his eyes keen and his voice strong. "Since I have lived more seasons than anyone in the tribe, heed my voice. You, Chief Tykota, were born to lead our people. It is not for us to say if you should turn away from your hereditary duties. We put our trust in you when your father asked it of us, and we will gladly follow you."

Tykota felt a surge of pride. "Are your feelings shared by the others in the tribe, Batera?"

"If any man feels differently, he has never said so to me. Since your father left us to walk with the spirits, all eyes turned beyond the valley, waiting for you to come and take up your rightful place among us. There has been strife and unrest among our people, but only because we had no one to settle our disputes."

"There is another matter I wish to put before you," Tykota said. "It is something I have done, and I want you to know about it. I have slain my half brother, Sinica."

Again Batera spoke. "We heard the Apache drums speak of this. Sadly, it had to happen. Sinica's blood was long tainted by his mother's hatred."

"I want accounts of my other brother, Coloradous. I know he still dwells in the valley, and I want to bring him back into the tribe. If any man can say why I should not do so, let him tell me now."

Mangas stood, his voice carrying to the far corners of the chamber. "I have known Coloradous to be an honorable man. He has honored his father's words and has not come among us. But I have sought him out over the years and judge him to be worthy."

The others nodded in approval.

"Then I shall go to my brother and embrace him. He should no longer have to bear the shame of Sinica and his mother."

Again the Old Ones nodded.

Tykota sat back on the white buffalo robe, wondering if his father would approve of his decision. He wanted to think he would have done so if he had lived.

When Huara removed the bandages from Makinna's eyes, she blinked against the bright sunshine that poured into the room. As she adjusted to the light, she looked at the woman who stood over her with concern on her aged face. She said something Makinna could not understand, but Makinna smiled and nodded and said, "I can see." She took the healer's hand. "Thank you for your tender care."

The medicine woman looked pleased and squeezed Makinna's hand.

Over the two days Makinna had been ill, she had grown fond of both the gentle healer and Tykota's sister. When a young Indian maiden entered the room, Makinna instantly knew it was Inea.

"I am sorry that I could not be here when your bandages were removed." Inea gazed at her inquiringly. "You can see?"

Makinna nodded and stretched a hand out to Inea, and when she came forward, they hugged. "I can see perfectly."

Inea was strikingly beautiful, with the same deep brown eyes of her brother. She also wore the leather headband with the golden eagle in her black hair. She was dressed in a fawn-colored leather dress and moccasins of the same color.

"Inea, will you thank Huara for me?"

Inea spoke to Huara, and the woman nodded and smiled. She picked up a waterskin and left the room, leaving Makinna and Inea alone.

Inea sat down on the soft fur rug beside

Makinna. "I have come to feel a strong friendship for you, Makinna. I know my brother admires you, and it is easy to see why. You have a sweet nature."

Makinna arched an eyebrow and laughed. "Your brother could not have given you that impression. He would *never* say I had a sweet temper."

"You met my brother on the stagecoach before the raid on Adobe Springs?"

Makinna nodded.

"I know what happened. We had word through the Apache drums. For a while, we feared that Tykota was dead."

"When will I see him?" Makinna asked.

"I have hardly seen him myself. He simply falls on his mat at night, too weary to speak. It is not easy for him to settle all the troubles of the Perdenelas."

"When you do see him, would you tell him that I would like to speak to him?"

"I will do this, Makinna."

Makinna smiled at the Indian woman. "Tell me about yourself. Are you married, and have you children?"

Inea shook her head sorrowfully. "I am a maiden still. I have waited for my brother to return so I would not have to marry a man I do not like."

Makinna could see that Inea was troubled. "Couldn't you just refuse the man?"

"No. His family is very powerful, and he is also a friend of my brother. Santo would not allow any other suitor near me. He threatened to kill anyone who looked on me with favor."

"Tykota has told me they were good friends and often went into the desert together to live by their wits and test their skills."

"That is so. And the only peace I knew was when Santo was away from the valley. I always dreaded his return."

"Was there nothing you could do to discourage him?"

Inea sighed. "I could not tell my father, because he wanted me to marry Santo. After my father died, Santo became more insistent. It was my right to refuse him when he asked me to become his woman, and I did that. I am afraid of him and always avoid being alone with him for fear of what he might do. I was happy when my father sent me to spend time with the Silverhorns so I could learn English. I hoped that by the time I returned, Santo would have found another to be his woman." She made a hopeless gesture. "But it was not to be."

"Is there someone you *would* like to marry?"

Inea's eyes became dreamy. "My heart has always turned to Kachee, and I am sure he returns my affection, though he has never spoken of his feelings to me. Since I am sister to the chief, Kachee would not dare aspire so high."

"But if you two love each other, why can you not be together? You must tell this to Tykota."

"There is little he can do for me because of our law. I must first get Santo to reject me before Kachee can look on me with favor." Inea ducked her head sorrowfully. "Santo will never reject me, and I shall never marry him."

Makinna was thoughtful for a moment. "Maybe we can come up with something to free you from him."

Inea looked doubtful. "Nothing will make Santo reject me."

Makinna thought of the story of Ruth in the Bible and wondered if Ruth's method of getting her dead husband's kinsman to reject her might provide a solution to Inea's troubles. She peered at Inea, who was looking so dejected. "I will see if I can help you. Don't despair."

Shaking her head, Inea said despondently, "I fear that no one can help me. Maybe not even Tykota."

"Don't be so sure." Makinna smiled. "I'm certain we can find the means to send Santo on his way."

Hope flamed in Inea's eyes. "If only it could be so!"

Tykota sat alone in his chamber, his thoughts troubled.

Mangas ambled in, his footsteps light, his

heart happy. "The children are eager to perform their dance."

Tykota stood wearily. He hardly had time to sleep, for all the ceremonies he had to attend and laws he had to act on. "I suppose they are waiting for me."

"Of course they are. This is in your honor."

Tykota moved to the door and gazed out at the campfires and the people who had gathered around them. "I am troubled, Mangas." He glanced at his old teacher searchingly. "I do not know what to do."

"It concerns the white woman?"

"Yes. I do not want to let her go."

"You must, Tykota," Mangas said sadly.

"Yet my father himself married outside the tribe."

"And you know what happened with that Apache woman. That is the very reason we now have a law to keep that from happening again."

"But Makinna is everything to me. I will not give her up. No one should ask such a sacrifice of me."

"Your people will ask it of you. You cannot take her for your woman. She is white. The law forbids it."

Fury burned in Tykota's eyes, and he turned his back on his teacher. "I am the law here now. I can change my father's ruling."

The old man inclined his head. "That is so, Tykota. You can change any law you want to."

Tykota whirled around. "And I shall."

"But before you do, ask yourself if you want to change the law for your own needs, or for the good of the people."

Tykota flinched as the words his father had spoken to him so long ago came back to haunt him. *"Everything you do must be for the good of the people."*

He drew in a painful breath. "The road set for me on the day of my birth is a hard one, Mangas. Never more so than now."

"Where the head rules, the heart cannot always follow, my chief."

Tykota sagged in defeat. "It will be a lonely road for me."

"I will walk with you," Mangas gently teased.

Tykota managed to smile in return. "While I love and respect you, Mangas, you are not exactly the partner I would have chosen."

Chapter Twenty

Tykota had been riding for over an hour. He was following the river in hopes of finding Coloradous. He had decided to come alone rather than bring Mangas when he told his half brother about Sinica's death.

He dismounted and let his horse drink from the stream while he walked along the bank, taking in the beauty of the land. Here were tall pine trees, and the wind weaving through the branches made its own music. He was drawn back to a time when he had been a carefree youth here in the valley. He had come here often with Coloradous, who did not seem to mind a younger brother tagging after him. Sinica, however, had always taunted him, calling him a weakling and accusing him of being their father's favorite.

"Is it as beautiful as you remember?"

Tykota had not heard Coloradous approach, and he turned to find a tall, lean, yet muscular brave not unlike himself. "It is even more beautiful than I remember. Remember when we fished in this stream?"

Coloradous moved closer and looked into Tykota's eyes. "I remember. You were destined for greatness even then."

Tykota reached out and clasped his brother's arm and was gratified when Coloradous returned the greeting with a firm hand on his arm. "I do not feel greatness, my brother. I am confused and a little uneasy about all the responsibility now thrust upon me."

Coloradous laughed and turned his gaze to the rushing water. "You will do well, Tykota. I have always known there was strength in you and that you would always do what is right for the people."

Tykota sat down on the grassy bank and lowered his head. "I have grave news to tell you." He lifted his gaze to Coloradous. "I will understand if you decide to challenge me."

Coloradous was silent as he sat down beside him. "I already know about Sinica. The word of the Apache drums reached me even here."

"I did not want to slay our brother, but I had no choice."

Coloradous rubbed his chin in thoughtfulness. "Put your mind at rest, my brother. Sinica was of my blood, but so are you. He was without honor, and you have much honor. Doubtless I would have done as you in like circumstances."

Tykota felt vastly relieved by Coloradous's words. There was sincerity and kindness in his older brother's eyes, and Tykota knew now for certain that their father had been wrong to expel him from the tribe. "I have come to bring you home."

Coloradous looked startled. "What do you mean?"

"I have gone before the Old Ones, and they agree with me that you should come home. All stain will be wiped from your name, and I will raise you up in honor as my brother."

Coloradous could not answer right away. When he did, his voice was gruff with emotion. "I have wanted this for so long, yet I had hoped it would come from our father."

"I know. I, too, wish it had come from him. And perhaps if he had not been so harsh with Sinica and your mother and you, Sinica might have turned out differently."

Coloradous placed a hand on Tykota's arm. "It would have been no different. Sinica was always bitter. He hated me because I was born before him and had the look of the Perdenelas, and you because you were born to the wife our father loved, then chosen to be chief." He ruffled Tykota's hair as he'd done when Tykota had been a child. "Put the past behind you, and walk into the future." He grinned and added, "O, mighty chief."

Tykota laughed. "Careful, or you will give me a swelled head."

Coloradous took Tykota's face and turned it toward him. "I suppose the women consider you quite handsome. *That* might well give you a swelled head."

They both laughed at the bawdy reference.

"Come, Tykota," Coloradous said, rising. He led them past the grazing horses. "I want to show you something."

Tykota followed Coloradous around the bend of the river and stopped, staring in awe at what he saw. There was a small earthen dam, not enough to keep the river from flowing down to the valley, but enough to feed ditches that led to a thriving field of corn.

"This," Coloradous said with pride, "is the way I have been spending my time. This can be done in the valley, and we can grow our crops even in years of drought."

"I saw something like this in England, but I never thought to apply it to our valley." He stared at his brother. "You are truly a man of vision."

Coloradous seemed pleased by the praise. "My vision tells me right now that I am in need of food. Come, my brother, we dine on fish and corn cakes."

Tykota's heart lightened. It was like old times to enjoy the companionship of his brother. He only wished that Coloradous was a bit less reserved. But Tykota knew that his brother was showing respect for his chief. He would have to become accustomed to such treatment not only from his Coloradous but from the rest of his people as well, no matter how alone it made him feel.

The first time Inea took Makinna about the village, the white woman received many curious stares. But as the days passed, people seemed to accept her and would even nod and smile at her. At first, she was embarrassed at how little clothing the men and male children wore, but she gradually became accustomed to it.

Makinna and Inea had been riding for hours through the countryside, and Makinna was enchanted by what she saw. Farmland, nut and fruit trees, and pastures rich with cattle.

It was almost sundown when Makinna reined in her horse and glanced up at the magnificent cave dwellings that had been masterfully carved out of the mountain.

"Inea, I never would have thought any civilization could exist in such perfect harmony with nature. I can see why the Perdenelas would want to guard their way of life from the rest of the world. You have everything you need here: crops, game, tranquility. It's like a paradise."

"Other than the summer I spent with Mrs. Silverhorn, this is the way I have always lived. But I saw many wondrous things in your world. Your roads and carriages, your wooden houses and split-rail fences, your dresses and suits of woven fabrics, your furniture and fireplaces."

Makinna nodded. "Our worlds are very different," she said, realizing just how deep the divisions were between her world and Tykota's.

They rode a little farther, and Makinna halted to gaze into the river. The water was so pure and clear that it reflected the valley on its smooth surface. She glanced up at Inea. "When am I to see Tykota?"

"I do not know. He has many people who need his advice."

"I . . . should speak to him about leaving." Makinna's gaze went to the cliff dwellings dug out of the mountain. Some had porches and open rooms attached. Wooden ladders and stone steps made them accessible. She wanted to remember everything about Tykota's valley, to burn it into her mind. "Will you tell Tykota that I'm ready to leave?"

"I wish you—" Inea broke off and smiled. "Look! You can speak to my brother yourself. He is riding toward us."

Makinna turned to see two Indians on horse-back emerge from the woods. She had not seen Tykota since the night he had taken her to the medicine woman. She wondered if he had been trying to avoid her, or if he was really as busy as his sister believed.

Tykota halted his horse beside them. He was no longer dressed in white man's clothing. He wore buff-colored breechcloth and knee-high moccasins. His long dark hair was circled by a wide leather band with a golden eagle. He was all Indian. And he was so handsome that her heart pounded in her breast.

"Makinna," he said, giving her a smile that would melt any woman's heart. "You are looking well." He glanced at Inea. "How are you today, little sister?"

"I am well, thank you." Her eyes went to the other man, and she cried out in joy. "Coloradous! Tykota has brought you home. I was sure he would."

Makinna looked at the second Indian, startled by how much he resembled Tykota.

Tykota introduced them. "Makinna, I would like you to know my brother, Coloradous. I am sorry, but he speaks very little English."

Coloradous smiled slightly and inclined his head. He spoke to Tykota in their own language. "Brother, if you do not want this woman, I will take her."

241

It was meant in jest, but Tykota's eyes glinted dangerously. "Ride on with our sister. I will remain to speak to Makinna."

Inea and Coloradous exchanged glances, surprised at their brother's jealous possessiveness of the white women.

Coloradous sobered as they rode away. "I fear Tykota loves that woman." He shook his head sadly. "She is certainly well enough to leave, yet Tykota keeps her here."

Inea frowned. "Our poor brother. Our laws forbid him to have her."

In the gathering darkness, Tykota lifted Makinna from her horse. He smiled when he felt the corset beneath her gown. "You are wearing too much clothing again."

She averted her eyes. "The same can't be said about you."

He set her on her feet. "Are you really feeling well enough to be out riding?"

"Yes. I was just telling your sister that I am well enough to leave."

He guided her down the riverbank and stood beside her. "Are you so anxious to leave us?"

She wanted to tell him that she never wanted to leave, that she would gladly stay here with him forever. But her stubborn pride formed her words. "My sister must be out of her mind with worry for my safety by now."

"I sent word to my mother to let your sister know you had come to no harm."

"Oh." She sat down and plucked at a long blade of grass. "It is lovely here."

He sat down nearby. "Yes, I think so."

She looked up at him and found him watching her closely. "You will remain here?" she asked.

"I must."

"I see."

He reached out and touched her cheek. He hadn't meant to; it just seemed necessary. "Will you leave so soon, Makinna?"

She fought against the tears that were forming behind her eyes. "You tell me, Tykota."

His hand dropped away. "Yes. I will make arrangements for you to go. In two days' time."

"Will you take me yourself?"

"As far as Biquera. My mother will see that you get to El Paso from there."

Her heart was breaking. He seemed so distant, and anxious to see the last of her. "Thank you."

They both fell silent, watching the water.

"Makinna, I suppose you will one day want to marry?"

She drew in a breath, wondering how he could ask her such a question. Wounded, she answered with bitter sarcasm. "Yes, of course. Every woman wants that, didn't you know? We are born to have children and please some man in bed." Upon making the outrageous statement, she saw the stricken look in his eyes.

He stood up, reached for her hand, and drew her up beside him. She was speechless as he took her into his arms. He laid his face against hers and said in an anguished voice, "Would that I were that man. I would sleep with you beside me at night so I could touch you as I am only able to do in my dreams." His mouth traveled down her cheek to the corner of her lips. "I would fill your belly with sons and make all your days happy."

A sob was building up inside her, and she threw her arms around him. "I want to lie beside you! I want to have your sons! I don't want to leave you!"

With an agonized murmur, Tykota tightened his arms around Makinna. "I have stayed away from you," he said, going down to his knees and pulling her down beside him, "because I knew I could not keep my hands off you if I saw you again."

Her eyes were wide with wonder. "You love me—you do!"

Her words were sobering. He could not let her know the depth of his love. Because he had to send her away. But he would taste her lips and hold her for a moment, then he would let her go. "It is desire I feel for you, Makinna," he said almost harshly.

She parted her lips and moved closer to him. "Then desire me, Tykota."

His lips were on hers, probing, covering, devouring. It was as if a floodgate had opened, and every emotion he had held back came spilling out. Makinna was ripe and ready for a man, and he wanted to be that man.

Makinna was quaking as he opened her gown and buried his mouth against her breast.

She found herself lying on the soft grass with Tykota beside her. Her tongue darted out to wet her lips.

He groaned her name and pulled her to him. At this moment, he would die for just one more taste of those lips.

Chapter Twenty-one

The last flicker of sunlight gave way to darkness as Tykota unhooked Makinna's gown and pushed it down over her shoulders, giving him full access to both her breasts. While his mouth settled on the one his fingers caressed the other.

Makinna writhed as burning desire overwhelmed her. She bit her lip to keep from crying out from the sheer ecstasy of it.

There was no moon and the only light came from the twinkling stars that sparkled in the heavens and reflected in the river.

Tykota moved back to her lips and kissed her with all the passion that had been locked in him for so long. She grasped his head, holding him tighter against her, feeling she would die if he did not take all of her.

"Beloved," he murmured in her ear, kissing her earlobe while he unhooked her undergarment with trembling hands. He dare not deflower her, dare not know the depths of her delicate beauty, but just once, before he sent her away, he had to look upon her, touch her, caress her, as if she were truly his woman, for all time. The sacrifice he had to make was great. At least this much he could grant himself, the memory of her naked in his arms.

He cupped her breasts, covered them with kisses. "I have ached to touch you in this way."

Makinna sighed as he removed the last of her clothing. Soon she lay naked beside him, and she felt no shame when he looked at her with admiration. When she felt one of his hands leave her breasts and spread across her stomach, she thought she would die from the unknown fluttering within her heart.

"Makinna," he said, his hand sliding lower, "you were created for a man to love and cherish."

Unable to speak for the tightening in her throat, Makinna reached out to him and placed her hand against his muscled chest, then slid it down to his taut stomach.

At her intimate touch he clasped her tightly against him, pressing her naked body against the throbbing erection beneath his breechcloth, trembling and gritting his teeth to hold himself in check. He knew he should not have gone this far, but he couldn't seem to stop himself.

Makinna moaned and threw her head back, biting her lip to keep from crying out as a powerful tingling started in her toes and worked its way up to the very core of her womanhood.

To gain control of his own desires, Tykota took her hand and raised it to his lips, kissing her fingers one by one, and then the palm of her hand.

Makinna shut her eyes, her entire body coming alive. Surely this could not be wrong when it felt so right. She was born to be loved by Tykota. Surely he must feel it, too.

Tykota raised his dark gaze and looked into her eyes, and the softness she saw there brought tears in her eyes.

"You know this is wrong," he whispered. "We are from different worlds. No one will accept that I love you."

Her fingers slid through his, and she arched toward him. "I don't care what the world thinks. I love you."

He inhaled a deep breath, despising himself for what he was doing. "We cannot be together, Makinna. I cannot do this to you and then send you away. What do I do about us?"

She placed a hand on his bronzed cheek, knowing that if he didn't love her, nothing in the world would matter. "Just love me, Tykota."

He closed his eyes, savoring her soft touch against his cheek. She would never know the depth of his love for her. She could never belong to him. His voice came out in a harsh whisper. "Love you? I can't take a breath without thinking of you. Nothing has any meaning if I am not with you."

Her heart was beating so fast, she could hardly breathe. "Oh, Tykota, Tykota," she said, tears now spilling down her cheeks. "I would have wanted to die if you did not love me."

He scooped her into his arms. "I cannot love you as you wish. But I will give you a gift to take away with you. It will show you the depth of my feelings for you, and it will leave me something to remember on those nights when I ache for you."

He waded into the river, kissing and caressing her. "We will swim with the stars tonight."

The river was dark and reflected millions of stars. And when he lowered her into the water, it did seem that she was surrounded by stars. They were above her, below her, all around her. It was magical.

But she forgot about the stars when Tykota pulled her against him, his hardness pressing against her and making her cling to him with weakness.

Slowly his hand went between her legs, and he caressed her there, creating a desire so strong that she collapsed against him.

"I will show you the depth of my feelings for

you, Makinna. I will worship your body. But when you leave me, you will be a maiden still, for I will not take my pleasure with you."

She did not understand. She only knew that he was carrying her to a higher plane of passion. He dropped his dark head to kiss and suckle her breast, while his wonderful hands worked magic on her trembling body.

Tykota knew it would take all his willpower to satisfy Makinna while leaving his own body unsatisfied. She could not imagine the restraint he was exercising over his own desires. But he was about to show her what the beauty of love could be like.

There, submerged in a river of stars, Tykota caressed, kissed, and gently stroked Makinna into submission. She gave little sobs as he touched her so intimately, her body quaked, and she fought to get closer still to Tykota, instinctively sensing there was even greater pleasure to be had if their bodies could be joined. But Tykota held her away from him.

Makinna stared into his passionate eyes. "Please," she whimpered. "I want—I want you to—"

"Shh," he said, bending his head to her lips. "Let yourself feel, Makinna. Let me make your body sing." He was fighting his own battle to keep his fierce arousal from taking over his thinking. Tonight was for her; he would deny himself in order to pleasure her. His lips moved over her face, tasting the saltiness of her tears.

She threw back her head as he slid a finger into her hot, moist core, and he watched her eyes widen with wonder, her breathing come out in small gasps. When he touched her maidenhead, he pulled back. That he would leave undisturbed, even though she should be his, and he should have the right to break through that barrier. Instead, he smothered her mouth with his.

He had not expected her to reach down, her hand to close around his thick erection. He gasped, closed his eyes, and slammed her body against his. "No, Makinna. You must not."

"Why?"

He let out a gasp when her hand softly stroked him, and he wanted to plunge into her and claim all she offered. He took a deep breath and tried to save them both. Said words he knew would wound her deeply and break his own heart. "Is this the way you will act with other men, Makinna? Will you offer yourself to any man who comes along with a bulge in his trousers?"

She froze. "I . . . what?"

He pulled away from her. "You heard me."

She was quiet for several moments, and when she spoke, her voice was trembling with bewilderment and anger. "Do you think because it was easy for you to undress me that

I would let another man do the same? No, Tykota, I will not offer every man what you do not want. I thought you knew me better than that."

"You were *too* easy, Makinna. I could have had all of you tonight if I had wanted too. You were more than willing."

Disillusionment, anger, and sadness fused together in her mind and wound their way through her heart. "Is this the gift you wanted to give me, Tykota?" she challenged, deep hurt in her tone. "If this is the best you can offer, then I reject you and your gift."

He wanted to speak, wanted to tell her what was in his heart, and that by hurting her, he had wounded himself. But he knew this was the only means he had to send her away. He must not give her any hope that they could ultimately be together. He had to kill his soul to let her go.

He said nothing.

Makinna quickly waded out of the river, scrambled up the hill, and retrieved her clothing. She heard Tykota beside her, but she refused to look in his direction. She managed to fasten all hooks and closures although her hands were trembling. She wanted to cry, but she would not.

"You do not need to come with me," she said, walking to her horse. "I can find my way back alone." In one smooth motion, she mounted the pinto. "Good night, Tykota. I hope you can make arrangements to get me away from here as soon as possible."

He was beside her, grasping her reins. "Makinna, wait. There is something I want to say to you."

"You have said quite enough," she said, backing away from him. "I will never forgive you for tonight."

Her cutting words wounded, but he forced himself to explain. "I can love no one, Makinna, as much as I must love the Perdenelas. Can you understand that?"

"I don't have to understand, Tykota. You can find another woman to torture."

"It was not meant to be torture, Makinna."

She jerked the reins from his hand. "But torture, it was!" She kicked her horse in the flanks and rode away at a gallop.

Tykota stared after her. He had never cried that he could remember. But he could feel tears in his eyes now. He had come to the realization that love was the most powerful emotion of them all, and he was desperately in love.

It was dark inside Huara's lodge, but Makinna managed to make her way across the room without bumping into anything. She removed her clothing and lay down on the soft mat. The tears she had kept in check now flowed freely. Oh, how cruel Tykota had been. At first he had been loving and kind. What had happened to make him lash out at her with words chosen to wound? And wound they had, deeper than he would ever know.

That she had also degraded herself by showing Tykota how much she wanted him to love her magnified her misery.

That would never happen again.

A coldness closed over her heart, and she turned her face to the wall, smothering a sob. She never wanted to see him again as long as she lived. She could not leave this valley soon enough to suit her.

Chapter Twenty-two

Makinna looked at Inea with compassion.

"Santo is becoming more and more aggressive. He cornered me near his lodge and put his hands all over me. When I protested, he said he had that right. He is going to my brother today to ask that I become his woman. He says he will no longer tolerate my coldness to him."

Makinna buried her own misery and took Inea's hand, wanting to help the gentle maiden she had come to care about. "If, as you say, Tykota is taking me away tomorrow, we must do something today."

"But what?"

Makinna frowned. "Tell me, what would happen if Santo saw you with Kachee in a pose that would make him look like a fool?"

"I do not know what you mean."

"Suppose you and Kachee were seen by many onlookers, including your brother, in a loving situation? What would happen?"

Inea's eyes widened with horror. "Santo would kill Kachee!"

"Not, I think, with Tykota looking on. And not if I am there to confirm how unhappy you are about Santo. Since I am not of your tribe, I am not bound to support your laws."

Inea looked hopeful but frightened. "If only we could do that."

Makinna nodded with assurance. "We can. Listen to me, and do exactly as I say. Tomorrow, Tykota and several of his warriors will be escorting me to Biquera Ranch. I would not be surprised if Santo is among them. This is what I want you to do . . ."

Makinna awoke feeling heavyhearted. Today she would leave Valle de la Luna, never to return. She would go to her sister in California and try to forget all that had happened to her since the raid on Adobe Springs.

She was about to put on the pink gown when Huara came to her, carrying a deerskin dress over one arm. She held it out to Makinna, saying something Makinna could not understand.

"You want me to take this dress?" Makinna asked.

The old medicine woman nodded and pushed the doeskin dress toward Makinna. Her pink gown was now ragged, and she was tempted to wear the soft Indian garb. She leaned forward and kissed Huara on the cheek, and the Indian woman looked pleased. She handed Makinna a pair of matching moccasins and smiled.

"Thank you so much!" Makinna said. "I wish I could make you understand what your kindness means to me."

Huara gathered up Makinna's tattered pink dress and motioned for her to put on the other.

Laughing, Makinna slipped out of her chemise and pulled the soft garment over her head. It felt wonderful against her skin. She sat down and slipped into the moccasins, delighting in the freedom such clothing gave her.

After she had eaten the corn cakes Huara brought her and drunk the sweet fruit drink, she hugged the dear woman and told her good-bye. "I will never forget your kindness," Makinna told her.

She hurriedly left, knowing she would miss this Indian woman with the hands and caring heart of a healer.

She descended the stone steps to the valley floor and found Tykota and Santo already standing beside their horses. She greeted them both with a mere nod, noticing the way Tykota was staring at her. *Well, let him!* she thought. Huara gave her the gown, and she was going to wear it, no matter if he approved or not.

She looked into Santo's eyes and felt an instant dislike for the brave. With his burning gaze boring into her, he appeared to be much more arrogant than Tykota, and she knew she would not like to meet him alone. She could see why Inea was frightened of him.

Though she no longer needed such assistance, Tykota stepped forward to help her mount. His strong hands went about her waist, and he lifted her onto the blanket. It seemed that his hands lingered about her waist, but she could be mistaken, for his manner was stilted and cold.

"This time our journey will not be so difficult, Makinna. We will not have to forage for food and water," he informed her.

She felt cold inside at his impersonal tone, and she hoped she appeared cold to him. "I have learned to thrive without creature comforts, Tykota. But I am ready to get back to civilization."

His eyes looked almost sad. "You will be there in no time at all."

She watched him mount his own horse, and she fell in beside him when he started off. As they rode along, several other warriors joined them. Apparently, they were going to have all the protection they would need.

Soon they were approaching the part of the village where Inea was supposed to be waiting with Kachee according to the scheme Makinna had hatched. But now that the time was upon her, Makinna was having doubts. What if she made everything worse for Inea by interfering?

She nervously glanced ahead, wondering if Inea had changed her mind. But then she saw Inea and her warrior beyond a group of women heading down the trail to go work in the fields. Kachee's arms were around Inea, and she was gazing up at him lovingly.

Tykota reined in his mount and glared at his sister. And before Makinna knew what was happening, Santo bounded off his horse and ran toward the couple. Chaos broke out as the other women crowded closer to see what was taking place.

Makinna quickly dismounted and ran toward Inea. Tykota followed her.

Santo grabbed Kachee and slammed him against the tree. When Inea tried to stop him, he shoved her away, and she landed hard on the ground. Makinna helped Inea stand, placing herself protectively between Tykota's sister and the threatening Santo. Makinna could not understand what the angered suitor was saying, and she was taken by surprise when Santo tore her away from Inea and shoved her to the ground, knocking the breath out of her.

Stunned and fearful for Inea, she tried to rise but could not.

Tykota stepped between his sister and Santo. "You will explain what you are doing, Santo. You dare to treat my sister and Makinna in this manner. Tell me now the meaning of your actions."

Santo spun around and pointed an accusing finger at Makinna. "That woman you brought among us is the trouble. She has planted ideas in Inea's head that are unbecoming in a Perdenelas maiden."

Tykota's eyes narrowed. "It is not for you to criticize my sister or to say these things about Makinna."

Santo turned on Tykota. "How would you know? You have not been here these seasons past to see what was happening. Your sister was going to be my woman before you brought that white woman to our valley." He looked at the people gathered around and said in a loud voice, "I challenge Kachee to a fight to the death!"

"Tykota, do not let him do this," Inea pleaded. "I never consented to marry Santo. He takes what he wants and does not ask." She placed a hand on Tykota's arm, hoping to make him understand. "I love Kachee, but Santo forbids any man to come near me."

Tykota frowned in thoughtfulness, trying to hold his temper in check. "It is true as you say, Santo, that I have been away too long. If I had been here, you would never have kept my sister from the man she chooses. I thought you were my friend, but you are not."

"It is that woman's fault!" Santo cried, pointing again at Makinna. "Your sister was not this way before she came."

Tykota turned to his sister. "Is this true? Did Makinna tell you to do this, to shame Santo before the whole village?"

Inea did not want to betray Makinna, but she could not lie to her brother. "She only gave me the courage to do what I should have done a long time ago."

"And was this her plan?"

Inea lowered her head. "I would never have been so clever." She looked up at her brother. "What are you going to do to us, Tykota?"

"How many times have you met with Kachee?"

"Never before today. We have barely spoken, but our eyes spoke of the love we could not confess." She tugged at Tykota's arm. "I know Kachee cannot number his wealth in horses, and his family members are not among the council. But he is a warrior of honor, and I love him."

Tykota glanced over at the young warrior, who was just getting to his feet. "Kachee, do you love my sister?"

Santo stepped forward, but Tykota motioned him aside. "Do you?"

"I do. I have not wealth to offer her, and I know that I reach high when I ask for her as my woman, but I will love her and cherish her. And if she belonged to me, there is nothing I could not do."

Tykota was silent for a moment, and those around him waited for him to speak, for his word was law. "Kachee, I give my sister to you, but you must increase your wealth by twelve horses and take a place on the warrior council."

Kachee glanced at Inea with joy spreading over his face. After all, twelve horses would not be hard to obtain once he was on the warrior council, where he could join in hunting outside the valley. "It will be as you say, my chief."

Tykota turned to the man who had once been his friend. "As for you, I believe your punishment has already started. Word of your behavior will run though the village, and you will know great shame."

Santo's gaze burned into Tykota's, and then he turned to Makinna with a look of such hatred that she recoiled. She had made a powerful enemy today.

"You will not accompany us, Santo. You will

wait here until I return, and I shall decide at that time what is to be done with you."

While Santo stalked away, Inea threw her arms around her brother. "Oh, thank you, Tykota, for giving me to Kachee. I would never have married Santo."

Tykota's dark gaze fell on the young warrior. "She is not yours yet. You will have to prove to me that you are worthy of her."

"It will be as you say," Kachee agreed happily.

"Let us go our way, then," Tykota said, watching his sister walk over to Makinna.

"What has happened?" Makinna asked, since she had not understood anything that was said.

"Your plan worked! Tykota has given me to Kachee."

The two of them hugged and laughed. "I know you will be happy."

"My happiness will not be complete, though, because you are going away. You will always be the friend of my heart."

"And you, mine," Makinna said. "But now I must leave." When she got to her horse and climbed on, she met Tykota's gaze, and it was dark and dangerous. She knew she would hear more about the happenings of this morning before the day was over.

Makinna waved to Inea as they rode away, happy she had helped Tykota's sister and that all had turned out well.

Chapter Twenty-three

Coloradous took Santo's place escorting Makinna to Biquera. He rode just behind Tykota and Makinna, and when she looked at him, she would find him studying her pensively. But there was nothing threatening about him; in fact, she found his demeanor calming and serene.

After a while, she kept her gaze forward. When they reached the narrow passage that led out of the valley, she halted her mount and glanced back down the mountain. The sun was high overhead, and she could see the people going about their daily chores. She wanted to imagine Inea married to her warrior and happy with her future.

Tykota's voice was harsh as he said, "We have

a long way to go, Makinna. It is best if we ride on, since we have already lost time."

She cast him a heated glance and urged her horse into a canter. "The sooner I get away from here, the better," she muttered beneath her breath.

They rode for three hours before they dismounted and rested the horses. Tykota went to speak to several of his warriors, and Coloradous came up beside her. He smiled, and it was almost painful to see how much he resembled Tykota.

"Makinna, it is a good thing you did for our sister. I did not know she was unhappy. Perhaps she would have been unhappy for the rest of her life if you had not helped her."

She was puzzled. "I was told you did not speak much English. Yet you speak it very well, Coloradous."

"I have practiced with my sister. She would come to my lodge in the woods and spend hours teaching me. I did not know even then that her heart walked with Kachee. Like the others, I believed she would one day be Santo's woman."

"I hope she will be happy."

"That is my wish, also." He watched her, as if deciding how to choose his words. "Are you sure you want to go away from our village?"

"What do you mean?"

"Do you want to leave my brother?"

Makinna tried to think how to answer him. "Why should I want to stay with Tykota? He does not want to be a part of my life, and I do not want to be part of his."

"Sometimes life is difficult for the chief of the Perdenelas, and our father made it more difficult still for the chiefs who come after him. Tykota is feeling the tightening of the laws our father set in motion. Although our father had the best of intentions, he has made a hard road for Tykota to walk."

Makinna recalled Mrs. Silverhorn saying almost the same thing. "We all have our roads to walk, Coloradous. Mine just happens to lead to California."

Tykota returned, his expression fierce when he saw Makinna talking to his brother. "Do you talk all day, or do we ride?" he asked his brother in their language.

Coloradous merely smiled, knowing Tykota would be jealous of any man who looked at Makinna. "We ride."

Makinna was silent for most of the day. By dusk, they made camp on high ground so they could see anyone who might approach. Guards were posted, and Makinna wondered if Tykota expected trouble.

Coloradous was standing on the edge of a cliff staring out at the desert when she approached him. "Will the Apaches still be searching for Tykota?"

"Not anymore. And if you are feeling uneasy, know this—no Apache or any other tribe would attack this large a force of Perdenelas."

"Why is that?"

"They fear us."

"Oh. It is hard for me to think of the Perdenelas as dangerous, since I have experienced so much kindness from your people."

"Do not be fooled by the reception *you* received. The Perdenelas are known to be the fiercest warriors in this land." He smiled. "But I pray *you* will always think of us as kind."

Tykota's shadow fell across Makinna's face, but his eyes were on his brother, and he spoke in their language. "Do you stand talking to the woman, or do you take your turn at guard?"

Coloradous laughed and gripped his rifle. "I stand guard, my chief."

Makinna refused to look at Tykota. She told herself she would be only too happy to get to her destination and see the last of him. He had become so different—hard, unreachable, and cruel. She turned to leave, but his voice stopped her.

"Now we will speak of what happened with my sister."

"I have nothing to say to you, Tykota. You were blind and heartless if you could not see that the man you called friend was hurting your own sister."

"Perhaps I was," he said regretfully. "I should have taken better care of my sister."

"You should have asked her what she wanted out of life. Did it not seem strange to you that she had never married though all her friends had done so and begun their families?"

He closed his eyes. "I should have known."

"Yes, you should have."

He gazed out on the apricot-colored sky and drew in a deep breath, letting it out slowly.

Suddenly, sympathy welled up in her, because she felt his spirit was tormented. After all, he had been betrayed by a friend. "I am sorry about Santo, but he has not proven himself worthy of your friendship."

He turned and stared at her, and her heart stopped beating. He was so handsome, his body so beautiful in his breechcloth. She tore her mind away from his physical appearance and tried to concentrate on their conversation. "You may as well know it, Tykota. I'm not sorry for helping Inea. She is a special person, and she needed a friend. I make no apology for being that friend and for helping her trick Santo into showing his true nature."

He surprised her when he started laughing. "I did not suppose you would be sorry, Makinna. I have learned enough of your character to know you will always champion those who need it—like the night you brought me food at Adobe Springs."

She attempted a haughty gaze. "I am glad that I amuse you."

His dark gaze swept her face. "It is good to have someone who can make us laugh in a world in turmoil."

"*Is* the world in turmoil, Tykota?"

"Perhaps only the place where I dwell." He breathed deeply and turned away. "You should place your bedroll away from the fire"—he pointed to his left—"beneath that rock wall. I will lay my bedroll between you and my warriors, so you will not feel uneasy."

Makinna could have told him that *he* was the one she felt uneasy around. She wanted so desperately to touch him, to have him kiss her, to go back to the way they had so briefly been.

She could have told him that, but she didn't.

Makinna's blanket was soft, and a cool breeze touched her cheeks. She folded her arms behind her head and stared at the endless sky, where a million stars were strewn like so many candles. She was aware when Tykota placed his bedroll, as he'd said he would, between her and his warriors. As she stared at the heavens, she wondered if he, too, was remembering the night they swam with the stars reflected in the river.

It was still painful for her to think about. She

turned her back to him and closed her eyes. He was so near, and yet she could not touch him. In a few days, she would be on her way to California, and she would never see his face again.

That thought was so agonizing, she could hardly bear it. To never see him again would be a living death for her. He had touched her heart, and their souls had joined. Didn't he know that?

"Makinna?"

She did not turn to face Tykota. "Yes?"

"Thank you for helping my sister."

Now she did turn to face him. His tall frame was stretched out on his bedroll, and she saw his rifle near his hand so he could grab it if he should need it during the night. "I do not want your thanks, Tykota. As it is, I could never repay all *you* have done for *me*. You saved my life many times, and often at the peril of your own."

"Do not mention that. I just wanted you to know that I have been considering what you said about my sister. I want you to know that from now on I will look more carefully to her happiness."

"I am glad." She shifted her weight and glanced back at the sky. "When will we reach Biquera?"

"Are you in such a hurry?"

"I . . . I am eager to see my sister."

"We will be there in two days' time."

"Good night, then," she said, closing her eyes and willing herself to sleep.

"Good night, Makinna. Fear nothing, and sleep in peace. You are in no danger tonight."

She did not answer. She turned away and clamped a hand over her mouth to keep Tykota from hearing her cry. She had nothing to fear—except living the rest of her life without the man she loved.

They broke camp and mounted before daybreak. Makinna watched the sunrise as they rode across a wide expanse of desert. This time she did not have to put mud on her face to keep from being burned from the sun. Huara had given her a salve to protect her skin.

Tykota rode beside her, and she could imagine them riding the wonderful pintos forever and never looking back.

The beauty of this land, with its wide canyons, red buttes, and giant cacti, now touched her deeply. Lofty mountains loomed in the distance, calling to her like some promised adventure.

"What are you thinking about?" Tykota asked. "From your expression, they seem to be pleasant thoughts."

"I was just thinking that I feel I was born to this land." She met his gaze. "I know it doesn't sound conceivable, but it's the way I now feel."

Tykota slowed his horse to a canter. "I am

271

glad you like this land. Perhaps you will forget the misadventures and hardships and dangers you found here."

She arched a delicate eyebrow at him. "You are the most dangerous animal I met in this desert."

He had been smiling slightly, but now his expression hardened. "I have never been a danger to you."

"No, not in the way you mean. I am sorry for what I said."

Tykota called back to one of his warriors. She didn't know what he said, but the brave rode forward to canter beside Makinna, while Tykota urged his horse into a gallop and rode on ahead.

Silently the group wound their way across the desert, taking Makinna ever closer to Biquera Ranch—and out of Tykota's life forever.

Tykota rode up a steep butte and looked over the land. He had a view on every direction. He watched as the wind seemed to gather the clouds overhead, grateful for the shade they cast.

The closer he got to Biquera, the heavier became his heart. Soon he would have to let Makinna go, and it wouldn't be easy. He was a man in love, a man who had found the perfect mate for him, and yet he must let her go. Makinna thought she loved him, but surely by now he had killed that love, or infatuation, which was probably what she'd felt for him. As soon as men from her own race began to pay homage to her, she would forget all about him.

"Why?" he whispered into the unrelenting desert wind. "Why must this be?"

Chapter Twenty-four

It was the last day of the journey. The Perdenelas warriors rode tirelessly behind their chief, a silent band rapidly making its way through the desert. By nightfall, they would reach Biquera Ranch.

At midday, they encountered a calvary patrol. The handsome Indian chief kept his gaze straight ahead, but the major who rode at the head of his troop was clearly startled to see a white woman in the other procession. He called for the Indians to halt, advising his men not to draw their guns but to stay alert. He spoke quickly to his second-in-command. "The woman is dressed like an Indian, but, as you can see, she's white. Be ready for anything."

The young officer rode up to Makinna,

touched his hat, and spoke guardedly, eyeing the Indian beside her, who looked like none he'd ever seen before. "I am Major Halloway, ma'am. Are you in any trouble? Do you need our assistance?"

Makinna smiled at his concern. The major was handsome, blond, and tall, with bright blue eyes and dimples that showed themselves when he spoke. "I'm Makinna Hillyard, Major, and I can assure you that I am in no need of assistance." She turned to Tykota. "These Indians are escorting me to Biquera Ranch."

The major looked astounded, and then relieved. "We have been searching for you, Miss Hillyard. We heard what had happened at Adobe Springs and feared you might be among the dead."

"This is Tykota Silverhorn, Major. He rescued me from the Apache raid. He saved my life."

"I saw your name on the Butterfield passenger log, Mr. Silverhorn, and assumed you were also dead." His eyes narrowed. "I did not know that you were an Indian."

Makinna, aware of Tykota's temper, spoke up quickly. "I owe my life to this man, Major. If it wasn't for his quick thinking, I would not be here today. He would have saved the others as well, if he could have."

Major Halloway glanced back to Tykota,

then ran his gaze over the other Indians. "I am not familiar with your tribe, Mr. Silverhorn, but I do know a Mrs. Silverhorn at the Biquera Ranch. Are you connected with her in some way?"

Again Makinna spoke before Tykota could voice his anger. "Mrs. Silverhorn is his adoptive mother, sir. She is also a friend of mine, which is why they are taking me to her ranch."

"Are you aware that your sister came in on the stage a week ago and is staying at Biquera Ranch?"

Makinna was shocked. She had not expected her sister to come looking for her. "My sister? Here?"

"That is why I took the patrol out to look for you. She believes you are still alive, but I admit I doubted the possibility." He smiled, and his cheeks dimpled. "I am glad to be wrong."

Makinna now felt an urgency to get to the ranch as soon as possible. "Thank you for your concern, Major Halloway. I will be happy to be reunited with my sister."

The major leaned closer to her and spoke in a low voice, glancing warily at Tykota's angry expression. "Would you like us to escort you to Biquera, Miss Hillyard?"

"Thank you, no. I am sure Mr. Silverhorn will want to see his mother. As I told you before, I am in no danger."

The young major tipped his hat. "Then I will

not hold you up any longer." He looked into her eyes and smiled. "I hope you are going to be staying at Biquera for a while. I have been invited there by Mrs. Silverhorn. If you are there, I shall certainly accept her invitation. I would like to hear all about your adventures."

"Then I shall see you there, Major Halloway."

She watched the troop of uniformed soldiers ride away. Her sister at Biquera—she had not expected Adelaide to come to Texas. She turned her gaze to Tykota. "I can't wait to see my sister."

The expression on Tykota's face was fierce. "That white man wants to see you again."

"Do you think so?"

"He admired you."

Makinna blinked her eyes in astonishment. Tykota was jealous! She smiled inwardly as she said, "I look forward to seeing him again. He seemed very nice."

Tykota kicked his horse in the flanks and rode forward. It had already started, he thought. The first white man she encountered was touched by Makinna's beauty. He had wanted to challenge that bluecoat for daring to look on his love with such open pleasure, but he did not have that right. "Like flies to the honey pot, they will come," he muttered in his own language.

It was almost sundown when they reached the outer perimeter of Biquera Ranch. Tykota told his warriors to camp beside the Rio Grande, while he and Makinna rode on to the house.

Tykota slowed his pace, as if making their time together last. "It is good that your sister is here."

"Yes. I am surprised that she would come all this way. She moved away when I was young, and I don't know much about Adelaide's life now."

"One does not have to be constantly with a brother or sister to be close to them. It is something in the blood that ties you together with an invisible string. I have found that with Inea and Coloradous."

"I suppose."

With his usual perceptiveness, he asked, "You are troubled?

"For the first time, I realize I have family. Adelaide must care for me, or she would not be here."

"You will soon see for yourself," he said, halting on a rise, where they looked down on the lights of the ranch house twinkling in the distance.

She turned to him. "This is the last time we will be alone, and I want to thank you again for all you have done for me."

His gaze met hers. "There is nothing to thank me for. I . . . want you to be happy. That will be my reward."

"I will never forget you."

"You will, Makinna."

She swallowed past the tightening in her throat. "One does not forget the person she shared so much with."

"Let us ride on and ease your sister's mind about your safety."

He nudged his horse forward, and she joined him. Each step the pinto took was taking her into a new life, but she wanted only to be with Tykota.

When they reached the ranch house, Makinna slid off her horse and went up the steps, pushing open the door in her haste to see her sister.

Mrs. Silverhorn rose from her rocking chair and advanced across the room to Makinna. "My dear, it is so good to see you!" She kissed her on both cheeks. "I must admit I have missed you."

"Thank you. I've missed you, too." She glanced around the room. "Is my sister here?"

"Indeed she is, she just went upstairs to—"

They both heard hurried footsteps on the stairs, and Makinna turned to face the sister she had not seen in years. Although less youthful, Adelaide was as beautiful as Makinna remembered her. She wore a cream-colored cotton gown trimmed in blue and looked like a breath of fresh air.

Adelaide rushed forward to hug her tightly, and Makinna responded to her warmth.

"When I think I could have lost you!" Adelaide said, shaking her head and plucking at the doeskin fringe on Makinna's dress. "And here I find you alive and well—and dressed like an Indian!"

"Oh, Adelaide, I am so happy to see you! It has been so long."

Tykota entered the room, and Adelaide gasped and stepped back.

Hannah Silverhorn went directly to Tykota and into the circle of his arms, which seemed to calm Adelaide's sudden fear.

"My son, it is good to see you again." She turned to Adelaide. "You must meet the man who saved your sister's life. Ty, this is Makinna's sister, Adelaide Johnson."

Adelaide nodded. "How do you do, sir." She tried to avert her gaze from his scanty attire. "I am indebted to you for bringing my sister back to me." She concentrated on his eyes and seemed surprised to find them alive with intelligence. "Your mother has told me all you have done."

He smiled slightly. "If I know my mother, she embellished the truth in the telling." He extended his hand, and Adelaide, warming to his grasp of English, gave him her hand.

"I doubt Mrs. Silverhorn embellished anything, sir. I am inclined to believe you are something of a hero."

His laughter was warm. "My mother, like

most mothers, believes me to be more exceptional than I am."

Makinna was astounded by the easy banter between her sister and Tykota. He was never that at ease with her. She frowned, catching Mrs. Silverhorn's gaze. The little English-woman simply smiled and nodded.

"My son does me credit in all things," she said with warmth. She guided Makinna toward the stairs. "Go and visit with your sister, since the two of you have so many years to catch up on. We will visit in the morning."

Makinna turned to Tykota. "Thank you."

He inclined his head, his dark eyes unreadable. "It was my pleasure," he said softly.

Makinna and her sister spent most of the night talking, becoming reacquainted and also crying over the deaths of their mother and brother. At last, around midnight, they fell silent, and Adelaide stared at her sister.

"You are so beautiful. Every man in California will come knocking at our door just to see you."

Makinna drew in a breath. "The last thing I have on my mind is meeting gentlemen."

Adelaide looked thoughtful. "Your Tykota is magnificent. Perhaps it would be difficult to find anyone who could compare to someone who looks like him, has the power of an Indian chief, and has, more than once, saved your life."

Makinna ducked her head, and when she

raised it, her eyes were swimming in tears. "Yes, very difficult. I love him."

Adelaide did not seem to be surprised or repulsed at the thought of her sister loving an Indian. "What woman wouldn't? Look at the man! What other man do you know that is as tall, handsome, and heroic?"

"There *is* no one like him."

"Well, how does he feel about you?"

"I don't know. He may care for me in his own way, but evidently not enough to commit his heart. He has told me that his tribe comes first with him."

"And you cannot live there with him—no, that would not be acceptable."

"I would have if he'd wanted me," Makinna said in misery. "I would have lived with him in a shack if he'd wanted me to."

Adelaide grasped Makinna's hand and gave her a look of compassion, and Makinna was surprised to find her sister so understanding.

"Did you tell him this?" Adelaide asked.

"No," she admitted.

"Then perhaps you should." Adelaide was thoughtful for a moment, as if she were deciding something. Then she said with feeling, "Makinna, I am married to a man who has given me everything money can buy—a mansion, clothes, carriages, jewels—and yet I would give it all away if Tom would look at me one time the way I saw that Indian look at you."

"You are unhappy, Adelaide! I thought—"

"Makinna," her sister broke in, "I knew that look of desperation and helplessness that I saw in Ty Silverhorn's eyes, because I see it in my own eyes when I stand before a mirror. If there is the slightest chance that your Indian loves you, go to him. Or you will spend the rest of your life like me—cold and unfeeling inside."

"Oh, Adelaide, I am so sorry."

"Listen to me, Makinna. If you don't, you may end up just like me, with only possessions to fill your lonely days—things that others may admire and envy you for, but nothing to touch your heart."

Makinna blinked tears from her eyes. "I am so sorry," she repeated.

Adelaide brushed a tear from Makinna's cheek and smiled. "I did not tell you this to make you pity me. I told you to keep you from making the same mistake."

"The choice is not mine, Adelaide. It was Tykota's, and he has already made that decision."

Her sister hugged her. "Don't be too sure, little sister. It is always darkest before the sunrise."

Makinna smiled. "Look at us. We should be celebrating our reunion, and here we are crying and moaning."

Adelaide said softly, "You are not going to end up like me if I can help it."

Makinna went to the window and pulled the curtain aside. "Even now, I am afraid that Tykota will go away without saying good-bye to me."

"Let us get ready for bed. Tomorrow will be soon enough to talk more and plan." She went to the trunk at the foot of her bed and withdrew a nightgown, which she tossed at Makinna. "You need your rest. You look exhausted."

Soon, wearing a fresh white cotton nightgown, Makinna fell into bed and was asleep almost as soon as her head hit the pillow, leaving Adelaide to lie awake, worrying about her little sister.

Chapter Twenty-five

The next morning when Makinna awoke, her sister was gone, but there was a beautiful green cotton gown with white lace on the collar and hem, with matching lacy undergarments and green leather shoes.

When Makinna had dressed, she looked in the large mirror over the washstand, examining the way the soft bustle flowed to the floor behind her. She had never had such a fine gown.

She hurried downstairs, fearing Tykota had left and wanting him to see her in the gown. Entering the dining room, she was relieved to see him sitting at the head of the table, dressed in a white shirt and buff-colored trousers. His hair was tied away from his face, and had it not been for his dark skin, he would have passed for a white man. Mrs. Silverhorn and Adelaide were on either side of him, and they both greeted her happily.

Tykota's gaze ran the length of Makinna, and he glanced back at his plate. His reaction did not escape notice. His mother and Adelaide exchanged knowing looks, as if it was obvious to them that Tykota was tormented by his love for Makinna, and the pity was that Makinna could not see it for herself.

"We let you sleep, my dear," Mrs. Silverhorn told her. "Sit next to me, and Frances will serve you."

"Did you sleep well?" Adelaide asked. "I know I kept you talking half the night." She looked at their hostess. "We had many things to discuss, since we have been separated for five years."

"I don't think I even turned over once," Makinna answered, smiling. "The soft bed was wonderful."

"You know, Makinna, I have been thinking," Hannah said. "If you and Adelaide will remain here for a few days, I would like to give a get-together for the two of you. There hasn't been any laughter in this house for a long time."

"Do you think that is a good idea, Mother?" Tykota asked.

Mrs. Silverhorn looked at her son quizzically. "Yes, I do. I know John Kincaid would attend.

John will be enchanted by you, Makinna." She took a sip of coffee and lowered her cup. "And what do you think? I just got a personal letter delivered by an army sergeant this morning after sunup.

"Was it from Major Halloway?" Makinna asked. "He was such a gentleman when we met him yesterday."

"Yes, it was from the major. He has asked to call on you. I told the sergeant I would let him know. Already your presence has the gentlemen in the area all stirred up, Makinna."

Adelaide was watching Tykota's face, and she saw his eyes darken, and his hand ball into a fist against the white tablecloth. "I would love to remain for a while, Mrs. Silverhorn. And a party would be wonderful. Thank you for being so generous to us."

Hannah Silverhorn's face brightened. "Excellent! I will have Frances bring out the good china and the crystal punch bowl."

Tykota stood so quickly he almost knocked over his chair. "I only remained this morning to tell you good-bye, Makinna," he said tightly as he moved to the door. "It seems you are in good hands."

"Ty," his mother said, rising and following him. "Surely you are not going to leave so soon. I was hoping you would stay for the party. You so seldom get to see John. There was a time when the two of you were inseparable."

He turned to the woman he called mother, wanting to yell at her for the first time in his life. But he exercised tolerance and spoke distantly. "I do not like parties." He nodded. "Ladies, I will be leaving now." And he was gone.

Makinna felt miserable. Her eyes were filled with sorrow as she said, "It seems Tykota could not wait to leave once I joined you at breakfast. He doesn't want to be in the same room with me."

She felt her sister's hand on hers. "I am not so sure." She smiled. "I wonder how long he can hold out."

"What do you mean?"

"Oh, nothing, really." She picked up the silver coffeepot and poured Makinna a cup. "Just thinking aloud."

Makinna resisted the urge to go to the front door and watch Tykota leave. How long would be the hours of each day when she could not see him, and how empty her heart would be without him.

Over the days that passed, Makinna and Adelaide became better reacquainted, and the always cheerful Hannah Silverhorn was a pleasant hostess. The sisters laughed, rode the ranch, and talked incessantly in the evenings with Mrs. Silverhorn.

Sometimes at night, in their quiet time, Adelaide and Hannah would find Makinna staring into space, and their eyes would meet, knowing she was thinking of Tykota. There was an unspoken alliance forming between them, because they had both come to realize that Tykota and Makinna were in love.

The night of the party was clear and hot, and the usual wind had died down, making it seem even hotter.

Makinna stood in the front room beside her sister and Hannah Silverhorn, being introduced to people as they arrived. She wore a wine-colored gown that revealed her shoulders, and its lace bustle dusted the floor in back. The dining room had been cleared of furniture for those who cared to dance, and many young couples were doing just that.

Makinna smiled when she saw a blue army uniform and recognized Matthew Halloway. "Good evening, Major Halloway. It's a pleasure to see you again," she said, offering him her gloved hand.

"Miss Hillyard, you are about the prettiest thing I've ever seen around here," he said, clasping her hand and smiling.

"Before you turn this poor country girl's head, Major, let me introduce you to the real beauty of our family, my sister, Adelaide."

"Miss Hillyard," he acknowledged, smiling and dimpling.

Adelaide laughed, having a wonderful time.

"She forgot to mention, Major, that I am Mrs. Adelaide Johnson."

The major gave a dimpled pout. "Well, Mr. Johnson's gain is our loss, madame."

"And you, Major, are more charming than you should be," Adelaide replied, smiling.

Major Halloway turned to Makinna, held out his arm, and asked, "Miss Hillyard, may I claim you for this dance?"

Makinna excused herself and went with the major to the dining room. The music was jaunty, and they joined the other couples, weaving in and out and circling in a country dance.

Makinna had never had a chance to be young and attend parties like other girls her age in New Orleans, and she was having fun!

After the dance ended, the major asked, "Would you like to go out on the veranda for a breath of air, Miss Hillyard?"

She arched an eyebrow at him. "I am not sure that would be proper."

He held up his hands. "I can assure you we do not stand on such ceremony out here in the country, Miss Hillyard. But, if it will make you feel better, I will tell you about the woman I am engaged to marry."

She nodded. "If that is your intention, then I will very definitely accompany you to the veranda. I would like to hear about this fortunate woman."

But as she leaned against the porch railing, Makinna remembered another night when she had stood in this exact spot with Tykota. She did not want to think about him and spoil her evening. She turned to her companion and asked, "Now, Major, tell me about your fiancée."

He gazed up at the stars. "You remind me of her a little. You are both about the same height and have the same color hair. You speak with the same soft Southern accent as Saber."

"Saber?"

"Saber Vincente. Her brother owns a ranch on the Brazos River. I haven't met him yet, and I don't know if he thinks I'm good enough for his sister. You see, they come from a very old Spanish line on their father's side."

Makinna liked the major, and she immediately guessed he was lonesome for the woman he loved. "You miss her a great deal, don't you?"

He smiled at her. "I shouldn't tell a beautiful young woman about another beautiful young woman. My mother did teach me better manners. It's just that you're so easy to talk to."

"Will you soon marry your Saber?"

"I hope to." He turned to brace his back against the post and folded his arms across his chest. "I'm being transferred to Ft. Worth at the end of the month, and I hope we can be married after that."

Makinna saw a tall stranger walk toward them. He smiled and shook hands with Major Halloway. "How are you, Matthew?"

"I'm fine. As you see, I'm with the prettiest girl here." He smiled at Makinna. "Have you met Makinna Hillyard, John?"

"No, but I came tonight for just that purpose. Will you introduce us?"

"Miss Hillyard, meet John Kincaid. He has the next ranch over. Of course, here in Texas, the next ranch over can be a hundred miles away."

Makinna recognized the name. This was Tykota's boyhood friend, who'd gone to school in England with him. He was tall and lanky, he needed a haircut, and he was rugged rather than handsome, but he had the softest gray eyes she'd ever seen. "I am pleased to meet you, Mr. Kincaid. However, I must tell you I do have the advantage over you—I have heard of you through a friend of yours."

"It's a pleasure to meet you, Miss Hillyard. But you have no advantage. Hannah has talked of nothing but you for weeks. I had to come and meet you for myself."

"Mrs. Silverhorn is too kind."

"So, tell me," he said, smiling, "was Tykota as kind when he told you about me?"

Tykota had tried to stay away, but a power stronger than himself had pulled him here tonight. He'd gone up the back stairs and dressed for the party. He walked through the house, greeting neighbors and stopping to speak to his mother and Makinna's sister.

"Ty!" his mother cried, joyfully. "I didn't know you would be here!" She winked at Adelaide over his shoulder. "How long can you stay, Ty?"

He looked about him, searching for Makinna. "I must return to the valley tomorrow." He frowned at his mother. "Where is she?"

Hannah Silverhorn feigned ignorance. "There are many young woman here who look upon you wistfully. Which one were you referring to?"

He let out an intolerant breath. "Mother, you know very well who I was asking about. Where is Makinna?"

"Why, I don't know. Have you seen her, Adelaide?"

Makinna's sister smiled. "I believe I saw her walk out the door with that handsome cavalry major. What was his name?"

"Oh, yes. I believe you're referring to Major Matthew Halloway. He couldn't wait to dance with her. John Kincaid was here a while ago looking for her, too. It seems that our Makinna will have no trouble getting gentleman to pay court to her when you take her to California.

That is, if one of the locals here doesn't snap her up first."

Tykota's expression was murderous as he stalked to the door. He did not see his mother and Adelaide Johnson grin at each other.

Chapter Twenty-six

"Since we're practically old friends," John said, smiling and extending his arm to Makinna, "would you honor me with the next dance?"

Neither of them had heard Tykota come out of the house and approach them. His hand fell heavily on Makinna's shoulder, and she spun around to face him. When she saw it was Tykota, her heart skipped a beat. Tykota looked so fierce, she almost recoiled. "I—I didn't expect to see you tonight." She hadn't expected to see him again ever, and her heart pounded with excitement.

"Ty," John said with genuine warmth. "I'm so glad you came. I've been wanting to talk to you."

Tykota's hand slipped to Makinna's wrist,

and he gripped her possessively. When he spoke to his friend, his voice was cold with anger. "We will talk at a later time. Right now, I want to see Makinna—alone."

Makinna wondered why his voice was so angry, and why he was ignoring the major. "You recall Major Halloway, Tykota," she said, hoping he would remember his manners.

Tykota heard the tone of her voice, and he knew what she was implying. "I remember him." He answered, dropping his hand to her waist.

Makinna was shocked by his rudeness.

"Come with me," Tykota said, and it was not a request—it was an order.

She hesitated for only a moment. Why was Tykota acting so strangely? She turned to the other gentlemen. "You will excuse me."

Tykota stalked away, leading Makinna down the veranda steps and across the path that led to the corrals.

The major took a chivalrous step forward. "Do you want to go with this man, Miss Hillyard?"

John reached out and restrained the major. "This is between them," he said in a low voice. "She is in no danger and needs no assistance from us."

"But that Indian—"

"I'll explain it to you later. I want to speak to his mother."

The major reluctantly followed John toward the front door, but he cast one final glance in Tykota and Makinna's direction. "Surely he forced Miss Hillyard to accompany him."

John held the door open. "As I said, Miss Hillyard is in no danger from Ty. I have reason to believe he loves her."

"But he's an Indian!"

John stared into the darkness that had already swallowed Tykota and Miss Hillyard. "Sometimes I believe he's more civilized than any of us. Put your mind at ease—Ty would never harm a woman."

Makinna was feeling somewhat as she had when Tykota had whisked her away from Adobe Springs and into the desert without so much as a by-your-leave. At first, when she'd seen him tonight, she had been overjoyed. But she would not tolerate his demanding ways. After all, he had rejected her utterly, and she no longer had to depend on him for her survival. And she certainly hadn't needed rescuing from Major Halloway or Mr. Kincaid.

What was he doing? Why was he here tonight?

He led her past the corral and toward the barn.

"Where are you taking me?" she demanded, trying to pry his fingers from her hand.

"Where I can speak to you without being

interrupted." He flung the barn door open and pushed her inside.

"It's dark in here," she said when he released her hand.

He lit a lantern and replaced it on a hook. Then he turned slowly toward her, silently assessing her. He had never seen her look more beautiful. Her hair was pulled away from her face and covered by some kind of sparkling net. The gown fit snugly about her small waist, and he frowned when he saw that the tops of her breasts were visible. It angered him when he realized that the other men had seen her this way, too.

"Why were you with John and that army officer? Did it ever occur to you that you were encouraging them?"

His face was half in shadows, but she could tell he was angry, and she didn't know why. "We were only talking. What do you mean?"

"I think you know."

Where she had only been confused by his actions before, now she became angry. "How dare you imply that I behaved improperly! Major Halloway and Mr. Kincaid were complete gentlemen. Which is more than I can say for you."

He flinched as if she'd struck him. "I have never aspired to be a gentleman."

"Well, if you had, you would have failed miserably."

"I am not the one who acted in an unbecoming manner."

She put her hands on her hips, glaring at him. "And just how did *I* do that?"

"You were alone with two gentlemen."

"No, I was not alone with two gentlemen! There was a houseful of people within the sound of my voice. I was alone with a man when I trekked across the desert with *you*. Was that wrong?" She moved closer to him, staring angrily into his eyes. "Who made you the keeper of my morals?"

He looked frustrated, but his own anger had not lessened. "Did you allow them to put their hands on you?"

"I—what!"

"Did the major want to kiss you? Did he touch you?"

His outrageous questions deserved no answer, but she made one anyway. "I danced with him, but he made no improper advances toward me. He was talking to me about the woman he is going to marry, Tykota. He is in love with a woman named Saber Vincente!"

Tykota spoke harshly. "I know Noble Vincente. I do not believe he would allow his sister to marry a mere soldier, and one in a blue uniform at that."

She was losing patience. "I don't know or care about that. If anyone is compromising my reputation, it's you, by bringing me here to the barn. Do you think people would not talk if they knew I was alone with you?"

He grabbed her and drew her tightly into his arms, his eyes filled with agony. "Do you not understand? I have not slept. Food does not appeal to me. Nothing matters when I am not with you. All I could think about was you in another man's arms." He raised his head and stared at the rafters, trying to gain control of his emotions. "What am I to do?" His eyes lowered to hers like a physical touch. "Tell me, Makinna."

Tears filled her eyes and spilled down her cheeks. She placed a hand on his cheek, and he closed his eyes at her touch. "Oh, my dearest," she said, her heart filling to overflowing at his admission, and compassion for him returning a hundredfold. "I, too, miss you desperately. But I don't want to be the one who stands in the way of your duty to your people. If I did, you would one day despise me. I would rather walk away from you and never see you again than to tear you apart like this."

He glanced down at her, and his eyes were misty. "My father calls out to me from the grave that I must not abandon my people. I know this, and I am willing to sacrifice much to that end. But, for just this one night, let me hold you."

He lowered his head, his lips touching her

eyelids, nuzzling her ear, and then sliding down her neck as he buried his head against her breast. "Beloved, I never knew there could be such a fire within me. It burns day and night."

Warmth filled her heart at the soft tone in Tykota's voice—and at his calling her *beloved*. She somehow knew that he had never called another woman by that endearment.

Makinna fought down the sob building in her throat. She must be strong for his sake. She forced her tears away, her heart gladdened because she knew, at last, that he loved her. But he was hurting inside, and only she could help him. It would take all her strength, but she would do it for him.

Tomorrow, she would walk out of his life and set him free to do what he had been chosen to do. But tonight she would give him everything she had.

She stepped back a pace, took off her gloves, removed the golden snood, and loosened her hair. Tykota stared at her when she began to unhook her gown. She pushed it off her shoulders to her waist, and the flickering lantern light illuminated her bare breasts. Gently placing her hands on either side of his face, she brought his head to her breast.

A strangled moan came from deep inside him as his mouth moved across her skin, his breath fanning the nipples into sharp points. "You stoke the fire inside me until it burns out of control, beloved."

"You once offered me a gift, Tykota. I now give one to you. Tonight, I belong to you." She blew out the lantern, the only light now was a faint glow from the moon coming in the loft door. She turned her back, saying, "I cannot reach the rest of the hooks."

He closed his eyes, trying to gain control of his feelings. He needed to touch her, to hold her to him, to feel her silken body, to kiss her until she wanted him just as much. Tykota shook his head to clear away such thoughts. He had to walk away from her. Now. "I cannot do this to you."

Turning, she wound her arms around his neck and brought her body closer to his. "It's what I want. I ask only this night from you. It will be our gift to each other."

Tykota's iron control snapped. He had never had a more painful arousal. He wanted to rip off her clothing and drive his hardness into her. He took a deep breath, his hands trembling as he unfastened her gown.

She turned to him as the gown floated to the floor, and she unfastened his coat, pushing it off his shoulders. Impatience clawed at him. All he could think of was burying himself in her body and finding ease for the fire that threatened to consume him. He quickly disposed of the rest of his clothing while she did the same with hers.

Lifting her into his arms, Tykota carried her to the tack room, where there was a cot for when someone had to stay in the barn all night with an ailing horse. His lips found hers, and he kissed her reverently, his hand moving gently over her breasts.

He lowered her to the cot and came down with her, hard, muscled, bronzed skin against white silkiness. He was on top of her, but he balanced his weight so he would not be too heavy. His mouth never left hers as his hand went between her thighs, touching, caressing, feeling the warm moistness and knowing she was ready for him.

"Makinna," he said in a husky voice.

"Yes," she breathed against his lips.

A groan started deep in his throat. "I want you. I want all of you."

"Yes," she whispered. "I am yours tonight."

"Tomorrow—"

She placed a finger across his lips. "Tomorrow will take care of itself. Tonight, we have each other."

He parted her legs, gently stroking her. She tried to pull him to her. She needed no caressing; she wanted him as much as he wanted her.

He positioned his hard arousal, knowing he must be gentle with her this, her first, time. She was moist, so he carefully entered her, going in only far enough that he would not cause her pain.

Makinna gasped and tried to move forward, to take more of him, but he gentled her with a hand on the small of her back. The feel of him inside her was golden, magical, something that was meant to be. In that moment, she knew she belonged to him—would always belong to him.

Tykota trembled with the intensity of his desire and love for this woman denied to him. He resisted the urge to give her all of him, knowing she had never been with a man, and he was so big.

"Do not try to hurry it, beloved. Trust me to guide you."

She arched her hips, and he bent forward, touching his mouth to hers. His tongue went around the shape of her lips and then darted inside, arousing her and stealing her breath.

Makinna felt her toes curl, and she whimpered against his mouth. She was sure she would die if he didn't give her more of him.

He eased deeper inside her, slowly, with control. He filled her emptiness with his throbbing erection, joining with her as he had only dreamed of doing.

Tykota did not move, but held himself still inside her, trying to beat down the desire to drive into her.

"Sweet, sweet," he murmured, gathering her to him, holding her closely, raising her body so her breasts were crushed against the hard wall of his chest.

He spoke some words Makinna could not understand, but she understood the soft tone and the huskiness of his voice.

"Tykota, I want—I need . . ."

"I know, I know," he breathed hotly in her ear. "I know what you need."

He inched forward to the barrier of her maidenhead, and again he told himself she was not his to deflower. But she chose that moment to arch her hips, and he broke through.

She buried her face against his shoulder, and he lifted her chin, pushing her hair out of her face, kissing her lips, whispering, "Let this be the only pain I ever cause you, beloved."

On the small cot in the dusty tack room, Tykota introduced Makinna to feelings she had never dreamed she could feel. She clung to him, riding a wave of impossible desire. Her mouth received his kisses, her body received his, she groaned when he suckled her nipples and stroked her hair. Floating on a sea of hot passion, they both realized that their bodies had been created for each other.

Just when Makinna thought she could not stand the aching tension inside her, Tykota would satisfy that ache and create another. He filled her, stroked the inside of her with his thrusts, and took her to new heights when he pulled back. Soon she understood the rhythm of his sensuous movements, and she thrust forward and pulled back in harmony with him.

The moment was so glorious, so sweet, as he continued to swell inside her, to give her more of himself.

Again he murmured something in his own language in her ear, and she turned to catch his mouth with hers. His kiss was intoxicating as he plunged faster and faster into her. She clung to him, feeling as if she might die from the pressing ache building inside her.

She gasped and trembled with surprise when her body climaxed for him. But Tykota did not stop. He took her to still new heights, pushing more of himself into her, until she had received all his length. When he pulled back and pushed forward, he awoke still deeper sensations.

This time her body erupted with his, and they both trembled. His lips crushed hers, and he whispered hotly in her ear, "*Corera con tomac meamore.*"

Makinna felt as if she were coming out of a silver mist. "What?" she asked, floating on a cloud of sweetness. "What did you say?"

"My heart is yours forever, my love," he replied.

For a long time, they held each other, neither knowing what to say but unwilling to lose these few precious moments they had left. Both also knew torment. Tykota, knowing he could not live without her, and Makinna, knowing that she had to set him free.

"My love for you is so deep, so strong, I cannot put it into words," he said, easing off her and lying at her side.

"I know. I feel the same."

He kissed her deeply, and she clung to him. Finally he untangled his legs from hers and stood. He disappeared only to return with a pail of water. He took Makinna's hand and pulled her to her feet, then gently, tenderly washed her. The intimacy of the act took her breath away.

When he had finished, he helped her into her clothing and kissed her cheek. "This type of clothing is something I will never grow accustomed to."

She smiled. "You seem very adept with it, making me think you have done this many times before."

He tilted her chin, straightening her hair and replacing the snood. "Not like tonight, Makinna. Never like this."

"I know." And, somehow, she did.

He ducked his head so he could see her face in the pale moonlight filtering into the room. "You do know I will never do this with another woman?"

"I . . . do not know."

"I could never touch another woman after

tonight. I would not even want to. You are all I will ever need or want."

"Don't make that promise, Tykota." Makinna laid her head against his shoulder, knowing that these were the last few moments they would ever have. "I won't hold you to it."

Something squeezed painfully at his heart, and a fierce sense of ownership surged inside him. She belonged to him now. "My love for you will never change, beloved." He turned her head so he could look into those blue, blue eyes. "Never doubt that."

Oh, why did it have to be this way? she cried inside, wishing she could hold on to this moment until the end of time.

Chapter Twenty-seven

It seemed like a lifetime ago that Tykota and Makinna had first entered the barn, and yet they could still hear the sound of music and laughter. The party was young yet. It was just that the two of them had changed.

Tykota was silent as he finished hooking Makinna's gown. He bent to kiss the back of her neck, then turned her to face him.

"You belong to me now."

She did not bother to deny it. "Yes. I will always belong to you."

He touched her face, his gaze soft as he looked at each feature. "My heart will never belong to another."

"I know."

His arms tightened around her, and he held

her fiercely to him. "I do not want to spend one day that I cannot see your face. We must be together. I will need to leave my tribe."

She slipped out of his arms and away from him. What she had to do was going to take all her strength and courage. "I want you to do something for me."

He took a step toward her, but she held up a hand. "Promise."

"Anything."

"I want you to go back to your tribe."

"Why?"

"If you remain there, for one month, it will give us both time to think. We can consider our lives and what we want. If, at the end of that month, you still feel the same way about me, then we will talk about what we are going to do."

"I do not need a month. I know I want you more than I want my own life."

"I feel the same way. But you must do this. For me."

"Do not ask this of me!"

"But I do ask it of you."

He lifted her chin. "Do not send me away like this." His gaze softened, and he spoke in his own language. "*Tutha mecata yethoa.*"

"What did you say?" She touched his face, her fingers sliding along his strong jaw.

"It translates to something like, If love is true, it will find a way."

She lay her head against his shoulder and closed her eyes to keep from crying. "I will not have you torn between love and duty. We must both be very sure of what we want. If we are meant to be together, one month is not so long when measured against a lifetime."

His dark gaze settled on her lips. "Even now, I want to take you back to the cot and make love to you."

Makinna stepped away from him, because his tone was so loving, and because she wanted the same thing. "You must go now, tonight."

Tykota took her arm and brought her to him. "If this is your wish, if this is some test I must pass before you will know how deeply I love you, I will do it."

"Perhaps it is a test. I'm not sure."

He dipped his head, and his mouth settled on hers, stirring her desire anew. "I will see you in one month. Then we shall never be parted again."

He turned to leave her, and she called out to him. "Tykota! Always remember that someone loves you—will always love you and wish you well."

Tykota paused and turned back to her. "That sounds very much like a final good-bye."

Makinna laughed, trying to sound light-hearted when her heart was breaking. "It is good-bye for now."

"You could come back to the valley with me, Makinna."

"No. You know I can't."

She gazed into his ebony eyes and saw what looked like tears. But how could that be? A man such as Tykota did not cry over a woman. Still, she saw that his throat was working, and he gazed upward, as if seeking control over his emotions.

"Makinna, why do I get the feeling that I am never going to see you again?"

She smiled and shook her head as tears spilled down her cheeks. "Until I touch you again, I will see you in my dreams."

He walked away from her, and she heard him mount his horse and ride away. She listened until she could no longer hear him.

"Carry him safely, Indian pony," she said between sobs. "Carry him back to Valle de la Luna."

Slowly she headed back to the house, and she frowned as she saw buggies being brought to the front. The guests were leaving, though it was still early.

She weaved her way between departing buggies. When she got to the front door, John Kincaid was there, his gaze somber.

"Mr. Kincaid, has something happened?"

He studied the tip of his boots for a moment, then looked up at her. "Well, ma'am, your sister got some bad news, and Mrs. Silverhorn thought everyone should go home. I'm sorta hanging around in case I'm needed."

John followed Makinna as she rushed inside, looking for her sister. "What kind of news?"

"It's her husband, Miss Hillyard. I'm sorry to be the one to tell you, but he was killed in an accident."

"Where is Adelaide?"

"Mrs. Silverhorn took her upstairs."

Makinna hurried up the stairs and burst into the bedroom she shared with her sister. Adelaide was lying on the bed, and Hannah Silverhorn had pulled up a chair and sat beside her, holding her hand.

Makinna ran to her sister, going down on her knees. "My sweet Adelaide, I am so sorry. I just heard."

Adelaide's eyes filled with tears, and she sat up, pulling her sister onto the bed and hugging her tightly. "Why did it have to happen to Tom?"

Makinna rocked her sister back and forth as she would a child. "We never know why these things have to happen, Adelaide."

She felt Adelaide tremble. "I feel so guilty because I wasn't with him." she sobbed.

"Hush, you don't know what you're saying, dearest." She brushed a damp curl out of Adelaide's face. "Hush. I will stay with you, and we will go through this together."

Adelaide clung to her, and Makinna met Hannah Silverhorn's sad eyes. "How did it happen?" Makinna asked.

"I believe it was some kind of mining accident. A cave-in."

Makinna shuddered. "Try to rest, Adelaide, I will stay right here."

"We will both stay with you," the older woman said.

It was almost morning when Adelaide finally fell asleep. Makinna dressed in a light cotton gown and stood at the window to watch the sunrise. This was a sad day for both sisters. Although Tykota was not dead, she knew she would never see him again.

She went downstairs and found Mrs. Silverhorn in the dining room. Hannah motioned for Makinna to sit beside her, then poured her a cup of coffee.

"I am sorry about your brother-in-law, Makinna."

"I hardly knew him. He and my sister married when I was quite young."

"Adelaide seems to be carrying a lot of guilt. You must help her get over it."

Makinna pushed the coffee cup away and leaned back in the chair. "Adelaide wants to go home tomorrow. I am going with her."

Hannah Silverhorn patted Makinna's hand. "Of course, you shall. You can get her settled and then come back. Or even better, help her settle her affairs and bring her back with you."

"Mrs. Silverhorn, I have grown very fond of you, and I thank you for all you have done for me and my sister. But I will not be coming back. Ever."

"But I thought you and my son—"

Makinna stood. "For Tykota, it is best this way."

Hannah lowered her head. "Tykota has had so many things forced on him, but you were the one person that he—"

"I know," Makinna said sadly, moving to the door. "I will always . . . He will always have my heart."

At breakfast the next morning Mrs. Silverhorn informed Makinna that John Kincaid would be driving her and Adelaide to El Paso. Makinna was sad to be leaving Hannah Silverhorn; she had become very fond of the kindhearted Englishwoman who had so generously taken her and Adelaide into her home and made them feel welcome.

Hannah walked Makinna to the door. John was already assisting Adelaide into the buggy. Tykota's mother took Makinna's hand. "Please remember, my dear, that you will always be welcome at Biquera Ranch. If you find that San Francisco is not to your liking, you will always have a home here."

Makinna kissed Hannah's cheek. "I will remember, and I thank you for all your kindness. But I shall not return to Texas."

"What shall I tell my son?"

"Will you do something for me?"

"You know I will. You have only to ask."

Makinna pressed a letter into Mrs. Silverhorn's hand. "Give this to Tykota for me."

Hannah glanced at the letter, then back at Makinna. "Is this the way you want to say good-bye to him?"

"It's the only way. You once spoke to me about how Tykota's two well-meaning fathers placed too much responsibility on his shoulders. I will not add to that burden. He must feel free to choose the road he will travel, and I know his heart is with the Perdenelas people."

"I saw him change with you, Makinna. I saw love and hope in his eyes. You gave that to him. Will you take it away?"

"He does love me, Mrs. Silverhorn, and I love him, but we walk in different worlds. I can't live in his, and if I asked him to live in mine, he would one day regret it."

Hannah pressed her hands to Makinna's cheeks. "What a wife you would have made for my son."

Makinna held back tears, not wanting Tykota's mother to see her cry. "Try to make him understand that I loved him enough to let him go."

"My dear, if it is meant that the two of you should be together, you will be."

She hugged the little woman and moved down the steps to the buggy. John helped her inside and urged the horses forward at a trot while three outriders rode alongside.

Although Makinna knew that Mrs. Silverhorn was watching them from the front veranda, she did not look back, because she knew she would cry if she did.

Adelaide squeezed Makinna's hand and Makinna gave her an encouraging smile. She needed to be strong for her sister.

Makinna was grateful that John was so sympathetic to Adelaide. He spoke to her in soft tones, and there was tenderness in his eyes when he looked at her. It wasn't long until Adelaide warmed to his kindness, and he even made her smile when he related some of the adventures he had had with Tykota in the London school they attended. He spoke of the difficulty his teacher had trying to teach a slow-talking Texan to speak what they considered "proper" English.

John laughed as he urged the horses up a hill, driving the buggy slowly and trying to avoid as many bumps as he could. "And, as you can hear by my speech, they failed miserably."

Adelaide joined his laughter. "They seem to have succeeded with Tykota."

"That they did. But I suspect that was

because he learned English from Mr. and Mrs. Silverhorn, who were British. Whereas my parents came to Texas from Tennessee." He winked at Adelaide. "We all know that Texans and Tennesseans can't speak English."

Makinna fanned herself with a handkerchief and shook away the dust that had settled on her gown. "I love Texas. I hadn't expected to, but I do."

"I suspect Tykota has something to do with your view," Adelaide remarked.

John studied Adelaide's face carefully. "How would you feel about making your home here, Mrs. Johnson?"

"Like my sister, I do love this land, when, like her, I had not expected to."

John looked pleased. "Could you . . . would you feel it an imposition if, after a while, I came to San Francisco and called on you ladies?"

Makinna realized that John Kincaid was developing a fondness for her sister, even though Adelaide was unaware of his feelings. She spoke up before Adelaide could answer. "We would be delighted, Mr. Kincaid, if you would call on us. We will want you to bring us all the news from Texas."

Chapter Twenty-eight

When they reached El Paso, Makinna stared at the mud-colored huts on either side of the narrow, dusty streets. In the distance she could see young children splashing and playing in the shallows of the Rio Grande. This was to have been her destination those many weeks ago, when the raid on Adobe Springs changed her life forever.

John stopped the buggy before the Central Hotel, helped the ladies with a room, and arranged for their luggage to be brought in. "I'll just go on down now and see to your tickets on the morning stage," he said, setting his hat firmly on his head. "I wonder, would you be wanting to eat in the dining room, or would you like me to arrange for something to be brought to your room?"

Adelaide smiled sweetly at John. "You are kindness itself. Speaking for myself, I would prefer the dining room. If you would care to join us, we will dine around eight."

"I would be right pleased, ma'am." He smiled and backed away. "Yes, ma'am, I surely would."

When she closed the door, Makinna walked to the window, watching drovers herding cattle down the street. "Texas is like nowhere else," she mused.

"Makinna?"

She turned to her sister.

"I . . . thank you for coming with me. We are alone in the world now, just the two of us."

Makinna went to Adelaide and put her arms around her. "We are fortunate that we have each other."

"I want to tell you something."

Adelaide looked dejected, and Makinna waited for her to continue. "Is something bothering you?"

"It's Tom. I can't feel anything for him."

"When Mother died, I felt numb at first. I suppose that happens when you lose someone you love."

Adelaide sat on the edge of the bed and buried her head in her hands. "It's nothing like that. I stopped loving Tom a long time ago."

Makinna knelt down beside her. "Do you want to talk about it?"

"Yes, I do. For so long I have had to keep this locked inside me, because there was no one to talk to."

Tears seeped out of Adelaide's eyes and ran down her face. "Tom . . . didn't love me. He had other women. He never bothered to be discreet but flaunted them in my face. He would take them to parties we were supposed to attend together. He drank too much, and I always made that the excuse for his behavior."

"Adelaide, I am so sorry! But he must have loved you if he married you."

"He said he never had, that he had married me to show off to his friends. He told me that when we had been married less than a year."

Makinna held her close, feeling her heartache. "This pain will pass with time, Adelaide. We will go through this together." She brushed the hair from her sister's face and wiped her eyes with her handkerchief.

"I don't want to stay in San Francisco. It is a town where I have been humiliated, and if I remain there, I will only be reminded of that humiliation."

"What do you want to do? Should we go back to New Orleans?"

"I want to move to Texas."

"What? Here?"

"I loved it here the moment I stepped off the stage. I want to sell everything Tom had in California. He was wealthy. I can do anything I want to do."

"But what would you do here in Texas?"

"I don't know. Make a new start. I have always wanted children, but Tom didn't. Maybe I will even find a new husband and start a family."

Makinna was troubled. "Let's go on to San Francisco and take it one day at a time. You may feel differently once you have had time to think."

Adelaide shook her head. "I will never feel differently about San Francisco. I was never happy there, and if I remain, I will always remember that unhappiness."

"You know I will do whatever it takes to help you."

Adelaide touched her sister's cheek. "I want you to be happy, too, Makinna. You deserve happiness. I know how many years you tended to Mother when she was ill. She wrote me letters telling me how you were always so cheerful and never complained."

"You should get some rest now," Makinna said, standing and fluffing up the pillow. "We have three hours before dinner."

Adelaide agreed with a weary nod, and she fell asleep the moment her head rested on the pillow.

Makinna stood at the window. She hadn't known what her sister's life had been like, and neither had their mother. Adelaide had suffered rejection and humiliation, but Makinna was determined to help her put her past behind her and start anew.

But, as far as Adelaide's wanting to come back to Texas, Makinna had every hope that she would forget that notion once they reached San Francisco.

San Francisco was bustling with activity. The noise from the crowded streets was a welcome sound to Makinna's ears.

When the stage stopped at the Butterfield office, both sisters were helped to the ground by an attendant. "Mrs. Johnson, I believe your carriage is waiting for you at the Golden Horn," the man informed her. "Accept my sympathy, and know that we all feel the loss of your husband."

"Thank you," she said, taking Makinna's hand and rushing across the street, dodging a heavy freight wagon.

Adelaide set such a fast pace that Makinna had to catch her breath when they finally stopped at the Golden Horn Hotel. Makinna thought they would go inside, but instead Adelaide approached an elderly Oriental man, who bowed respectfully to her.

"Hong Lee, see to our luggage. We want to leave right away."

"It shall be as you say, mistress." He bowed again and hurried across the street.

In no time at all, the two sisters were seated in a carriage lined in red velvet. Two matching black horses took them on the journey up to Knob Hill.

The house was imposing, massive, almost Gothic, with gables, arched windows, and ornate overhanging eaves.

Adelaide shuddered. "Isn't it hideous? I detested this house from the moment I first set foot in it. It never was a home."

Makinna tried to find something positive to say about the monstrosity. "It bespeaks wealth."

"It does that. It was exactly right for Tom. He loved the garish house and grounds. I can't wait to sell it."

Makinna stepped down from the carriage and helped her sister. Seven servants stood lined by the door waiting for them.

"Don't you feel like royalty?" Adelaide asked almost hysterically, tears brimming in her eyes. "Tom always insisted that we be greeted by all the servants whenever we returned from a journey."

Makinna gripped her sister's arm. "What you need to do is lie down. You are exhausted."

Adelaide stopped before one woman who stood apart from the other servants, her arms folded front of her, her demeanor somehow arrogant. "Caroline, now that my husband is dead, there will be no further need for your services."

The woman's lips curled in a smirk. "I expected it."

"I'm sure you did. Be out of my house before sundown."

"I can help you," the housekeeper said in a slightly softer manner. "You don't know how to manage such a large household."

Years of frustration poured angrily out of Adelaide's mouth. "The house will be sold, Caroline. My husband no longer needs you in his bed, so leave!"

The other servants bowed their heads as their mistress spoke. "Paula, you will take on the duties of housekeeper, and stay with Caroline while she packs. Make certain none of the family silver finds its way into her hands." She raised her head proudly. "Paula will choose three of you to remain to close up the house. The rest of you will be given six month's pay and references." Her eyes hardened as she glanced at Caroline, who looked as if she'd like to strike her mistress. "You, of course, will be given only the wages coming to you."

Makinna gripped her sister's arm and led her up the steep steps to the front door. "What was that all about?" she asked when they were out of earshot.

"That woman was one of my husband's mistresses. He made her the so-called house-keeper and flaunted her in my face every day. I had to suffer the indignity of her presence in my home, where she did little but be surly and disrespectful."

Makinna smiled brightly. "Well done, then. Bravo! I like your spunk. Who knew you had it in you?"

Adelaide's eyes suddenly twinkled. "I admit, what I just said to Caroline gave me a great deal of satisfaction." When they entered the formal sitting room, Adelaide smiled and wiped angry tears away. "I was good, wasn't I?"

"You were magnificent!"

Three weeks had passed since Makinna and Adelaide arrived in San Francisco, and Makinna was amazed at how strong her sister had become.

Adelaide had hired a young lawyer, Robert Darwood, newly graduated from law school back East and settled in San Francisco only three months. In fact, Adelaide was Mr. Darwood's first client. As it turned out, the young attorney was very idealistic and took on Adelaide's affairs with a vengeance.

Between the two of them, the stream of businessmen who had associated with her late husband went away with a new respect for the young widow. Some of them had thought they could take advantage of a mere woman. Mr.

Darwood soon set them straight, and Adelaide not only sold Tom's house, mines, and other businesses in short order, but she also made a tidy profit.

Makinna and Adelaide stood on the balcony of the upstairs sitting room gazing out over the blue Pacific. It was a cool, crisp evening, and it appeared that the sun was dropping into the ocean.

Makinna walked back inside, where most of the furniture was draped with dustcovers. The new owners would soon be taking possession of the house and furnishings. She found a chair without a covering and sat down, watching her sister with concern. Everything had happened so quickly, she wondered if Adelaide had truly done the right thing.

When her sister stepped from the balcony onto the thick Persian rug, she was smiling. "Soon this will only be a bad dream that I can put behind me."

"Have you thought what you really want to do, Adelaide? You are a very wealthy woman now. You can do anything you want to."

"I still have not changed my mind about moving to Texas."

"Then that is what you should do if you feel that strongly about it."

"You will come with me, won't you?"

"No. I can't."

Adelaide dropped down in a chair beside her sister, looking distressed. "I can't go without you. I want us to be together."

"I have to keep distance between myself and Tykota. For more reasons than one." She averted her eyes. "You don't know what I did."

"I think I do. I can only imagine how it would feel to love a man and know he loves you, then face the realization that you could never be together. You don't have to tell me what happened between the two of you."

"I love him so much. I will always love him. But there can never be a happy ending for the two of us."

"Mrs. Silverhorn told me about the law preventing Tykota from taking a bride outside the tribe."

"I know he will eventually have to marry. He will want a son."

"Makinna, nothing was ever solved by running away. What may look impossible today may be reality tomorrow."

"Not this, Adelaide. Nothing can change the fact that Tykota is chief of his tribe, and the Perdenelas' law says he can't marry me."

"What do you want to do, Makinna?"

Makinna shook her head. "I don't know. It seemed that my life stopped the night I sent Tykota away, knowing I would never see him again."

Adelaide went on her knees and raised her sister's chin. "There is always hope. That's what you've been telling me."

"Not in this." Makinna shook her head. "I should be comforting you."

"I don't need comforting, Makinna. You may think me coldhearted, but I don't miss Tom, and I no longer feel guilty for not being the kind of wife he wanted. I even have hope that I may find the kind of love I always needed."

"John Kincaid," Makinna said softly.

"How did you guess?"

"I saw the way he looked at you, and I knew he was developing strong feelings for you. But you must be sure that you love him."

"The feeling is new for me, and it's too early to call it love, but I have never felt such softness toward a man, this need to be closer to him and learn all about his life."

Makinna stood and pulled her sister up with her. "Then by all means you should return to Texas."

"Not without you."

"No, you don't, Adelaide. You are not going to trick me into returning to Texas."

"Sometimes I believe you are too smart for your own good, Makinna. But I do like John more than any man I know."

Makinna kissed her cheek. "Then go back."

"How would you like to sail around the

world, visit exotic places, and stay as long as we want to?"

"I wouldn't want to any more than you do."

"Then what will we do? We have to be out of this house within two days."

"I don't know. I wish I did."

Chapter Twenty-nine

Tykota stared at his mother long and hard. "What are you saying—that Makinna is not coming back?"

"I don't think she will, Ty." She wanted to hold him and comfort him as she had when he was small, but he was a man now, and he would not welcome such a display from his mother. "She left this letter for you."

He ignored the letter. "Just what did she say?"

"Makinna wanted me to make you understand that she loved you enough to let you go."

"What is that supposed to mean? I know that if I loved someone, I would not let her go."

"But you did, Tykota. Right from the first, you let her know that there could be nothing between the two of you," Mrs. Silverhorn reminded him.

"I later learned that I could not live without her. Everything else became meaningless." There was desperation in his voice. "I want Makinna with me for the rest of our lives."

"Make me understand, Ty. What were your plans for the two of you? Were you going to take her back to your valley and shut her away from the only world she knew?"

"No. I was going to live in her world. I was going to live here at Biquera."

Hannah Silverhorn blinked back tears. "That's what I wanted for you. But Makinna was wise enough to realize that too many people made demands on you, even I, with the best of intentions. She did not want her love for you to interfere with your duty or your own choices. She was afraid that if you walked away from your people, you would one day resent her for it."

"Interfere with my life? She has done that since the first day I met her! If I had known that she was leaving me forever the night she asked me to go, I would have taken her away with me."

"And what would the two of you have done, Ty?"

He glanced at the ceiling. "I have found it difficult to live among my people. No matter how well Mangas taught me our ways and laws, I have lived too long apart from them, and I feel a restlessness stirring within me."

"Is there no woman of the Perdenelas that you could, if not love, at least respect, and who could one day bear you fine sons?"

"There are too many women at Valle de la Luna who would be only too willing to do just that. But none of them touch my heart. None ever will."

Hannah Silverhorn nodded sadly, feeling his pain deep in her own heart. "I will leave you alone to read your letter. Later, if you feel like it, we will talk." She pressed Makinna's letter into his hand and quietly left the room.

Tykota stared at the letter. At last he went to the chair by the lamp, opened it, and began to read.

My dearest Tykota,
When you read this, I shall be gone. Do not be angry with me, and try to understand why I do this. Never doubt that I love you with all my heart and always will. But, loving you as I do, I could never be the one who stood between you and your people. What happened between us was beautiful and rare. I will always remember our last night together and put it in a secret place in my heart to be cherished always. As you go through life, I know you will realize that my leaving was best for you. Just know that there will always

*be someone somewhere who loves you with
all her heart and wishes you only happiness.*

The letter was unsigned. Tykota crushed it in
his fist and hung his head. She did not love him
as much as he loved her, or she never would
have left him. And he felt hopeless and bereft
that he would never see her again.

How would he live without her?

He smoothed the letter out and read it again.
Then he sat motionless until the lamp grew
lower and the night grew darker.

Then he got on his horse and rode away.

It was after midnight when Tykota returned to
the ranch house. He found his mother waiting
for him in the parlor.

"Are you all right?" she asked, going to him
and slipping her arms about his waist.

"I have been trying to think what to do."

"And what have you decided?"

"I do not have the answers. But I do know
that I am no longer capable of leading the Perdenelas. My father's spirit must cry out that I
have failed him."

"And what do you think of this?"

"I think my father did not understand that
when he sent me away from our valley, he placed
me in a world so different that I can never truly
feel a part of my people. I think and love and act
and feel differently than they do. They come to

334

me with their problems, and I have no solutions for them."

"What do you do?"

"I have Coloradous stand beside me as an adviser. He seems to know just what the people need. He has already begun building a dam to irrigate the crops. He is the one who should stand in my place. He is the one who knows how the people feel."

"So Coloradous is a good and wise man?"

Tykota looked at his mother for a long moment. "Yes. Yes, he is."

"You changed your father's law and brought him back into the tribe?"

Tykota felt his heart lighten. "Yes, I did that."

"Then what is your answer?"

Tykota looked thoughtful. "I know what I must do." He hurried to the door and called over his shoulder. "And I know what will be best for the Perdenelas!"

Tykota faced the council. "I have two reasons I called you here today. One concerns my brother, Coloradous, and the other concerns Santo. First, bring in Santo, and I will put his deeds before you."

By now, everyone in the village had heard about how Santo had brought shame on his family. The Old Ones nodded.

Santo wore a surly expression as he was led before Tykota.

Tykota spoke. "You know why you are here?"

"I know that we were friends." Santo's rage was simmering below the surface. "I know that you have turned away from that friendship."

"While I was away, you took it upon yourself to make my sister, Inea, your intended wife. She was afraid of you, and yet, since she had no protector, you treated her as if she did belong to you."

"I was only taking care of her until you, her brother, returned to see to her well-being. She was a maiden alone and needed someone to keep other men away from her."

"Enough!" Tykota said, standing so he would be eye-level with the man he had once loved like a brother. "We both know you kept the other braves away because you wanted her for yourself." Tykota's voice was hard, his tone menacing. "You are fortunate that I do not kill you for what you did. But I do demand that you leave this valley in shame and never return."

"You will be sorry for this," Santo hissed. "You will regret this day!"

Tykota grabbed the bear-claw necklace around Santo's neck and jerked him forward. "You dare to threaten the chief in this council room? Men have been put to death for less."

Santo lowered his eyes so none could see the hatred and defiance there. "I was wrong. It is right that I should be expelled from the tribe. I brought dishonor upon myself and my family."

Tykota flung him backward, and he landed hard on the stone floor. "Get out of my sight. Never let me see your face again."

Santo was helped up and escorted to the door by two warriors. He did not look back, but hatred burned in his heart, and he would know no peace until Tykota was dead.

Tykota took a steadying breath. "Now, before I bring my brother in, I have something I want to say to all of you. Hear me out before any of you speak."

The room grew quiet, and all eyes were on Tykota.

"I love this valley, and the Perdenelas will always be my people. My father taught me that my wants and needs must come after those of my people, and I believe this."

Heads angled in puzzlement.

"I have come to know in my heart that I cannot give the people all they need from their chief. The fact is painful but true. I have walked too long in the white world to recognize the wants and needs of each of you."

There was a long silence.

"I have come to see that my father was misguided when he sent my brother, Coloradous, away. Coloradous was my father's oldest son, and he has remained true to the tribe even when he could not be a part of it. All of you know of the irrigation ditches he has dug for our fields. He is strong of spirit and honor. It is he who should stand in our father's shoes."

"No!" cried one brave.

"You are our chief!" said an Old One.

"It was your father's wish that you lead us," Mangas said, standing. "You were raised to do this. Would you go against your father's wish?"

Tykota held up a hand for silence. "Know this. I would die for my people, but it has become clear to me that I cannot live for my people."

Mangas shook his head. "Do you say this because you want to be with the white woman?"

"No, old friend. The white woman has gone from my life forever. But it was she who made me see that I am more like the white race than I am like the Perdenelas. I want what is best for all of you and your families. Coloradous is the best man to stand where I stand."

There was a murmur among the warriors and the Old Ones. At last, Batera, the most senior of the tribe, spoke. "We have waited a long time for a wise chief to lead us. By your actions today, you have proven that you are both wise and worthy. It is you we want to lead us. We believe that as the years pass, you will become less white and more Indian."

Tykota was touched by their loyalty. "I honor

each of you. I wish I could be the chief you deserve. But that man is my brother."

Tykota walked among the council and spoke to each one individually, convincing them that Coloradous, and not he, was the one they should honor.

Sadness hung heavily in the chamber when at last Tykota spoke to the guard at the door. "Bring in my brother."

Coloradous had not been in the council room since the night his father had stripped him of all honor. He did not know why he had been called now. There was a worried frown on his face as he stood before Tykota.

"I have questions to put to you, my brother. I will ask you to answer them with a true heart."

Coloradous nodded.

"Will you always put the good of the people before any wishes you might have for yourself?"

Coloradous was more puzzled than ever, but he did not hesitate. "Yes. Always. Why do you ask?"

"Think carefully before you answer me, Coloradous. Would you be willing to stand in my place if it was for the good of the Perdenelas?"

Coloradous shook his head, his gaze pained. "No, brother. I have never wanted to stand where you stand. I am content to do what little I can to help our people, but not as their chief."

"If it fell to you to lead the people, would you

do it with truth and wisdom? Would you make any sacrifice in your life for their good?"

Coloradous frowned. "What are you asking of me? I love you, my brother. I would never do anything to harm you."

Tykota reached up and removed the leather headband with the golden eagle and slid it over Coloradous's head. "It is my wish, and that of the council, that you become chief of the Perdenelas."

Coloradous reached up and removed the headband, handing it back to Tykota. "No, never! It was our father's wish that you be chief. I honor my father, and I honor you."

Tykota clasped his brother's arm. "You may very well be one of the wisest chiefs the Perdenelas will ever have."

Coloradous was stunned into silence as the warriors and the Old Ones gathered around him.

Tykota smiled. "Have I your word that you will look after my sister and see that she becomes the wife of the warrior who has her heart?"

"Yes—but—"

Tykota placed the headband of the chief around Coloradous's hair once more. "I honor you as chief. Your word is law, and I will obey."

Chapter Thirty

Makinna watched the servant pack the last of her clothing and close the trunk. She glanced around to make certain she hadn't forgotten anything, but the room was as clean as it was impersonal, and she had left nothing behind.

She and Adelaide were moving to a hotel until they could decide what they were going to do.

Going down the stairs, Makinna saw her sister close the front door. Adelaide's face was ghostly white as she turned to Makinna and held out a folded piece of paper.

"It's a telegram for you. They always mean bad news. The last telegram I received was that my husband had died."

Makinna was afraid to reach for it for fear it did contain bad news. "You read it. I can't."

Adelaide's hand was shaking as she unfolded the paper, and her voice trembled as she read.

Please come. You are needed.

Adelaide raised her head. "It's signed *Hannah Silverhorn*."

Makinna placed a hand to her heart to stop the furious beating. "Something is wrong with either her or Tykota." She took the telegram and read it as if it would reveal its secrets to her. "Oh, something is terribly wrong!"

"Let us make arrangements to return to Texas at once. Mrs. Silverhorn would never have sent such a message unless she needed you desperately." She ran through the house, calling for the housekeeper. Then she turned back to Makinna. "We will send her a telegram telling her we are coming, and we will take the noon stage tomorrow."

Tykota bid his sister farewell, and he could see that she was fighting to keep from crying. "Marry your young warrior, and be happy, Inea."

"I will miss you."

He touched her cheek. "Name your first son after me."

Inea nodded and turned away as Tykota

mounted his horse. Mangas had insisted on accompanying Tykota, while Coloradous rode with them as far as the twin peaks.

The brothers dismounted and stared at each other, both knowing that an old wrong had been righted.

"I never wanted it this way, Tykota. You were the chosen one."

Tykota smiled. "Sometimes the chosen one is the wrong one, my brother. You are the one who should have been chief all along."

"Will you return?"

"I believe I will for visits." He gripped his brother's arm. "My only sister and brother are here. I will want to see you from time to time."

"Will you marry the white woman and settle down at Biquera?"

"I do not know, Coloradous. But I will try. For if I do not find her, I will be empty inside." He looked at his brother. "Have you ever felt that way about a woman?"

Coloradous smiled. "For a very long time. Before I was disgraced and sent from the village, I wanted to make her my wife. She loved me and would have come with me, but her father would not have it—he wanted her to marry a war chief. And I did not want her to share my disgrace. She never married, and I hope it is because she still loves me."

Tykota smiled. "I believe her father will have

a change of heart. He will crow if his daughter marries the chief of all the Perdenelas." Then Tykota became serious. "I will need to reveal to you the sacred treasure."

Coloradous turned away. "This is hard for me, Tykota. Our father showed you the treasure."

"And I am revealing the secret to you."

Coloradous turned back to his brother. "There is much that I must do to establish my right to be chief, so I cannot leave the valley just now."

"I know. At next full moon, meet me at the cave where our father took us as boys."

"The treasure cannot be there. I have explored that cave, and there are but the two caverns."

Tykota smiled. "Things are not always what they seem."

Coloradous nodded. "I will meet you there."

Tykota mounted his horse. "Until then, my brother. I know the people will prosper under your wise guidance."

Coloradous reached up and placed a hand on Tykota's arm. "I want to warn you to watch out for Santo. He was making threats against you. I do not know if he will do anything, but a man eaten up with anger is not to be trusted. We know this from our brother, Sinica."

"Have no concern, my brother. I have no fear of Santo."

"Do not dismiss him so easily. In his eyes,

you denied him the woman he wanted and drove him from the tribe."

"I will look out for him."

The two brothers looked into each other's eyes and saw love and respect reflected there. "Take care, my chief," Tykota said, smiling. He turned his horse, and he and Mangas rode out of the valley and into the desert.

The sun was low in the west when Tykota swung to the ground and spoke to Mangas. "We will camp here for the night."

Mangas dismounted and took the reins of Tykota's horse before he spoke, following him up the mesa. "Why do we come this way? This is the place where Sinica died."

"I need time to think, so I am going to a cave two days' ride from here. You cannot go with me, but tomorrow you can ride on to Biquera."

Mangas staked out the horses while Tykota stood at the edge of the mesa remembering the last time he'd been there. He touched the mesquite tree where Makinna had been tied that day, and he remembered that he had died a little when he'd killed his own brother.

Later, when they sat before the campfire, Mangas spoke. "I still think of you as my chief, and so will many of the others."

"You will think of me as such less and less as time passes. Coloradous will make a much better chief than I."

345

"That may be so, but my heart does not accept anyone but you to stand in your father's shoes. When do you want me to leave?"

"In the morning, old friend. I will be gone for a while, and I must show Coloradous the secret of the treasure."

Mangas nodded, but his mind was troubled. He knew that Coloradous was a good warrior, and his heart was true, but Tykota would have been the greatest chief that the Perdenelas had ever had. "I will do as you say. But what will I tell your white mother?"

"Tell her I will be home soon."

Mangas met Tykota's glance. "Do we stay at Biquera?"

"I do not know."

"I have grown to like it there. I have my own dwelling, and I have become accustomed to the white man's comforts."

Tykota's eyes were troubled. "I do not know where the future will take me."

"You want the white woman for your wife."

"Yes. But she is gone, and I do not know where to find her."

Mangas stood up. "I am an old man. I am going to my—"

A rifle shot rang out, and Tykota watched Mangas lurch backward as if some unseen hand had jerked him against the cliff wall. Tykota ran to him and knelt beside him. He had been shot in the chest!

Mangas spoke in a whisper. "You cannot save me." He grasped Tykota's arm with a blood-stained hand. "Save yourself."

Tykota fell to his stomach and crawled toward his rifle. Grasping the weapon in one hand, he cocked it and glanced back toward Mangas. Fighting to contain his rage, he inched away from the campfire and into the shadows just as a bullet whizzed past his head.

"Santo!" he called out, knowing who the shooter was. "Do you hide like a woman, or will you face me like a warrior?"

He was met by silence.

"Show yourself!"

This time his answer was a bullet ricocheting off the side of the stone cliff. From the direction of the bullets, Tykota gauged that Santo was hidden in the clump of sage bushes to the left of the mesa.

Cradling his rifle, he crawled back to Mangas. Blood had spread over his chest and onto the rock face of the mesa. "Mangas, I believe it is Santo. I am going after him. I will come back for you."

The old man raised a hand and let it fall limply by his side. "Go from me. Save yourself, Tykota."

Tykota felt grief rip through his heart. Anger coiled within him, and his gaze went to the horses. Touching Mangas's limp hand, he crawled toward his horse. He slid onto the mare's back and, keeping to the shadows, rode quietly down the slope.

When he was clear of the mesa, he urged his horse into a gallop. Bending low over the animal's neck, he headed for the place he was sure Santo was hiding.

Tykota did not hear the bullet that tore through him, knocking him off his horse. He landed hard on the ground and rolled down a small hill. Pain made it hard for him to breathe, and he felt warm, sticky blood run down his shoulder.

He raised his head in time to see Santo standing at the rise, his rifle aimed at him. "If only the Perdenelas could see their great chief now, Tykota. They would know that I am greater than you, because I have slain the dog, Mangas, who trails after you, and I have killed you."

Tykota clutched his own rifle and fired. The bullet struck true. Santo tumbled down the hill and lay beside him.

He jerked Santo up, cursing, "You are not fit to lie even with dogs. You hide in the darkness like some wild animal."

But Santo did not hear Tykota's words. He was already dead.

Tykota managed to stand, and, using his rifle to lean on, he made his way up the hill and pulled himself onto his horse.

Each step the horse took caused Tykota's

wound to throb and bleed. He wanted to go to Mangas but he knew he could not make it. Nor could he lift his old friend's body. He pointed his mount in the direction of the cavern and slumped forward into unconsciousness.

The moon was low in the sky when Tykota woke. He groaned and sat up straight on his horse. His mouth tasted like metal, and his shoulder hurt so fiercely that he gritted his teeth to keep from crying out. The bullet was still in him, and there was no one to remove it. Even his food and waterskin were back at the campsite. Struggling to stay upright, he urged his horse forward. He had to make it to the cave.

Then he shook his head at his own befuddlement. Coloradous would not be at the cave until the full moon, and that was three weeks away.

No one else knew where to find the cave.

He slumped forward, not afraid to die— death had no sting for him. But he would have liked to see Makinna just once more.

Chapter Thirty-one

Makinna stepped down from the stage, surprised to see John Kincaid. He offered her his arm and smiled. "Didn't your sister come with you?"

Makinna nodded, turning to watch as Adelaide stepped to the ground. She glanced back at John and saw the warmth creep up his face. She had little doubt John was in love with her sister, or certainly well on the road to it.

"Can you tell me how Mrs. Silverhorn is?"

"I saw her just this morning, and she was doing fine."

Makinna drew a relieved breath. "When I got the telegram, I was afraid she might be ill."

"No, ma'am. She's fit as ever."

"Then I wonder why she asked me to come."

"She didn't tell me, ma'am. You'll have to ask her when you get to Biquera."

Makinna was puzzled and a little frightened. What if something was wrong with Tykota?

John held out his other arm to Adelaide, and she blushed prettily as she placed her hand there. "You look as pretty as a summer rose, Mrs. Johnson," he said, smiling. He glanced over at Makinna. "And so do you, Miss Hillyard."

Makinna laughed softly and raised the hem of her gown to climb the wooden steps to the stage office. "Thank you, John."

He touched his hat and grinned. "You ladies wait here in the shade while I bring the buggy around and load your trunks."

After he walked off, Makinna looked at her sister's flushed face. "He's in love with you."

"Do you think so?"

"I'm sure of it."

"I must be awful to be thinking about another man with my husband so recently buried."

Makinna glanced up at the deep blue sky, where high, thin clouds were scattered across the heavens. "Love seems to pick its own time, Adelaide. We, as mere humans, seem to have no control over that emotion whatsoever."

"You don't think I am wrong to care for him?"

Makinna glanced at John, who was just getting out of the buggy. He was rangy and a bit gruff, but she had seen the softness in his eyes and heard the gentleness in his tone. "No, I do not think it is wrong. Here in Texas people seem to be always reaching out for life. They're a breed apart from the rest of the world. They have their own rules, and they go by those, not what the rest of the country expects from them."

Adelaide nodded toward John. "He is wonderful, isn't he?"

Makinna laughed. "Yes. Yes, he is."

Adelaide looked at her sister. "Oh, I know he isn't as magnificent as your Tykota, but, to me, he is the best of all men."

Makinna was taken aback. "Tykota is not mine." Then she smiled sadly. "But as for you and John Kincaid, well, if love is true, it will find a way," Makinna said, repeating what Tykota had said to her.

"I am almost afraid to love again. I was mistaken when I married Tom."

"Then give yourself time to know John. There is no hurry." She moved toward the buggy, where John had just stowed the last trunk. "Let's go. I want to find out why Hannah Silverhorn sent for me."

* * *

Tykota had used up his strength climbing the hill toward the cave. He was so thirsty that his throat was parched, and his shoulder throbbed. The mouth of the cave seemed a long way off.

He gritted his teeth and stood erect. With the last bit of strength he had, Tykota climbed higher, his gaze set on his final goal. At last he reached the overhanging ledge and stopped to catch his breath. He was weak and shaky, and he wasn't sure he had the strength to go on.

He was so close to water, and yet his strength was ebbing away. Drawing on his innermost determination to survive, he made it over the ledge and into the cave. He stumbled toward the narrow pathway to the inner cavern. He fell forward into the water, closing his eyes as the cool water washed over him. He turned his head into the stream that trickled over the rocks and drank thirstily.

Then he fell to the floor of the cave and closed his eyes.

Hannah Silverhorn was waiting on the veranda when they arrived. Makinna quickly got out of the buggy and ran up the steps to her.

"Are you all right?"

"Yes, my dear," Hannah said, slipping an arm

around Makinna's waist. "There's nothing wrong with me."

"But your telegram—I was afraid you were ill."

"I'm sorry if I caused you concern." She smiled at the young woman and kissed her cheek. "It wasn't for myself that I contacted you. It's Tykota."

Fear whitened Makinna's face. "Has something happened to him?"

"I believe Tykota's malady is more one of the heart."

Makinna watched her sister approach, then turned back to Hannah. "I don't understand why you would ask me to return if no one is ill."

"Don't you, my dear?"

"No, I don't."

"I believe Ty needs you now more than ever. He has made some difficult choices, and I know he is feeling very alone."

Makinna stared into Hannah Silverhorn's soft eyes. "I can't give him what he needs."

By now, Adelaide had joined them, and she happily greeted Tykota's mother.

Hannah gestured to the door. "Let's get inside where it's cooler. John, you can get one of the men to help you with the trunks."

Makinna caught her sister's gaze and shrugged. Then they both followed their hostess into the house.

* * *

The house was quiet. John had left earlier after enjoying a good meal with the ladies. Adelaide had gone up to bed, and Makinna and Hannah sat in the parlor.

At last Hannah broke the silence. "Word came to me that Tykota left the Perdenelas and made his brother, Coloradous, chief."

"How can that be?" Makinna stood and walked around the room, tears blinding her. "I never wanted him to make such a sacrifice."

Hannah patted the settee. "Makinna, sit beside me."

Makinna did as she asked. "That's why I left, Mrs. Silverhorn. I didn't want to interfere with his life."

"Makinna, I don't think that's solely why he passed rule to his brother, although it may have played a big part in his decision. I truly believe he thought it was for the best of the tribe. I know my son; he must be feeling devastated at the moment. I am sure he feels he failed both you and his people."

"He must go back." Makinna closed her eyes to settle her thoughts. "Where is he? I will make him go back."

Hannah gave a helpless gesture with her hands. "I don't know where he is." Her eyes were swimming with tears. "You should have seen him when he read your letter, Makinna. I have never seen him so distraught."

"It wasn't meant to bring him pain. I had intended only to set him free to live his life as he wished to."

Suddenly, there was a banging on the door, and Hannah hurried to answer it. Makinna heard her speaking to one of the ranch hands.

When Hannah reentered the room, her face was white, and she looked terrified. "Mangas just rode in. He's been wounded and is asking to see me."

"Mangas. Wouldn't he be with Tykota?"

"Yes. That old Indian never stirs from my son's side. Something is terribly wrong."

Makinna grasped Hannah's hand. "May I speak to him?"

"They have put him in his cabin. Let us hurry!"

Makinna held the lamp for Hannah while she removed the bullet from the old Indian's chest. Mangas met Makinna's gaze and moved his mouth. She grasped his hand, knowing he was in pain.

"She has the bullet out now," Makinna told him. "She has only to clean and bandage the wound."

He blinked his eyes, and she would have sworn his mouth curved into a smile. "I have had worse wounds and lived."

"And I've taken worse bullets out of you, you old Indian," Hannah said with affection. "I think you will live this time, too."

Suddenly Mangas's grip tightened on Makinna's with a strength that startled her. "Tykota. He is in trouble. He needs help."

Makinna held her breath while Hannah spoke to Mangas. "What has happened to my son?"

"After I was shot, Tykota was too, or he never would have left me. I saw the blood, and I saw Santo's dead body. There were hoofprints. I believe Tykota has gone to the sacred caverns, and I do not know where they are. No one knows but Tykota and perhaps Coloradous."

"I know!" Makinna cried. "At least I was there. I'm not sure if I could find them again on my own. But if someone could take me to the mesa where the Apaches held me captive, I believe I could find the cave from there."

Mangas rose up, his eyes bright. "Send John Kincaid to me. I will tell him how to find the mesa. You must hurry!"

Hannah took Makinna's arm. "You are my son's only hope. I would go with you, but I would only slow you down. I will prepare food and everything you will need if you find him wounded."

Makinna felt fear for the man she loved.

What if she never found him, or found him too late? "Pray for me that I might find him alive."

Makinna rode away from Biquera just before sunup. John Kincaid and two heavily armed ranch hands galloped at her side. One of the men led a packhorse. Makinna wished she was riding an Indian pony so she could simply race across the desert to Tykota.

On the third day out, they were in sight of the wide mesa. Makinna halted her mount and studied the lay of the land. She looked to the south. She remembered Tykota telling her that the cave was two days' ride south of this mesa.

"In the morning we ride south," she told John.

He nodded and prepared to make camp with the ranch hands.

"John, wait. I have to tell you something, and I don't know if you will understand."

"I will try, Miss Hillyard."

"Tomorrow we will ride for a day and a half. Then I must ride on alone."

He looked worried. "It could be dangerous for a woman alone."

"That's the way it has to be, John. You and the others can't come with me."

"This cave Mangas and you were talking about—could it be the sacred cave of the legendary Perdenelas?"

"I don't know. It could be."

"And Tykota took you there?"

"I saw nothing of value there. But I know Tykota has strong feelings about that place. And if there is the slightest chance that it is the sacred cave, I can't take you or anyone else there." She looked into his clear, honest eyes and knew she could trust him. "Do you understand, John?"

"I do. And I surely don't want those two"—he nodded to the cowhands, who were drinking coffee from tin cups—"to learn about the cave."

"Neither do I." She was quiet for a moment. "I ride the last few miles alone."

"Yes. But what will you do if Tykota is injured?"

"I'll have to manage. I promised him I would not share the secret of the cave with anyone, and I cannot break that promise."

"Miss Hillyard, I do believe you'll accomplish whatever you set your mind to do."

She nodded, though she felt utterly inadequate to the task at hand. "I can." She straightened her shoulders. "I can do anything if it will help Tykota."

When they had ridden for the appointed time, Makinna told John that they would make camp, and that she would go on the next morning alone.

As dawn broke, Makinna was ready to ride.

She turned back to John, who had been loading the packhorse for her, as he finished securing the supplies. "Tell me the truth, and I will know it if you lie. Do you think he's alive?"

John smiled at her. "I can tell you that Tykota is a stubborn man and one hard Indian to kill."

"Yes." She let out the breath she'd been holding, feeling a glimmer of hope. "He is stubborn."

Chapter Thirty-two

Makinna had been riding for hours, and she was becoming frantic. Where was the cave? Tykota had told her it was in this direction. She would recognize the mountain if she saw it.

She halted her mount and uncapped her canteen, taking small sips as Tykota had taught her. Somewhere out there he might be severely wounded, and she had to find him.

What if she never found the cavern? What if she wandered aimlessly and was lost in the vast desert?

It was almost sundown when she spotted the mountain looming out of the sand. Urging her horse forward, she began laughing and crying at the same time.

She had found the cave!

* * *

Tykota woke slowly to the sound of the water spilling into the pool. He groaned and tried to sit up, but pain seemed to pin him to the ground. He licked his dry lips, wondering how long he'd been there. He had no sense of the passage of time.

He closed his eyes, wondering if Coloradous would come in time to save him. No, probably not. His thoughts turned to Makinna. Makinna laughing. Makinna angry. Makinna soft and loving in his arms.

If he was going to die, his last thoughts would be of her.

Tykota heard her calling his name, and he smiled. He felt her soft touch on his burning forehead. He felt her near him, bending over him.

Yes, he thought wistfully, *let the memory of her essence walk with me into the shadow of death*.

Makinna placed a hand on Tykota's forehead. He was feverish. She saw the rise and fall of his chest and called out his name.

He was alive!

She saw the angry wound in his shoulder where he'd been shot. "Tykota, open your eyes. Talk to me!"

He listened to her voice as if in a dream.

"Tykota! Open your eyes!"

It took great effort to raise his eyelids. Yes, there she was, looking frantic. She was as perfect in his imaginings as she had been in person.

"Tykota, I need to ask you something."

He blinked. Her hand on his skin felt so real. "Are you a dream?" he whispered through dry, cracked lips.

"No, I am here, Tykota. I need to know if the bullet is still in your shoulder."

He tried to concentrate on what she was saying. "I . . . was shot." He tried to rise, but he was too weak. "Santo . . . killed Mangas."

"Tykota, listen to me. Mangas is not dead. He is the one who told me I would find you here."

"I was coming to you," he said, closing his eyes. "I just had . . . one more thing to do before we could be together."

"We are together now."

"You left me."

Tears gathered in her eyes, and she bent to kiss his lips. "I will never leave you again unless you ask me to."

Suddenly, his eyes opened, and he gripped her arm. "Makinna, you are not a dream?"

She gently touched his face. "No, I am not a dream." She pushed his dark hair away from his face and smiled through her tears. "Tykota, is the bullet still in you?"

He licked his dry lips, feeling joy spread through him. If she was a dream, he didn't want to awaken. "The bullet is still there."

She sat back on her heels, gathering her thoughts. She had watched Hannah dig the bullet out of Mangas. But could she do the same? Yes, if it meant saving Tykota's life. She could do anything.

"Tykota, I have supplies at the bottom of the mountain. I am going to get them. I will be right back."

His hand tightened on hers. "You said you would not leave me."

She placed a quick kiss on his lips. "Only long enough to get what I need to remove the bullet."

She hurried out of the cave, unwilling to dwell on the difficult task ahead of her. She prayed that God would give her a steady hand and a strong will.

When she reached the bottom of the hill, she gave the horses water from a waterskin, unsaddled hers, and took the supplies from the packhorse.

All the while she was praying silently that she could save Tykota.

Makinna placed a blanket beneath Tykota's head, then turned to the fire she had built. She gripped the handle of his knife and thrust the blade into the flame. Gathering her courage, she turned back to Tykota to find him watching her. His dark eyes were liquid, and she saw the love shining there.

"Tykota, I have never done this before. I don't want to hurt you."

His lips formed a smile. "You are too stubborn to let a little thing like a bullet stop you."

She nodded, feeling her stomach tighten in dread.

"Just do it, Makinna," he urged.

"I think your wound may be infected."

"That is because I did not have the strength to remove the bullet. You must do it for me."

He watched her swallow hard and nod.

Makinna's hand was shaking, and she felt sick inside. She avoided Tykota's eyes as she called on all her strength.

"Just do it, Makinna."

She knew in that moment that this was the hardest thing she'd ever been called on to do—cause him pain.

When the blade touched his wound, he flinched. "No," he said between clenched teeth. "You are not a dream. This is all too real."

Makinna knew she had to do it quickly, so she wouldn't prolong his agony.

With a downward probe she felt the bullet against the blade of the knife. She became dizzy but would not give in to weakness. She probed deeper and felt him go limp.

Tykota had passed out.

She had to get the bullet out before he regained consciousness. She dug deeper and was finally rewarded for her efforts when she felt the bullet move. Slowly, painstakingly, she glided the offending object out. Then she eased away from Tykota, blotting the sweat from her forehead with her sleeve.

She saturated the wound with alcohol and washed most of the blood away. Then she bandaged his shoulder and arm. Now she could do no more than wait. Her hands were shaking so violently that she had to clasp them together to still them.

She went to the pool and washed her hands and face, then wet a cloth and placed it on Tykota's forehead because he still had a fever. When she made him as comfortable as possible, she prepared him something to eat. Hannah had thought of everything—her basket was overflowing with biscuits, dried meat, apples, and cheese. Tykota probably hadn't eaten in days.

Makinna sat quietly watching Tykota. He could be unconscious, but he seemed to be sleeping peacefully. Her gaze ran the length of him, his masculine perfection. He was lean yet beautifully muscled and undeniably handsome. His thick, dark hair fell to his shoulders, and she wanted badly to touch his bronzed cheek.

Sitting there in the waning light, she knew

that she would never love anyone the way she loved Tykota. He was a man of honor, in his commitment to the Perdenelas, in his love for her. She didn't know exactly why God had brought her back into Tykota's life, but she was glad He had.

She reached forward to touch his cheek. She wasn't sure, but it felt a bit cooler. She rewet the cloth, washed his face and chest, wet the cloth again, then reapplied it to his forehead. It was so difficult to just wait.

Makinna stood and walked to the outer cavern. She moved to the entrance and stood on the ledge as she had done when she and Tykota had been here before.

The sunset bathed the desert in golden light, and she closed her eyes, absorbing the beauty of this land that now called to her and it gave sustenance to her spirit. She was not the same person she had been when she first came to this land.

Fearing that Tykota would wake up and need her, she went back to the inner cavern. He had not moved, so she sat down beside him and braced her back against the wall. Laying a hand on his, she closed her eyes and drifted into sleep.

Makinna felt a presence and opened her eyes. From a darkened corner, an Indian emerged, and at first, she thought it was Tykota. But a quick glance showed her that Tykota was still sleeping.

She scrambled to her feet and hugged the wall. Then she saw it was Coloradous!

"What are you doing here, white woman?" he asked in a cold voice.

"I . . . Tykota was wounded, and I . . . took the bullet out."

"How did you know of this place?"

"I . . . Tykota brought me here."

Coloradous bent down and laid a hand on his brother's chest. "How bad is he?"

"I don't know."

"How did this happen to him?"

"Mangas told me that Santo did it."

Coloradous nodded. "Yes, Santo would have done this." He rose to his full height, and she was struck, as she had been before, by how much he looked like Tykota.

"I don't know how bad his wound is. He has not regained consciousness since I removed the bullet," she said.

"His breathing is very shallow."

"Is that bad?"

"It could be." His dark gaze settled on her. "You removed the bullet and bandaged him?"

She nodded.

"You did well. But I will look to my brother now. You may leave."

"I can't leave without knowing if he is going to live."

"You do not belong here. I will take care of him, and when he is well enough to travel, I will take him to the healing woman, Huara."

"He must not be moved," she argued. "It could kill him."

He took her arm and led her to the narrow passage. "I will do all I can for him. He is my brother, and I would give my life if it would save him."

Makinna had no choice but to do as Coloradous said. "Will you send word of him to Biquera?"

His voice was kinder now. "I will do that. Assure my brother's white mother that Tykota is strong and has the blood of chiefs in his veins."

She raised her gaze to his headband. "You now wear the symbol of the chief."

"I do."

She glanced back at Tykota. "When he wakes, will you tell him that—"

He seemed impatient to have her gone. "I will tell him you were here, and what you did for him."

Makinna nodded. Her footsteps were heavy as she moved down the passageway and out of the cave. It was difficult to leave Tykota, but Coloradous would know better how to help his brother than she did. She saddled her horse and mounted, turning to the north.

* * *

Five days later a very fatigued Makinna rode through the gate of Biquera Ranch. Her sister, Hannah Silverhorn, and a surprisingly spry Mangas rushed toward the corral to greet the returning travelers.

Adelaide was the first to reach her. "Are you all right, Makinna? Did you find Tykota?"

Makinna looked at Hannah. "I found Tykota. He had been shot, but I took the bullet out of him. When I left him, he was still unconscious but alive."

"Why did you leave him?" Hannah asked, her hand at her throat.

"His brother, Coloradous, came to the cave. He asked me to leave and said he would take care of Tykota." Her gaze sought the old Indian's. "He will help him, won't he, Mangas?"

Mangas nodded. "Coloradous will do well by Tykota." He studied the ground before he looked back at Makinna. "Was he wearing the chief's headband?"

"Yes."

The old man walked off murmuring to himself, and Hannah hustled Makinna toward the house. You can bathe and eat, then I want you to get some rest. You look done in."

Makinna turned to John and the other men. "Thank you. I could never have found Tykota without your help."

John touched his hat, and then his eyes went

370

to Adelaide. "You Hillyard sisters have hidden strengths. You look so fragile, but you aren't."

Makinna smiled and turned toward the house.

Chapter Thirty-three

Later Makinna slipped out of the house and hurried toward the barn. She closed the wide door behind her and walked purposefully toward the tack room, where she stood in the doorway, staring at the cot, remembering Tykota. She walked around, touching the splintery wall, then a leather bridle that hung on a rusted hook. Silence surrounded her until she heard a horse nicker and stomp.

She heard the barn door swing open and Adelaide and John Kincaid talking as they walked in. She started to call out to her sister, but suddenly John swept Adelaide into his embrace.

"I wanted to wait to tell you how I feel about you, knowing you were but recently widowed, but I can't wait. I'm too afraid some other man will come along and take you away from me . . ."

Adelaide lay her head against his broad shoulder and looked into his rugged face. "It wouldn't matter who came along, John. I could never feel about them the way I feel about you."

Makinna moved away from the door and stood in a corner. It was too late to make her presence known now.

"Can you really care about me the way I do about you?" John asked in a voice filled with wonder.

Adelaide's voice was playful as she said, "I don't know, John. You haven't told me how you feel. You only said you were afraid some other man would take me away."

He held her at arm's length. "I love you. I love you so damned much that I can't pass an hour without thinking about you."

Adelaide rested her hand on his chest. "I'm not a young girl, John, and I don't play games. I love you, and I'm not too shy to admit it."

He let out a loud whoop, gathered her about the waist, and swung her around, laughing. "I am the luckiest man that ever lived! I love the lady, and she loves me!"

They became quiet, and Makinna guessed they were kissing. She definitely couldn't make her presence known now. She smiled with happiness for her sister. Adelaide was going to be all right. John would be good to her. Her sister had wanted to live in Texas, and now she could.

She heard John speak.

"When can we be married? I don't want to wait."

"But you must, John. I have been a widow but four months. It would not be proper."

"Here in Texas we do things differently. No one holds much with convention. We're too busy raising cattle and children. I want to increase my herd, and I want children. Do you like children, Adelaide?"

"Yes, I do, John."

"Then it's settled. I won't stop kissing you until you agree to marry me."

Adelaide's laughter was beautiful to Makinna's ears. "Let's go ask Hannah and see what she thinks."

"All right, but I warn you, Hannah has been telling me for years that I need to settle down. The Bar K is a big ranch, and it's good land. I have money, Adelaide, so I want you to put yours in a bank somewhere and live off mine. You can set yours aside for our children if you want to."

Again Adelaide laughed. "If that's what you want. Just how wealthy are you?"

"Not nearly as wealthy as the Silverhorns, but I make a better than good living."

Makinna heard them move out the door, and she felt tears on her cheeks. She smiled wistfully. "Oh, Adelaide, you are going to be so happy," she whispered.

Adelaide and John made an unusual-looking couple, he tall and raw-boned, looking uncomfortable in a suit and tie, she delicate and pretty in a lacy apricot gown.

But as they stood in Hannah Silverhorn's parlor but a few weeks later, their eyes shone with love when the preacher pronounced them man and wife.

The wedding was small, the only guests Hannah, Makinna, and John's sister and her husband.

When the ceremony was over, Makinna hugged Adelaide, smiling through her tears. "Be happy."

Adelaide's laughter bubbled. "I am! Oh, Makinna, I love him so much. Is it right for anyone to be this happy?"

"Yes, it is. If anyone deserves to be happy, it's you."

Adelaide squeezed Makinna's hand. "If only you could be as happy as I am. If only—"

"This is your day. We will not speak of anything but your happiness. A bride should have only happy thoughts on her wedding." Makinna forced a laugh. "Go to your bridegroom. He is looking this way."

And she watched her sister move across the room and into her new husband's embrace.

The house seemed so quiet without Adelaide. Makinna watched Hannah mending one of her gowns, not realizing she had sighed aloud.

Hannah looked at her over her spectacles. "It was a lovely wedding."

"Yes, it was. I am so glad my sister found John."

"He's a good man."

"I think so, too."

"Mangas is up and about. He seems to have recovered nicely."

Makinna laughed. "He is a loveable old man. His eyes twinkle, and he almost seems full of mischief."

"He likes you."

"How do you know?"

"He told me so."

Makinna was thoughtful. "I consider that a compliment. I have a feeling Mangas doesn't give his approval easily."

Hannah studied Makinna's face as she said, "I had word from Coloradous today."

Makinna sat forward. "How is Tykota?"

"You will be glad to know that he is healing nicely."

Makinna closed her eyes in relief. "I'm glad. I have been so worried about him."

"So have I. But not so much for his injury. I

knew in my heart that he would heal from that wound."

"You are concerned because he stepped down and allowed Coloradous to be chief of the Perdenelas."

"Not even that. I am more worried about why he did it."

"I don't understand."

"If Ty stepped down because he did not feel capable of leading his tribe, he will find no peace."

Makinna thought about what Hannah said, and she understood. Tykota might always carry guilt that he didn't fulfull his promise to his father. She stood up and walked restlessly to the window.

"Something is bothering you, isn't it, Makinna?"

She turned to Hannah. "I have to tell you something, and I don't want to."

"You are going away, aren't you?"

"Yes. I have decided to go back to New Orleans. At least for a while. I feel if I go back to my roots, maybe I can find who I am. Adelaide insisted on lending me enough money to open a small book shop there."

"I don't want you to leave."

Makinna went to Hannah and took her hand. "I will miss you. But you know I have to do this."

Hannah nodded. "Knowing it and liking it

are two different things. I would like to keep you with me."

"I shall certainly miss you."

"When do you plan to leave?"

"I thought I would go as soon as Adelaide gets back from her honeymoon."

"Then I still have you for two more weeks."

Makinna kissed the little woman's cheek, knowing she would miss her dearly.

Chapter Thirty-four

The sun had gone down hours ago, and dark clouds were gathering on the eastern horizon.

Makinna and Hannah had settled on the veranda after dinner, enjoying the coolness of the evening. Hannah sat in a rocking chair, and Makinna was seated on the steps, watching flashes of lightning in the distance.

"Did you finish packing?" Hannah asked.

It was painful for Makinna to think about leaving. "Yes. Everything is ready to go."

"You can still change your mind," Hannah said hopefully.

Makinna wanted to stay, but she couldn't. If she remained, she would only watch for Tykota every day, and she could not live that way. "I have to go. You know I do."

"Looks as if it might rain hard," Hannah observed. "We could use some rain."

Makinna's heart wrenched in pain as she remembered how Tykota had taught her not to fear the thunderstorm. "The earth being reborn," she muttered sadly.

Hannah set her sights on the sky. "More than likely it will pass us by."

Makinna heard footsteps coming up the walkway, and she assumed it was one of the cowhands coming to speak to Hannah. She stood up to give the man room.

She walked to a corner of the veranda and stared up at the sky, leaning her head against a wooden column. She was overwhelmed with melancholy. She was happy for her sister, but, unlike Adelaide, she would never know the joy of marrying the man she loved.

As Tykota stepped onto the veranda and approached his mother, he placed a finger to his lips and nodded toward Makinna. Hannah understood immediately and smiled as joy burst through her heart. She knew why he had come. In fact, she'd been expecting him. "I'll just go inside," she whispered. "Convince her to stay, Ty."

Makinna heard the door open and shut, but she kept watching the sky, still remembering that other storm so long ago when she had first begun to realize that she loved Tykota.

"Were you, perhaps, thinking of me, Makinna?"

She whirled around to find Tykota standing behind her. She pressed a hand to her stomach to stop the fluttering there. Then lightning flashed, and her gaze collided with Tykota's.

"Are you well enough to have ridden a horse here?" She immediately felt foolish for asking such a mundane question, but it was all she could think of to say.

He held out the arm that was in a sling. "So it would seem."

To keep him from knowing she was falling apart inside, Makinna tilted her chin upward. "Your brother sent word as he promised. We knew that he'd taken you back to your tribe."

Makinna's hair glistened in the soft light, and Tykota wanted to reach out and touch it, but he restrained himself.

"I wasn't sure you would come back to Biquera, Tykota."

His voice was deep with feeling. "Why would you think that, Makinna?"

Her words were almost inaudible. "I don't know. I thought . . ." She paused. "Well, I'm glad you came now, or I would have missed seeing you."

"Oh. Why is that?"

"I'm going away tomorrow. Oh, you probably don't know yet that John Kincaid and my sister married."

"There is nothing that happens on this ranch

that I don't hear about, Makinna. I even heard that you were leaving. But I do not think you will."

"And why is that?"

He stepped closer but still didn't touch her. "What makes you think I will allow you to leave?"

A flash of lightning made a jagged pattern across the sky, and he held out a hand to her. She stared at him, then gave him her hand. His clasp was warm, and she trembled when he raised her palm to his lips and placed a passionate kiss there.

"I forgot to thank you for removing the bullet from my shoulder, Makinna."

She could not speak because he was gathering her closer to him. When she would have pulled away, he glared at her, and she relented. Blissfully, she lay her head against his shoulder.

"I have been so worried about you," she admitted.

There was uncertainty in his voice, a trait he had seldom displayed before. "When Mangas told me you were going back to New Orleans, I feared I would not get here in time to stop you."

Makinna's heart was thundering inside of her, and there was a tightening in her throat. "I don't know what you mean."

He tilled her chin up and smiled down at her. "Do we play games, beloved?"

"No, I—"

"Your lips beg to be kissed."

"You shouldn't say things like that." She shook her head. "Don't do this to me, Tykota."

"I will never hurt you again, Makinna."

There was something different about him, but she didn't know what it was. He seemed calmer and somehow . . . lighthearted. "If you were to speak the truth, Tykota, we have both hurt each other."

"I always speak the truth with you." He smiled. "Well, almost always. Some thoughts about you are private, and I keep those to myself."

She moved away, not trusting herself to be so near him. "What about the tribe, Tykota?"

"They will do much better with Coloradous to lead them."

"But your father—"

Reaching out, he touched her face lovingly and stared into her vivid blue eyes. "My father was sometimes wrong, Makinna. I never want our sons to be burdened with the secret of the Perdenelas' treasure."

His statement brought a gasp to her lips. She wanted to feel Tykota's arms around her, but she still did not trust her own heart. "Our son?" she echoed weakly.

His dark gaze probed hers. "Yes, our son. For this I swear, Makinna, you will have no man's sons but mine."

A sob escaped her lips as he tore off his sling and hugged her to him. "Tykota! she cried.

"I want to fill you with sons and daughters," he whispered against her hair, closing his eyes and absorbing her essence. "I do not believe that any man has ever loved a woman as I love you."

She raised her head and saw the passion in his dark eyes. "If I can't have your children, Tykota, I will have no other man's child."

He growled as his arms tightened about her. "We had better have the wedding soon, because I do not think my mother will like what I am thinking."

She laughed. "The tack room?"

"How soon will you marry me?"

She placed a finger over his mouth. "Tykota, are you sure this is what you want? I know how you felt about your tribe and safeguarding them and the treasure."

Tykota reached inside his vest and withdrew something, which he placed in the palm of her hand.

Makinna glanced down at the two leather armbands with the golden eagles, and the significance of his gesture struck her like lightning. "Oh, Tykota."

"Beloved, I have found in you something more precious than any treasure, and a love more timeless than the sacred mountain."

His lips brushed hers, and he held her tighter

against him. Neither of them spoke. It was enough to touch, to feel, to let their love for each other transcend the pain of the past.

Finally Tykota raised his head and lightly kissed her lips. "Makinna, you are so much a part of me, that when you breathe, I take a breath; when you are hurt, I feel pain. Say you will walk through life with me."

Happiness flowed through her, and she pressed her cheek to his. "Yes, oh, yes, Tykota."

He took her hand and led her toward the house. "Come, let us tell my mother." He stopped and quirked an eyebrow at her. "Unless, of course, you would rather I take you to the tack room."

She steered him toward the front door. "No. I think that will wait until I am Mrs. Tykota Silverhorn."

"You had better plan a wedding quickly then, because I do not intend to wait much longer to take you to bed." He slid a hand across her breast, and she felt him tremble. "I have known the joy of your body, and I want to know it every day of my life."

He gave her a long, drugging kiss, but finally Makinna broke it off and moved a safe distance away to look up at him. "You have no doubts?"

"None."

"Where will we live?"

"Here, Makinna. Here on Biquera Ranch we will raise our sons and daughters." He looked down at her. "With you, I have found peace for my restless soul. You have brought true love into my life." He closed his eyes for a moment. "Peace is wonderful."

"Oh, I do hope so, Tykota," she said with feeling. "That is what I want for you above all else. I have watched you struggle, watched you torn between two worlds. The pain of your struggle has been like a knife in my heart."

Tykota raised his eyes and stared at the distant lightning as the first drops of rain begin to hit the roof of the ranch house. "I like to think my father knows and would approve. If he loved my mother half as much as I love you, he is smiling from the Spirit World right now."

Makinna closed her eyes as Tykota enveloped her in his arms. "If there is love," she said softly, "it will find a way."

Epilogue

Makinna shaded her eyes against the glare of the Texas sun and laughed down at her daughter, Yalinda, a dark-eyed, dark-haired little beauty who looked so much like her father. The child was giggling and tugging at Makinna's skirt.

She lifted her into her arms and walked toward the corral. She braced Yalinda on the top rung of the rail fence, and they both watched Tykota instruct young Coloradous.

"My son," he said, "you must never have any fear of a horse. Here in the desert country, your horse will be your best friend. He will often be your only hope between life and death."

Makinna watched Tykota place their three-year-old son, Coloradous, on the back of a pinto. Unlike his sister, who had the coloring of her Indian heritage, Coloradous looked more like Makinna. His hair was light brown, and his eyes were a startlingly beautiful golden color.

With pride shining in his eyes, Tykota stood back and watched his son clutch the reins. He caught Makinna's gaze and called out to her. "Our son fears nothing. Do you see the way he sits his horse?"

Makinna felt pride and love well up in her. She and Tykota had been married for four years, and they had been wonderful, loving years. "Our son may not fear horses, but he might have reason to fear his grandmother. Hannah wants both children to bathe—she's taking them to visit their Aunt Adelaide."

Tykota lifted the boy from the horse and set him on his feet. "You had better run along. I learned early in life that it is not wise to keep your grandmother waiting."

While Coloradous scampered toward the house, Tykota reached for his daughter and hugged her to him. His expression softened when she threw her arms around his neck. After a quick kiss on her cheek, Tykota put her down and watched the child run after her brother.

Makinna linked her arm through her husband's and lay her head against his shoulder. "We make wonderful babies together."

His dark eyes suddenly flamed with desire. "We could always make another one."

"Oh, I am certain we will." They walked toward the house, and he stopped her, encircling her in his embrace. "We could start this weekend, since we will have the house to ourselves."

She looked into his bronzed face, watching the way the wind rippled his long hair. There was contentment in his eyes, his spirit no longer seeking and restless. "Then let us get your mother and the children on their way."

He touched her hair and let his hand drift through the silken strands. "My lovely Makinna, what joy you have brought to my life. I wake up each morning not knowing what to expect out of you. And"—he arched an eyebrow—"I can't keep my hands off you. I wait for the night so you can be completely mine."

"Tykota, I never knew that life could be so good. Sometimes I am afraid."

"Of what?"

"That no woman should be this happy, that it will be taken away from me."

He rested his chin on the top of her head. "Take each day as a gift, Makinna. We have been blessed as few people ever are."

Her hand slid into his, and they walked toward the house. "I'd better help your mother get the children ready."

"Uh-huh. The sooner they leave, the sooner I can take you to bed."

She laughed, feeling her stomach flutter at

the thought of their lovemaking, which was so exciting and good.

He stopped her at the door and swung her around, his mouth covering hers in a passionate kiss.

She turned her head, untangled his arms, and scolded. "Not here in front of everyone."

He laughed and pulled her back to him. "Why not? Everyone already knows how I feel about you." He caught her face and raised it to his. "They all know I am in love with you."

Tears brightened her eyes. "Oh, Tykota, never stop loving me."

"Not until the day I close my eyes in death, and even then, I believe I will love you from the Spirit World."

They kissed long and deeply, and then they heard the children's laughter from inside. Tykota opened the door for her, and they went into the ranch house—a house where two worlds had once collided, then come together, bonded with love.

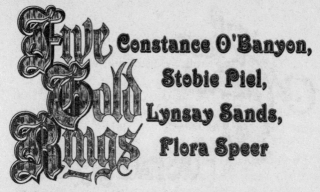

Five Gold Rings

Constance O'Banyon, Stobie Piel, Lynsay Sands, Flora Speer

In the Year of Our Lord, 1135, Menton Castle is the same as any other: It has nobles and minstrels, knights and servants. Yet from the great hall to the scullery there are signs that the house is in an uproar. This Yuletide season is to be one of passion and merriment. The master of the keep has returned. With him come several travelers, some weary with laughter, some tired of tears. But in all of their stories—whether lords a'leapin' or maids a'milkin'—there is one gift that their true loves give to them. And in the winter moonlight, each of the castle's inhabitants will soon see the magic of the season and the joy that can come from five gold rings.

___4612-1 $5.50 US/$6.50 CAN

Dorchester Publishing Co., Inc.
P.O. Box 6640
Wayne, PA 19087-8640

Please add $1.75 for shipping and handling for the first book and $.50 for each book thereafter. NY, NYC, and PA residents, please add appropriate sales tax. No cash, stamps, or C.O.D.s. All orders shipped within 6 weeks via postal service book rate. Canadian orders require $2.00 extra postage and must be paid in U.S. dollars through a U.S. banking facility.

Name_____
Address_____
City_____State_____Zip_____
I have enclosed $_____ in payment for the checked book(s).
Payment <u>must</u> accompany all orders. ❑ Please send a free catalog.
     CHECK OUT OUR WEBSITE! www.dorchesterpub.com

San Antonio Rose
Constance O'Banyon

Sam Houston knows he needs all the help he can get to defeat Santa Anna's seasoned fighting men. But who is the mysterious San Antonio Rose, who emerges from the mist like a ghostly figure to offer her aid? Fluent in Spanish, Ian McCain is the one man who can ferret out the truth about the flamboyant dancer. Working under Santa Anna's very nose, he observes how the dark-haired beauty inflames her audience, how she captivates El Presidente himself. But as she disappears with a single yellow rose, he knows that despite the tangled web of loyalties that ensnare them, he will taste those tempting lips, know every secret of that alluring body. And before she proves just how effective she can be, he will pluck for himself the San Antonio Rose.

___4563-X $5.99 US/$6.99 CAN

TEXAS PROUD

CONSTANCE O'BANYON

Rachel Rutledge has her gun trained on Noble Vincente. With one shot, she will have her revenge on the man who killed her father. So what is stopping her from pulling the trigger? Perhaps it is the memory of Noble's teasing voice, his soft smile, or the way one glance from his dark Spanish eyes once stirred her foolish heart to longing. Yes, she loved him then . . . as much as she hates him now. One way or another, she will wound him to the heart—if not with bullets, then with her own feminine wiles. But as Rachel discovers, sometimes the line between love and hate is too thinly drawn.

___4492-7 $5.99 US/$6.99 CAN

Dorchester Publishing Co., Inc.
P.O. Box 6640
Wayne, PA 19087-8640

Texas Empires: Lone Star

Evelyn Rogers

The Lone Star State is as forthright and independent as the women who brave the rugged land, and sunset-haired Kate Calloway is as feisty an example as Cord has ever seen. A Texas woman. He has not dealt with one in a long time, but he recognizes the gumption in her blue eyes. He would be a fool to question the threat behind the shotgun leveled at his chest. He would be still more a fool to give in to the urge to take her right there on the hard, dusty ground. For though he senses they are two halves of one whole, Kate belongs to the man he's come to destroy. That they will meet again is certain; the only question is: how long can he wait before making her his?

___4533-8 $5.99 US/$6.99 CAN

EVELYN ROGERS

TEXAS EMPIRES: Crown of Glory

It is nothing but a dog-run cabin and five thousand acres of prime grassland when Eleanor Chase first set eyes on it. But someone killed her father to get the deed to the place, and Ellie swears she will not leave Texas until she has her revenge and her ranch. There is just one man standing in her way—a blue-eyed devil named Cal Hardin. Is he the scoundrel who has stolen her birthright, or the lover whose oh-so-right touch can steal her very breath away?

___4403-X $5.99 US/$6.99 CAN

Cinnamon and Roses
Heidi Betts

A hardworking seamstress, Rebecca has no business being attracted to a man like wealthy, arrogant Caleb Adams. Born fatherless in a brothel, Rebecca knows what males are made of. And Caleb is clearly as faithless as they come, scandalizing their Kansas cowtown with the fancy city women he casually uses and casts aside. Though he tempts innocent Rebecca beyond reason, she can't afford to love a man like Caleb, for the price might be another fatherless babe. What the devil is wrong with him, Caleb muses, that he's drawn to a calico-clad dressmaker when sirens in silk are his for the asking? Still, Rebecca unaccountably stirs him. Caleb vows no woman can be trusted with his heart. But he must sample sweet Rebecca.

Lair of the Wolf

Also includes the second installment of *Lair of the Wolf*, a serialized romance set in medieval Wales. Be sure to look for future chapters of this exciting story featured in Leisure books and written by the industry's top authors.

___4668-7 $4.99 US/$5.99 CAN

Dorchester Publishing Co., Inc.
P.O. Box 6640
Wayne, PA 19087-8640

Please add $1.75 for shipping and handling for the first book and $.50 for each book thereafter. NY, NYC, and PA residents, please add appropriate sales tax. No cash, stamps, or C.O.D.s. All orders shipped within 6 weeks via postal service book rate. Canadian orders require $2.00 extra postage and must be paid in U.S. dollars through a U.S. banking facility.

Name_____
Address_____
City_____State_____Zip_____
I have enclosed $_____ in payment for the checked book(s).
Payment <u>must</u> accompany all orders. ❏ Please send a free catalog.
CHECK OUT OUR WEBSITE! www.dorchesterpub.com

BRIDES OF DURANGO: ELISE
BOBBI SMITH

Elise Martin will do anything for a story—even stage a fake marriage to catch a thief. Dressed in a white lace gown, she looks every bit the bride, but when her "fiancé" fails to show, she offers ten dollars to the handsome gentleman who just stepped off the stage to pose as the groom. As a fake fiancé, he is all right, but when he turns out to be Gabriel West, the new owner of her paper, the *Durango Star*, Elise wants to turn tail and run. But she can't forget the passion his unexpected kiss at their "wedding" aroused, and she starts to wonder if there is more to Gabriel West than meets the eye. For the more time they spend together, the more Elise wonders if the next time she says, "I do" she just might mean it.

___4575-3 $5.99 US/$6.99 CAN

Dorchester Publishing Co., Inc.
P.O. Box 6640
Wayne, PA 19087-8640

Please add $1.75 for shipping and handling for the first book and $.50 for each book thereafter. NY, NYC, and PA residents, please add appropriate sales tax. No cash, stamps, or C.O.D.s. All orders shipped within 6 weeks via postal service book rate. Canadian orders require $2.00 extra postage and must be paid in U.S. dollars through a U.S. banking facility.

Name_____
Address_____
City_____State_____Zip_____
I have enclosed $_____ in payment for the checked book(s).
Payment <u>must</u> accompany all orders. ❏ Please send a free catalog.
        CHECK OUT OUR WEBSITE! www.dorchesterpub.com

GUNSLINGER
Connie Mason

He blows into Trouble Creek on a raw April wind, a fast gun for hire to the highest bidder. But when Chloe Sommers offers him a job protecting her herd, she has no idea Desperado Jones has a hidden agenda as deadly as his Colt .45. All she sees is a man packing even more raw sex appeal than firepower. She senses right away that his dark good looks and blatant virility are a threat to her peace of mind. But she never guesses what she will discover after a night of explosive loving: Desperado holds a secret claim on her ranch and a far more binding claim on her wayward heart.

___4532-X $5.99 US/$6.99 CAN

Dorchester Publishing Co., Inc.
P.O. Box 6640
Wayne, PA 19087-8640

Please add $1.75 for shipping and handling for the first book and $.50 for each book thereafter. NY, NYC, and PA residents, please add appropriate sales tax. No cash, stamps, or C.O.D.s. All orders shipped within 6 weeks via postal service book rate. Canadian orders require $2.00 extra postage and must be paid in U.S. dollars through a U.S. banking facility.

Name_____

Address_____

City_____State_____Zip_____

I have enclosed $_____ in payment for the checked book(s).

Payment <u>must</u> accompany all orders. ☐ Please send a free catalog.

CHECK OUT OUR WEBSITE! www.dorchesterpub.com

Spirit's Song

MADELINE BAKER

She is a runaway wife, with a hefty reward posted for her return. And he is the best darn tracker in the territory. For the half-breed bounty hunter, it is an easy choice. His was a hard life, with little to show for it except his horse, his Colt, and his scars. The pampered, brown-eyed beauty will go back to her rich husband in San Francisco, and he will be ten thousand dollars richer. But somewhere along the trail out of the Black Hills everything changes. Now, he will give his life to protect her, to hold her forever in his embrace. Now the moonlight poetry of their loving reflects the fiery vision of the Sun Dance: She must be his spirit's song.

___4476-5 $5.99 US/$6.99 CAN

Dorchester Publishing Co., Inc.
P.O. Box 6640
Wayne, PA 19087-8640

Please add $1.75 for shipping and handling for the first book and $.50 for each book thereafter. NY, NYC, and PA residents, please add appropriate sales tax. No cash, stamps, or C.O.D.s. All orders shipped within 6 weeks via postal service book rate. Canadian orders require $2.00 extra postage and must be paid in U.S. dollars through a U.S. banking facility.

Name_____
Address_____
City_____State_____Zip_____
I have enclosed $_____ in payment for the checked book(s).
Payment <u>must</u> accompany all orders. ❑ Please send a free catalog.
    CHECK OUT OUR WEBSITE! www.dorchesterpub.com

ATTENTION ROMANCE CUSTOMERS!

SPECIAL TOLL-FREE NUMBER
1-800-481-9191

*Call Monday through Friday
10 a.m. to 9 p.m.
Eastern Time*
**Get a free catalogue,
join the Romance Book Club,
and order books using your
Visa, MasterCard,
or Discover**®

Leisure
Books